J.M

The WONDER GIRLS *Resist*

THE
Cindy
PRESS
SOUTHAMPTON SO15

Text © J. M. Carr 2021
First published in Great Britain in 2022
This edition published 2022
by
The Cindy Press
Southampton SO15 5DR
United Kingdom
www.thecindypress.com

J.M. Carr has asserted her right
under the Copyright, Designs and Patents Act 1988
to be identified as the author of this work.

Cover artist: Anne Glenn,
anneglendesign@gmail.com

Contents

Dedicated to the 99 wonder-full people
who funded the first edition of this book
on kickstarter.com.

Who's in the story?

This story is about lots of people – gangs, networks, and not least of all 4000 child refugees! They all have stories to tell, but these are important characters for this one.

THE WONDER GIRLS
Baby
Fingers
Letitia Zara Ketton
Brian (Brenda) Shaw
Ida Barnes

THE ORPHANS
Ramón, *a lost Spanish orphan*
Bonnie Barnes, *Ida's little sister*
Robert Perkins, *not really an orphan – he's sure he has a mum somewhere*
Aggie, *definitely an orphan*
Frank, *Robert Perkins' small white dog*

THE SPANISH TEENAGERS
Regina, *fashionable young woman 1*
Maria, *fashionable young woman 2*
Alfredo, *a bully*
José, *Alfredo's reluctant associate*

THE ADULTS
Miss June Lovelock, *orphanage matron*

Mr Easton Fitzgerald, *a teacher, sometimes drives a black van*

Miss Rosamund Grenville, *Fitzgerald's well-to-do fiancé*

Harry Miller, *a pilot, walking out with June Lovelock*

THE OLDER GENERATION
Mr Alexander Shaw, *Brian's dad, recently released from Nettlefield Asylum*

Hortensia Maud Ketton, *Letitia's grandma*

Sir Hugh Sinclair, *a friend*

Mrs Lovelock, *June's mum*

HELPFUL (mostly)
Elsie, *Letitia's maid*

Leonard Cook, *(not a cook) has a useful laundry van*

Sergeant Ted Jackson, *Nettlefield Police*

Constable Spencer, *Nettlefield Police*

William Teasdale, *unreliable kitchen boy*

DEFINITELY BLACKSHIRTS
Mrs Tatler, *Harry Miller's landlady*

Mr Moles, *a council official with a cream-coloured car*

The Lillie & The Story so far

...

The Lillie is an abandoned railway carriage from the last days of Queen Victoria. It's where Baby, a smallish girl from India, and her friends made their home.

That was until that Blackshirt devil, Arthur Underwood, stripped it of its blanket of ivy and brambles, tore off its roof and scooped out its cosy heart.

Well, Baby and the other Wonder Girls, a gang of girls, boys and a little white dog put an end to his devilish schemes to send Nettlefield orphans to Adolf Hitler.

And in return The Lillie was repaired and spruced up with curtains and shutters and rugs, a brand-new roof and front door. And in all the ways that were helpful (hot dinners, the odd hot bath and stories round the fire on winter evenings), the nearby Nettlefield Grange Orphanage took The Lillie under its wing.

1

Letitia Zara Ketton

Coronation Day, Threep

LETITIA ZARA KETTON SAT ON THE ROOF above her bedroom window. It was her favourite place to think. She could see the church, the woods where she still loved to play even at sixteen years old, and at shortly after four o'clock on 12th May 1937, she saw her grandma.

Like a stately Bahamian galleon, Hortensia Maud Ketton was on her way home from the council meeting in her biggest and best Sunday hat.

Letitia slid on her belly over the slates, still damp from the morning's rain, and grabbed the guttering. She pushed against the eaves with her feet and swung through the open window, landing gracefully on her bedroom floor.

Elsie, their maid, sat upright on Letitia's bed with a little gasp. 'Is the madam coming home?' The thermometer waggled in her mouth like a conductor's baton.

'She certainly is. But we still have a few minutes,' said Letitia, removing the thermometer as Elsie adjusted her wire-rimmed spectacles.

Letitia struggled to remember what the correct reading should be. Why was it that when she was so good with numbers, Letitia could never remember that particular figure?

'Were you having a nap?'

'Ooh, no Miss,' said Elsie.

The head-shaped dent in the pillow suggested otherwise, however, the rolled-up copy of Detective Weekly sticking out of Elsie's apron pocket confirmed that she was probably telling the truth. Letitia really couldn't begrudge Elsie a little break when she was such a willing patient.

'Let me check your pulse.' Letitia took hold of Elsie's wrist.

'Ooh, Miss Letty! That hurt a bit.'

'Sorry, Else. I couldn't find it but there's no doubt you're alive, so that's good.' Letitia replaced the thermometer in its box and tucked it inside her father's old doctor's case with his medical textbooks and some grubby bandages. She slid the case under the bed.

The toasty smell of a burnt cake wafted up from the kitchen two floors below.

Elsie sniffed. 'Oh botheration! Sorry miss, got to go …'

'I'll get the door for Grandma,' said Letitia. 'Don't worry.'

Elsie scurried away with cries of fiddlesticks and botheration over the tap tap tap of her well-heeled shoes on the backstairs.

Letitia checked for any tell-tale moss on her school tunic, which was as grey as the slates, before walking downstairs.

Grandma, magnificent in purple and green, having at last been persuaded out of mourning for Grandfather, stepped inside the front door. The delicate scent of a dab or two of Yardley's Lavender entered with her. She unpinned her hat. It was a flamboyant affair more suitable for the coronation of George V in 1911, than George VI in 1937. 'What a splendid occasion that was,' she said. 'I thoroughly approve of the council's decision to acquire a television set. To think I watched the coronation of His Majesty the King as it happened in London, while I remained here in Threep!' She pulled at the fingers of her gloves. 'I am reassured that the council are maintaining a due respect for your dear Grandfather's work as mayor and are mindful of his memory.' She handed her hat to Elsie, red-faced behind foggy spectacles after dashing up from the kitchen. Grandma continued, 'I feel that the time has come for me to finally take his dear ashes back to The Bahamas. To that end, Letitia, I have booked a passage for myself from London to Nassau.'

'When are we leaving?' asked Letitia, an inch taller with excitement until she reminded herself of the sad reason for the trip. She sighed and tried to adopt a more sensitive attitude.

'I don't think you heard me correctly, my dear. I alone will be leaving Threep a week on Friday. I will stay with cousin Amelia in London before getting on the boat the following morning. Elsie will be here to look after you while I'm away. But of course, for much of the time, you will be at school.'

Any excitement Letitia still had dissolved. 'But couldn't I come too? I want to say goodbye to Grandfather.' She closed the front door trying not to be grumpy and hoping Grandma wouldn't notice she was doing Elsie's job.

'Dear girl, we agreed that you will be taking your school certificate. It was what you wanted and, whatever you choose to do in life, you will need it.' Grandma flapped her gloves to emphasise her point. 'So no, I'm sorry Letitia. You cannot come on this occasion. You'll be staying here, in Threep.'

Letitia would need qualifications to follow in her father and grandfather's footsteps and become a doctor. But she didn't really need to go to school for those. She could take the examinations tomorrow and pass with flying colours. Her teachers said so. They did exaggerate for Grandma's benefit, she believed, but perhaps not in maths. Though how could a series of entertaining puzzles be considered a serious subject?

'However, who knows what or who I might find for you on my trip?' continued Grandma with a twinkle in her eye. 'I shall be away for some weeks at the very least. I am aware that some young people your age and much younger are forced to work, but they are not of your class, my dear.'

'But I think I am sure that I do want to be a doctor, like Grandfather!'

'Yes ... but don't close your mind to other opportunities.' Grandma gave her gloves to Elsie, waiting patiently with the hat. She patted her coiffure of grey hair, arranged as well as Elsie could with pins and clips, and left Letitia in the hall.

Grandma wore her hair naturally. She didn't hold with relaxers, pomades or oils. Just a simple black bow for Grandfather's passing a year ago, nestled near her brow. Letitia's own curls grew down and were much looser. Grandma often said that Letitia took after her mother in so many ways, her hair being just one of them. Grandma said it was much to be admired and she was sure that at the right time, some young Bahamian man would too.

Letitia really didn't like the sound of that. Her grandmother's aspirations and her own were very different. Grandma would often complain about the deplorable lack of good young Bahamian men in Norfolk and now it was sounding like she was going to import a few, or at least one. No, Letitia didn't like the sound of that at all!

She knew for certain that she wanted to do some good in the world, to help people, to make a difference. Wasn't medicine the way to do that? Plus, it would have made her grandfather so proud. But she was all fingers and thumbs with the practical side. If only there were another way. Though for the life of her, she couldn't see one.

What did Grandfather always say? 'See Letitia, practice makes perfect.' Though that was usually after he'd watched her on the tightrope he'd rigged up in the woods. Letitia was six years old when Grandma had finally had enough of her balancing on the furniture and Grandfather had stretched a sturdy rope between two tall fir trees. It was just a few inches off the ground at first. 'When you can walk along that without a tumble,' he'd said, 'we'll make it a little higher.' Which is exactly what happened until the rope was well above Grandfather's head. Letitia could still hear him, 'Bend your knees, Letitia. You must lower your centre of gravity.' Then, when she succeeded, 'Bravo, dear girl! Bravo!', his arm warm across her shoulders. If Grandma had her way and married Letitia off to a Bahamian import, 'practice' would become impossible.

'Why are you still daydreaming out there in the hall?' Grandma had already settled herself with her sewing in her chair by the fireplace. 'Come in here and get your sewing out too. Then you can tell me about your day.'

Letitia joined Grandma and sat on what had been her stool since she was a small child. She took a wrinkled piece of fabric from the sewing box on the occasional table between them and examined it for her needle.

She had often watched Grandfather sew up a wound and had assisted him, scrubbing her hands in the way he showed her, passing him the needle and twine and watching carefully as he expertly brought the clean edges of the skin together. She didn't mind the sight of blood but, although she was taking every opportunity to practise doctoring, she had to admit that sewing up a wound was beyond her.

She missed her grandfather dreadfully. He was like a father to her and she loved him as she would have a father. Her actual father died the year she was born, her mother too. They survived the war and then got themselves killed in a motor car accident when Letitia was only a few months old in 1921. Her parents met at the front, so they had very little time together. Her mother, a white woman, had run away to nurse though she'd had no training, and that was how they met. Letitia wished she could remember them, but she couldn't, so their deaths were just a fact of family history that brought an irritating sympathy to people's faces. Letitia didn't feel she deserved it. As interested as she was in her mother and father, she couldn't attach an emotion to people she never really knew. And she was fully aware how much, for Threep at any rate, she lived in the lap of luxury with her dear grandparents, who, to all intents and purposes, were her parents.

Letitia found the needle stuck through some uneven stitching, already threaded with a grubby length of yellow silk. But the thread had mysteriously tangled. Letitia unthreaded the needle and tried to undo the knot but, in the end, decided just to give it an extra hard tug to pull the needle through the fabric.

Letitia was sure it was her grandfather's wish that she follow the family profession. He always said that she should follow her talents. He said that she had the skills and talents to change the world. Hadn't he given her that card, with the name and address in London of an old friend of his, should she ever need help – a Sir somebody or other? It made her sad to look at the card. It was the last thing Grandfather gave her. So Letitia kept it in her purse and tried to forget it was there.

Grandfather had been so weak at the end, so surely saving people's lives was what he meant her to do. The Sir was probably someone influential at Grandfather's old hospital, therefore doctoring had to be Letitia's destiny. Why was Grandma so half-hearted about that? Oh yes. In spite of her suffragette sympathies, Grandma was a Victorian woman whose top priority was to find Letitia a husband!

Sitting in her chair, more a throne than a fireside chair, Grandma rummaged through her own sewing box. 'In council today we were also hearing about the awful trouble in Spain. Can you imagine it? Planes flying overhead at all hours of the day dropping bombs without a care for who they're dropping them on! But a committee's been set up to bring the poor children to Britain. We may take some in Threep, once they've gone through the necessary examinations and checks.'

What examinations, wondered Letitia, pricking her finger. You didn't actually have to sit an exam to stay in the country now, did you?

'Suck that clean, my dear. You don't want a bloodstain on your work, do you?'

Letitia watched it bubble, waiting for it to clot – only the other day had she been trying to read about haemophilia, where the blood doesn't clot. She was beginning to wonder about her own, when there was a knock at the front door – an official sounding rat-tat.

Grandma dropped her sewing in her lap.

'I'm getting it, madam,' said Elsie from the hall, pulling off her apron on the way, as Grandma had showed her.

The voice at the door had the kind of accent that came from centuries of aristocratic English ancestors.

'Who shall I say is calling, madam?' asked Elsie.

'Miss Grenville, from The Hall,' said the woman at the door.

'Miss Grenville from The Hall is here to see you, madam,' repeated Elsie at the door to the sitting room.

'Well show her in, Elsie!' said Grandma.

Letitia noticed a flush to her grandma's cheeks.

With a sweep of her arm, Elsie ushered in Miss Rosamund Grenville.

In her late twenties, Miss Grenville wore a silk jacket with embroidery on the pockets. Wide-eyed and pale, she appeared to float in with the jacket. The green silk was faded and a little old-fashioned, not at all like Grandma's vivid colours. Surely Miss Grenville could afford something new?

Grandma invited her to sit down on what used to be Grandfather's fireside chair. Letitia wished they had an alternative chair for visitors.

'Thank you,' said Miss Grenville in a breathy voice, 'I am most appreciative of you seeing me on the hop, as it were. But I'm sure you've heard about the mercy mission some of us are getting up to help the poor Spaniards?'

'We most certainly have,' said Grandma. 'I was only telling Letitia here ...'

'Yes. We expect the boat about the twenty-second of this month,' interrupted Miss Grenville. 'I'm actually on my way to Southampton in the next few days, to meet my fiancé, Easton. He's been teaching in Spain and has volunteered to be part of the advance party. I must show you his photograph.' Miss Grenville rummaged in her bag, which rattled with its contents.

'Oh, here it is,' said Miss Grenville with a sniff and produced a curled-at-the-edges photograph of the handsomest man that Letitia had ever seen – and that included film stars like Paul Robeson or Errol Flynn. He even had that same thin line of moustache sitting on his top lip.

'That is surely admirable, Miss Grenville. I hope that here in Threep, we can do something to help the poor children,' said Grandma.

'Yes, we can ...' agreed Miss Grenville, suddenly vague and absent-mindedly smoothing the silky folds of her jacket. She sniffed in a way that made Letitia think she might cry.

Then, as if Miss Grenville had just remembered where she was, she continued, 'What I am actually here for is to ask if you have any medical supplies that you

11

might care to donate to the cause – from your late husband? The children will no doubt need all kinds of things. They'll have been living in very cramped conditions for the duration of their journey from Bilbao and goodness knows how they're managing now – the news is that some of those places on the north coast have been utterly devastated, flattened even. Coming to England is only a temporary measure to keep the children safe but one does wonder what they'll return to.'

'Most certainly, Miss Grenville. We'll have those sent over shortly. When did you say you were leaving?'

'Most kind. Oh, sometime in the next week or so.' Miss Grenville sniffed again and stood up.

The sniff was becoming quite off-putting.

'I won't keep you any longer Mrs Ketton, Miss Ketton ...'

Letitia had a thought. 'Miss Grenville, how will you understand the children?'

Miss Grenville frowned quizzically. 'I beg your pardon?' She sniffed again, three times in quick succession. 'My apologies. The English atmosphere so disagrees with one. One often longs to be back in India.'

'I mean, what language will they speak?' asked Letitia.

'Oh, Spanish, I guess. Though I do believe the Basques in the north have their own language ...'

'So how will you understand them?' asked Letitia.

'I'm sure Miss Grenville will manage.' Grandma rang the bell for Elsie.

Elsie arrived, her hands all floury. 'Yes, madam?'

'Miss Grenville is leaving now, Elsie.'

'This way, madam.' Elsie wiped her hands down her apron as she led Miss Grenville out to the hall and opened the front door for her.

As soon as the door was shut, Grandma said, 'No, Letitia Zara, you are not going to Southampton.'

Letitia huffed and pricked her finger again.

With some tears and many one-sided conversations with her dear departed husband, Grandma spent the rest of the week in his old consulting room, parcelling up supplies such as the refugee children might need. These were sent up to The Hall to go on a lorry whose drivers were gathering supplies from all of Norfolk as the county's contribution to the Spanish rescue.

Letitia tried to persuade Grandma to allow her to go to Southampton with Miss Grenville. 'I could help. Couldn't that be the point of Grandfather making me speak Spanish?' When Letitia was really quite young, he told her that it was a family tradition to learn the language of the oppressor. In the case of The Bahamas, this was Spain.

'But Grandfather, that was hundreds of years ago!' Letitia used to argue.

'Never mind, and now in Spanish, dear girl,' he'd always reply.

So, Letitia learned to speak Spanish almost as soon as she learned to speak at all.

Grandfather often used to say, 'You have an aptitude for languages, Letitia, this will stand you in good stead in whatever path you choose.' But Letitia found it hard to value something that came so easily.

Grandma refused to listen to Letitia's pleas and turned her attention to the preparations for her trip to Nassau. She left reams of instructions, all in her very clear hand, easy for Elsie to read.

And equally easy for Letitia to copy.

Letitia laid her pen in its groove on her desk, now returned to its place in front of her bedroom window and blew on the ink. 'Think about it Else, you'll have the whole place to yourself. All you have to do is pretend that I've been called to The Bahamas too. It's that simple.'

'But Miss Letty, the madam – what if she discovers ...' Elsie stood behind her, nervously twisting her apron around her hands.

'But she won't, will she? She won't be here and I'm not going to tell her. Are you? With these letters for school, it will all be absolutely fine.' Letitia held up her forgery next to Grandma's list. 'Look, you can't tell the difference, can you?'

Elsie squinted at the two pages of handwriting. 'No, Miss Letty.'

That was good enough.

Very early on Friday morning, 21st May, sunny at last after weeks of dismal grey weather, a large black taxicab parked outside The Manor.

It was one day before Letitia believed the huge ship loaded with refugee children was due to dock at Southampton. Letitia Zara Ketton was fit to burst with excitement.

Grandma, in her best summer hat and a dress suitable for the Bahamian sun under a warm jacket suitable for the English one, eased herself into the back seat. She was clutching the urn containing Grandfather's ashes.

The sadness at seeing the urn and saying a final goodbye to Grandfather helped Letitia contain her excitement. She was going to follow in her mother's footsteps and get some practical experience at last. She might be dressed for school, but she'd laid everything on her bed for a super-quick change.

As the driver was piling cases into the boot, the post office boy on his bike rattled up the drive waving a piece of paper. 'Telegram for Ketton!'

Grandma reached out of the taxicab window, took it from the boy and fumbled in her handbag before giving him a coin.

As the post office boy rattled back down the path, Grandma read, 'Oh dear, Amelia cannot have me, something dreadful to do with the plumbing.'

Letitia's excitement tumbled to the ground like a coconut knocked off its shy at the fair. Grandma had to go today but here she was opening the taxicab door again.

'No wait, what am I doing? I shall simply stay in a hotel,' said Grandma.

And with relief, Letitia watched the driver close the door and check it was secure with Grandma safely inside.

'Now remember,' said Grandma through the window, 'I will write once a week. I expect to be away some time and will let you know when I'll be returning.' She then ran through her list of reminders for Letitia, for the umpteenth time ... 'Watch Elsie when she boils the potatoes – she boils them to death and don't let her iron anything of mine – she always forgets until it's far too hot. Don't be late for school and remember to change your tunic at least once a week and for heaven's sake, Letitia Zara, please consider your age and station. If you must play in the woods on that tightrope of your Grandfather's, wear something suitable.'

'Yes Grandma.' She kissed the old lady's cheek through the window.

Letitia waved the taxicab out of the gates, trying hard not to leap for joy. She dashed upstairs, tore off her school tunic and put on her most grown up clothes – a smart blue jacket and skirt, but over a close-fitting pair of blue bloomers. She grabbed her father's case, well stuffed with supplies. And with a 'Goodbye Elsie, have fun!' Letitia Zara Ketton was on her way to the station for the very next train.

It was already pulling out of the station. Through clouds of white smoke, she ran and grabbed the rail. With her case firmly gripped in her other hand, Letitia hauled herself inside, past the guard and his harrumph of disapproval.

But she had a horrible feeling she was missing something.

She opened the catch on her case and riffled through the various compartments. At the bottom, her father's old medical manual weighed the bag down. Piled on top were clean bandages, ointment, iodine, tweezers, safety pins, scissors, twine, her father's stethoscope, and a sling. She even had aspirin and some more bandages just in case. So what was it?

Her purse? No, that was there, tucked safely under the extra bandages containing the neatly folded five pound note with a few coins and the ticket to Southampton, purchased in advance. Her pocket Spanish/English dictionary, a very compact wash kit in a floral bag, a second pair of bloomers and some clean underwear had all been packed and hidden away for more than a week.

What was she missing?

Of course, if the Spaniards only spoke Basque she'd be scuppered. Though she was sure she'd be able to pick it up fairly quickly, so it wasn't that.

And then she knew what it was.

Apart from going to school every day, which didn't count somehow, for the first time ever Letitia was independent. Neither Grandma, nor Elsie would be checking up on her or running around after her. Would she miss that? She'd miss them and she'd miss home, of course she would, but she was ready to explode with joy because: This. Was. It.

Letitia Zara Ketton was on the verge of her very first adventure.

2

Mr Movie Star

About 2 o'clock, Friday 21st May, Nettlefield

BABY PUSHED OPEN The Lillie's new front door and kicked off her even newer shoes.

But she didn't want to seem ungrateful, so she picked them up, undid the bows and left them neatly by the step between her sister's unworn pair and her own old boots. She hung her green silk jacket on the hook above and curled her toes into the thick pile of the colourful new rug that now covered much of the floor.

At the table, where the sun poured bright and warm through the window, Baby sat down and let her feet dangle against the chair. She cupped her chin in her hand and puffed a long, lip-burbling sigh.

She'd had some fine times in this old railway carriage these last few months.

Baby gazed at the polished stove filled with fir cones for the summer, and the jug of bluebells sitting on top. She admired the freshly painted cupboards where Brian's dad's books were lined up, the ones that survived the wrecking before Christmas. And she stroked the fresh new wallpaper covered with birds and trees, just like the outside.

But Baby had an itch she couldn't shift, like a flea had made its home on her and was going nowhere no matter how many baths June Lovelock, the kindly new orphanage matron, made her have. And the three good meals a day, prepared lovingly by the orphanage cooks and Wonder Girl, Brian, whose real name was Brenda and was learning the trade, meant the fullness in Baby's belly was weighing her down.

Baby was used to hitching up her skirt with a bit of rope or rolling her sleeves until they were doughnuts around her wrists. She was used to the slick-slock of old worn boots. She was used to finding a barrel to sleep in, not a giant bed that filled a whole room, with pillows and quilts and hot water bottles when the frost sparkled outside.

The plan had always been to go to America, where the pickin's were like you'd never seen.

Maybe, it was time to go at last.

She took a scrap of newspaper from her pocket. It was a picture of the Nettlefield Hands Across the Sea Coronation Tea Party, a week or so back. Kids sat at long trestle tables in the church hall, eating tea and waving little union jacks with Nettlefield's Blackshirts and Mrs Tatler, June Lovelock's old landlady, all looking on. Baby didn't like it, but they seemed to have given up marching and if tea parties was all they were doing, perhaps she could leave them be ...

She screwed up the paper, closed her eyes in the warmth and tried to imagine how she would tell them all, Brian especially, that she and Fingers were leaving. Brian had Down's syndrome, which meant that sometimes she understood things a bit differently.

A train whistled on its way out of the station, sparrows squabbled in the bushes that grew round the clearing outside, and a twig cracked.

Now they knew it was here, Nettlefield folk did come for a look at The Lillie from time to time. They were generally polite. Baby waited for the knock on the door.

A coolness on her cheek, as if a cloud had hidden the sun, made her shiver.

Her muscles tightened and goose pimples popped up on her arms.

Against the brightness, a dark outline of a man in a panama hat almost filled the window. He pushed his hat further back on his head, shaded his eyes, pressed his nose against the glass and peered in.

Baby jumped down from her chair and backed away from the bright blue eyes, the perfect row of white teeth and the thin line of moustache. 'What d'you want Mister?'

21

'Oh, hello there,' he said, 'so somebody is at home.' He disappeared from the window.

Baby heard the click, click, of the doorknob being twisted open.

The man, in a pale grey suit and an open-necked shirt, took off his hat and strode in.

'I didn't hear you knock, mister.' Baby stretched to her tallest. Though she still only reached his shoulder, she wasn't putting up with him just waltzing in like he owned the place.

The man was like nobody she'd seen in Nettlefield before, unless it was at The Embassy Cinema, stepping down off the silver screen. And she hadn't seen that happen, not ever. His oiled hair shone like a copper's boots. A bit of her wanted to touch him make sure he was real – but the smell! It reminded Baby of waiting outside the theatre up west when the toffs came out.

'Well, well, well, what a nice place you have here,' he said.

'What do you want?' said Baby, standing in his way.

'The facilities are that way?' He pointed to the door next to the kitchen sink at the far end of The Lillie and brushed past Baby as if she wasn't there.

Baby tried to push past him but the man was already leaning in through the open door to the lav where they'd put a new toilet, and a basin with a mirror on the wall too.

'More than adequate,' he said.

'I should think so,' said Baby. 'Now would you mind ...'

Baby was all for running for the coppers but this man, this invader, would be long gone before Sergeant Ted Jackson could heft himself out from behind his desk.

'Now that must be the bedroom.' He brushed past Baby again to the 'room-bed', the floor of mattresses piled high with colourful quilts and pillows. 'Hmm, we'll have to do something about this, but otherwise all very satisfactory.'

Baby puffed herself up. 'What for?' she asked with as much authority as she could muster.

But at that moment the thud, thud of galumphing steps across the clearing took Baby's attention away from the man.

'Baby! Baby! Come quick!' Brian grabbed The Lillie's doorframe and bent over puffing and panting to catch her breath. 'She's stuck!'

'Who's stuck, Bri?'

'Fingers, of course,' said Brian, as if that was the most reasonable and obvious thing in the world. 'And June's out shopping,' she added, straightening up, showing off her cook's apron, splashed with brown stains. A wooden spoon dripped gravy in her other hand.

The man, Mr Movie Star, put his hat on, pulled the brim lower over his face and pushed his hand deep into his trouser pocket, rucking his jacket, as he slipped between them, out through the door.

'Who was that?' asked Brian.

'I don't know.' Baby pulled Brian round to look her square in the face. 'What about Fingers? Where's she stuck?'

'Fingers! Yes! She's stuck!'

'But where?'

'On the railway! Come on!'

'Oh Gawd, what's she been doin' now?' Slipping her feet into her old boots, Baby followed Brian out of The Lillie across the clearing and through the bushy tunnel to the station.

Baby ran for the gap between the sheds, straight for the tracks.

'No, not that way,' Brian grabbed Baby's arm and pulled her out of the way of a dark-red car heading out of the station towards West Street.

Brian ran, all arms and legs, away from the sheds and the mountain of coal, past the stationmaster's office, where the stationmaster filled his doorway.

'And where are you off to in such a hurry, young ladies?' he said, sticking out his chest to inspect his pocket watch.

'Oh, nowhere,' said Brian, scurrying past and picking up speed at the same time.

Baby shrugged her shoulders at the stationmaster, as if to say she had no idea what Brian was up to either.

Baby followed Brian to the top of the bank that, if you dared, you could roll down through the long grass all the way to the road. Baby scanned the bank. 'Where is she?'

Brian tugged on Baby's sleeve and pointed to the top of the railway bridge that carried trains over the main road and into or out of the station. 'Up there.'

Baby followed the line of Brian's arm. She had to squint in the afternoon sun but could just make out Fingers's head of messy ginger curls over the top of the bridge.

'Fingers, what are you doing? Get off the bridge!'

'Didn't she tell ya? I'm stuck! I can't get me foot out!' shouted Fingers.

Baby ran across the top of the bank to where it joined the bridge. Brian galumphed behind her.

William Teasdale, a young man of seventeen, was sitting there, leaning against the signal post with his head in his hands.

'You wait here with 'im, Bri, in case a train comes.'

Baby nudged his shoulder. 'What's wrong with you?'

William looked up. His shirt was buttoned up to the wrong buttonholes, his face was dirty, and Baby caught a whiff of bad breath through his crooked teeth. 'It's not my fault. I bet she's joshing anyway!'

25

Baby wanted to smack him round the head and ask why on Earth he wasn't helping, but at that moment she heard a train whistle on its way into the station. It wouldn't be long before it would be heading out again.

Across the bridge.

She climbed over the parapet wall onto the bridge itself.

In the space between the tracks and the low wall, Fingers was tugging away on her laces, trying to pull her foot out from under the track. 'We was playing dare, 'e said I couldn't jump the tracks I said I could, 'e said 'show me' and when I went to do it, 'e pushed me and I dunno how, but when I turned round to push him back, me foot stuck.'

Baby wanted to give her a right old telling off for not only messing around on the railway tracks but on the bridge too. What was she playing at? But along the track, billows of steam told her the train had arrived in Nettlefield station.

'We gotta leave your boot there.' Baby kneeled down in the gravel and weeds and picked at the knots that were keeping Fingers's foot firmly in her boot.

'June Lovelock did 'em up but they kept coming undone, so I did 'em up some more,' said Fingers.

And she surely had. Baby fumbled with the little sausage of knots, but they weren't loosening.

She heard the creak of the train signal on the post where William Teasdale was still leaning, like the useless lump of idiot he was. The signal went up. The train was coming.

'Right, I'm going to pull.' Baby positioned herself between Fingers and the parapet, wrapped her strong brown arms round Fingers's middle, positioned her own feet against the track, dug her heels into the gravel, and with one big heave pulled her sister ...

... free of the railway track, boot and all.

Baby fell backwards onto her bottom and into the parapet wall, which was just high enough to stop her falling over the edge.

But not high enough for Fingers.

Fingers rolled backwards over Baby, over the wall ...

... and over the bridge.

With gravel-dented hands, Baby tried to grab her, but Fingers had momentum and as if in slow motion, Baby watched her sister fall to the road below.

The engine smell of soot and burnt coal filled her nostrils. The hot steamy wind of the three o'clock Portsmouth train tried to suck her in as it thundered past. Baby pressed herself against the wall, as far away from the tracks as she could.

As soon as the last carriage had passed, Baby got up, leaned over the parapet and peered through the smoke.

Fingers was lying lifeless in the middle of the road! The look of it made Baby feel as sick as sick. She ran past William, who was slumped in a guilty heap, to the top of the bank. She tumbled down through the grass to the street where Fingers lay.

Brian tumbled behind her.

But a girl, brown skinned like Baby, in an expensive-looking blue suit, had beaten Baby and Brian to it. She carried a bag like the one Baby had seen the doctor carry. She also had a fine head of black curls that bounced just above her shoulders

The smart girl was unclipping her bag.

Like she'd swallowed a boulder and been soaked in concrete, Baby couldn't move a muscle ... apart from the one round her mouth.

'Is she ... dead?'

3

The New Matron of Nettlefield Grange

Friday 21st May, Nettlefield

BABY WATCHED THE GIRL kneel beside Fingers's body, pick up Fingers's limp wrist, and listen to Fingers's chest.

The girl beamed like she'd won the cup and said, 'She's got a pulse. I think I felt it! And she's breathing.' The girl glanced at her wristwatch. 'But to be doubly sure I need to check her heart too,' she said.

Baby dropped to her knees. 'Fingers, don't you go and die on me!' She felt Brian's hand squeeze her shoulder.

The girl drew out a long tube with ear plugs, the kind doctors use. Baby held her breath while the girl pressed the end of the tube in different places on Fingers's chest.

At last, the girl punched her fist in the air and declared to the small crowd including a car that had stopped, rather than swerving around the scene, 'She's definitely alive!'

Baby shouted, 'Fingers, Florrie, wake up!'

Fingers opened one eye, groaned and shut it again.

'You little tyke, what you go and scare me like that for?'

'I don't think she meant to,' said Brian.

The girl pulled the listening tube off her neck. 'I don't think her leg is broken, but she has received concussion from a nasty bump on the head. Time will tell how bad it is.' She stuffed the tube back in the bag from where a posh pair of drawers was escaping.

'Oops,' said the girl pushing the silky underwear back in the bag with the listening tube.

Baby leaned over to try to see what else was in the bag, but the girl was pulling out reams of bandage. She eventually found the end and started wrapping it around Fingers's head.

In her half-awake state, Fingers groaned and winced some more.

Baby pulled on the girl's arm. 'Do you think she really needs a bandage?'

But behind them, hurried footsteps made by sensible shoes clacked on the pavement.

'Oh, Fingers. What have you done?' June Lovelock dropped her shopping bags and pushed her way through the small crowd.

'It's all right, she's alive,' said Brian.

'Yes, but in what state?' said June, 'We must get you inside! And the doctor, we need the doctor. Brian, dear, can you go and fetch him, please.'

Brian got up and, with her wooden spoon leading pointing the way, charged up West Street. Brian's real name was Brenda, like Fingers's was really Florrie or very, very occasionally, Florence. Miss Lovelock's name was June and that's what she liked to be called. It was all a bit 'progressive' to Nettlefield folk but since the important part June played in the goings on last Christmas, most of them put up with it.

'She'll be absolutely fine, I'm sure,' said the girl, 'I study medicine. My father and grandfather were both doctors. Well, my grandfather was the town's mayor too, but that's beside the point.' She held out her hand for June to shake it. 'Letitia Ketton, and I'm mostly here to help with the Spanish Relief Committee.'

'Oh, that's good,' said June, 'perhaps you can first help us get her off the road? Baby, can you go and ask Cook for the stretcher? It's at the back of the kitchen broom cupboard. I'm so glad we kept it. I never expected us to actually need it.'

Nettlefield Grange, the town orphanage was a large old house with an East Wing and a West Wing and an imposing front door in the middle. Curtains billowed through a row of tall windows, open to catch the early summer breeze. Baby dashed through the gates – always open now. No children would ever want to run away with June Lovelock in charge. She ran past the playground that June had had installed, the swings, slide, roundabout and see-saw, to the kitchen door at the side of the building.

Baby and the cook rummaged in the cupboard, brooms and mops clattering out on to the kitchen tiles, as Baby burrowed to the back.

'Your Fingers is a right one, isn't she?' said the cook, a sturdy woman, but soft as sponge pudding with jam tart cheeks, mopping her brow with her apron.

'Is this it?' At the back of the cupboard, Baby pulled on two poles wrapped in canvas, much taller than she was. The canvas smelled musty. During the war, Nettlefield Grange had been an overflow military hospital. Though the whole place had been spruced up a lot since then, especially since June took over last Christmas.

'Oh, that brings back memories,' said Cook. 'I'll take it out while you put the bits and bobs away.' She reached over Baby for the rolled-up stretcher and hurried out with it under one arm.

Cook had gone before Baby could extricate herself from the muddle.

When Nettlefield Grange was a hospital, the nurses probably didn't have time to clean and tidy cupboards. A smelly old greatcoat hung up there with a collection of old aprons that previous staff had used. Underneath, where the stretcher stood propped against the wall, Baby could see a wooden box.

It was about the size and shape of the box that June used to store her typewriter. Not that she did much typing anymore. 'Just to keep my speed up – I can't get rusty, typing is such a useful skill.' This box, at the back of the broom cupboard, looked fairly clean, unlike all the other stuff.

She couldn't stop to investigate, but she'd be back for a look as soon as Fingers was better.

Outside, there was a cry of pain.

Baby wriggled past the brooms and mops and buckets and pulled the cupboard door shut. There was a key in the lock, but no time to fiddle with it to lock the door. It was only a broom cupboard after all. She dashed out from the kitchen to her sister.

Fingers moaned and groaned on the old stretcher being carried through the orphanage front door by Cook, at Fingers's feet, and June at her head. They set the stretcher down in a patch of sunlight on the hall floor. The girl, Letitia, came in with them and a tangle of unwound bandage, some of it still attached to Fingers and the rest trailing behind the stretcher over the doorstep.

Cook returned to the kitchen while Baby, June and Letitia waited with Fingers in the hall for the doctor.

'Baby,' said June, 'this is Letitia. She's a medical student. How lucky she came by.'

The girl smiled full of excitement. Baby felt a frown wrinkle her forehead. This girl was too excited; excited in a pleased I've got away with it way. On the stretcher, Fingers was frowning too. Her eyes were shut.

Fingers opened one eye. 'Is she still here?'

The girl, Letitia, pulled on the bandage that was still attached to Fingers.

'She is!' said Fingers fully awake now. 'Keep her away from me!'

'It seems,' said June Lovelock, 'that Letitia has only just started her training. Is there any sign of Brian and the doctor?'

'I'm actually on the way to some practical experience,' said Letitia.

'Oh, the Spanish refugees, of course. I'm sure they'll need all the help they can get,' said June.

'Not that sort of help, they won't,' said Fingers grumpily from her stretcher.

'Well, I'd better be going,' said Letitia, clipping her bag shut but not quite catching all the bandage inside.

'Let's give your bandage a wash first,' said June. 'It did get a bit dirty trailing across our playground didn't it?'

'Thank you, that would be good. Hygiene is extremely important, you know.' Letitia pulled the bandage out of her case.

'Where's the patient?' The doctor was peering in through the open front door with Brian. 'Lovely bright afternoon out there, quite a change in the weather. Shame the sun didn't come out for the coronation, what?'

'She's down there,' said Brian, pointing helpfully. 'You can't see because your eyes haven't got used to how dark it is in here.'

'Quite,' said the doctor and rudely turned his back on Brian as he attended to Fingers.

June sent the bandages to the kitchen with William. She put Letitia's case by the orphanage telephone. 'Let's leave that there while the doctor examines the patient, and have a well-deserved raspberry bun.' A tray of them had appeared, as if by magic, on the table in the main living room.

A disappointed whine came from the stretcher on the floor.

'Don't worry, Florrie Fingers, there's plenty,' said June, shooing Baby and Letitia through the double doors where all sorts of lovely things had happened since June Lovelock took over. Vases of bluebells decorated the long table where they all sat down for breakfast, dinner and tea. Over the huge fireplace, the grim picture of a stern Victorian man with mutton chop whiskers had been replaced with the children's own paintings in bright colours. Shelves of books and games lined the walls under the windows and at one end, a pile of cushions, like The Lillie's room-bed, were piled in nests round a wireless and a cosy armchair – June Lovelock's story chair.

The doctor came in, pulling off his stethoscope. 'Well she's a very lucky girl. I'm astonished how every bone in her body isn't broken after a fall like that, and after being moved as well, and, may I say, rather inexpertly, too.'

Sitting at the table with the others, Letitia stared into her lap.

'The girl must be made of rubber,' said the doctor, 'However, she did receive quite a bang on the head. So, as I gather that the er ... young lady is one of the group, who lives independently in the er ... orphanage annexe, I think she should be supervised tonight.'

'I'll keep watch over her,' said Baby.

'Yes, and you'll both stay here for the next few days,' said June.

'She's resting now,' the doctor unclipped his black bag. 'I advise you to check on her every fifteen minutes.' He looked at it more closely. 'Is this my bag?' He drew out the silk drawers Baby spotted earlier.

Letitia got up and snatched them off him. 'I'm sorry, I think you've picked up mine.'

'Yours must still be in the hall, doctor. Thank you very much for coming out so promptly, shall I show you out?' said June.

A stream of orphans coming home from school bustled in through the front door, round the doctor who was caught in the flow.

'Children, wash your hands for buns,' said Miss Lovelock, signposting them to the bathrooms and the doctor to the door.

June saw Fingers settled in the sickroom next to her office. June then sat down at the table with Baby, Brian, all the orphans, as one by one they returned from the bathroom, and this new girl, Letitia. 'Letitia, do you have a story to tell us?'

Letitia looked puzzled.

'How old are you, for instance?' asked June.

Letitia slumped over the table like all the air had gone out of her. 'I'm seventeen ... nearly. I want to help. I want to make a difference in the world. I'm trying to work out how. I told you my father and grandfather were doctors, so I think that's what I ought to do too, if only I were better at it. Though I have learnt a lot from watching, especially watching my grandfather. My father died when I was baby.'

'Like mine,' said orphan Bonnie Barnes. Her golden blonde hair, tied in two bunches, made ringlets like fat sausages that Baby always admired.

Bonnie perched onto June's lap and showed off her clean hands.

A very pale arm reached up from underneath the table and, on the end of it, a spidery hand felt about for the buns.

'Is that hand clean, Robert?' asked June Lovelock of the boy who owned it.

Not strictly an orphan, Robert Perkins peeked out from under the tablecloth. 'Not yet, but they'll all be gone if I go and do that.'

'No, they won't, I'll make sure of it. Now off you go.' Albino Robert, too blonde for Arthur Underwood and the Nazis, scurried off to the bathroom, followed by a similarly white little dog.

June turned to the would-be doctor. 'Letitia, would you like to stay for some supper, before you set off for Southampton? Perhaps you'd like to stay the night too?'

'Ermm ...' said Letitia, biting her lip. Then with a smile of relief she said, 'Yes please, Miss er ...'

'It's Lovelock,' said June, gently lifting Bonnie off her lap and getting up from her chair, 'but everyone calls me June.'

'I was going to go directly to Southampton,' said Letitia, 'but um ... this place, Nettlefield looked er ... interesting.'

Letitia reminded Baby of Bonnie's big sister Ida, someone else who didn't always stop to think.

'Could I call you Miss June,' asked Letitia, 'if I may? It feels more respectful.'

'If that would make you feel more comfortable, but isn't respect as much about how you say a thing as what you say? June is my name, but I can be Miss June to you if you like.'

Yes, Letitia was as goody-goody as Ida, or as goody-goody as Ida used to be, at any rate.

In the hour after school and before supper, in the large orphanage living room, Baby played with the kids on the floor, while going to check on Fingers every fifteen minutes as instructed. It didn't take much effort to persuade Letitia it was best that she, Baby, did the checking on Fingers. Letitia made herself comfortable in Miss Lovelock's story chair. She drew out from her case the thickest, dullest book Baby ever did see. Some of the kids tried to peek over Letitia's shoulder, but when they saw there were hardly any pictures, they left her alone.

Supper was steak and kidney pie with carrots and mashed potatoes, Baby's favourite. Fingers had hers sitting up in bed in the sickroom next to June's office.

Brian helped dish up. She was wearing the chef's hat that June got for her to celebrate her apprenticeship. 'I made the pastry today,' Brian told everyone, and in return she received a ton of compliments, the biggest one being: 'Is there anymore?'

To the sound of dinner plates being scraped, June stood up and told everyone that she would be out for the evening and that Cook would be staying on to sit with them. 'And of course, Baby is more than able to take care of Fingers.'

Baby felt a pang of guilt. If she'd taken care of her properly, Fingers wouldn't have fallen off the bridge. She wouldn't have been on the bridge in the first place.

The children liked Cook. She wasn't as good as June at storytime, but she did make extra buns for a bedtime snack, which she served with warm milk, without Ovaltine. Cook knew very well that none of the kids liked it.

'Where are you going?' asked Brian.

'Oh, just to the Assembly Hall,' said June, 'I won't be long. They have a new band there and they're going to be playing some Benny Goodman tunes from America.'

Baby wondered if, at this rate, she and Fingers would ever get there.

'Look, he's here.' Brian pointed at the double doors.

Harry Miller, the man June was walking out with, was peering through one of the porthole windows; all the doors had them in the Grange. When June had finished speaking, he walked in with a big bunch of flowers.

June's cheeks flushed bright pink at the sight of this man in a dashing flyer's leather jacket with a sheepskin collar. When he gave her kiss on the cheek, some of the older kids went a bit giggly.

The littl'uns, however, clamoured round him. 'Make us fly, Harry! Make us fly!'

This was when Baby wished she was just that bit smaller. Harry flew planes in the war and was a hero by all accounts. He was certainly a hero for them before Christmas. Now he only flew his aeroplane for rich people.

'No! They've only just had their tea!' said June. 'I'm going to get my hat, back in a jiffy.' Behind June's back, Harry put his finger to his lip. The small kids sniggered. As soon as June had dashed out the door, Harry picked up each one in turn, tossed them in the air and caught them again like they were pillows in a pillow fight.

'Again! Again!'

'Now that really is enough,' he said, 'you'll be sick!'

'Ooohh!' whined the small kids all together.

Harry straightened his jacket and pushed his flop of hair back in place.

June returned with her hat. 'Harry, could you put the stretcher back, please. Baby, perhaps you could show him where it goes?'

'Stretcher? What's that all about?'

'Oh, I'll tell you later. It was quite a drama but fortunately Fingers is fine.'

41

Harry followed Baby to the sickbay, where Fingers was snoring loud as the elephant at London Zoo. Harry took the rolled-up stretcher from where it was propped against the wall, 'Where did you find this?'

'In the broom cupboard,' said Baby, 'the one in the kitchen. It was right at the back.'

'You stay with Fingers, I'll put it away again.'

'I'll help.' Baby grabbed the other end of the stretcher.

Harry yanked it out of her grasp. 'No, no need,' He said sharply. Then he looked Baby up and down. 'Baby, I think you have ideas well above your height!' he said, the sharpness in his voice gone.

Baby left Fingers snoring, and with her empty plate followed Harry across the corridor to the kitchen, where Brian and Cook were supervising William with the washing-up. William was still in the doghouse, and Baby reckoned he would be there for a quite a while too. Without his older brother Bill around, William Teasdale seemed to have a new confidence for mischief.

Baby followed Harry to the cupboard.

Harry spun round to face her. 'What are you doing? Didn't I tell you?' the sharpness in his voice back, and a deep frown on his face that Baby hadn't seen before. She felt like she'd been nabbed.

Baby had thought to ask him about the box at the back of the cupboard but instead showed him Fingers's

42

plate. 'Putting this in the washing-up,' she said. Harry's manner reminded Baby of all her old suspicions about him being a Blackshirt.

But seeing the dirty dinner plate, his face softened again. 'Oh yes, of course.'

She took it over to the sink and slid it into the dirty water, where William had his arms plunged up to his elbows.

When Baby turned round, Harry had gone, and the broom cupboard door was shut.

But something was missing.

The key, the old key that was in the door when Baby got the stretcher out, was gone.

Baby tried the door.

It was locked.

Those old suspicions about Harry fluttered round Baby like fruit flies around a box of apples on the turn.

And it occurred to her, that that box, at the back of the cupboard, hadn't looked so much left behind, as hidden.

4

The South Western Hotel

Saturday 22nd May, to Southampton

ONLY A FLIMSY CURTAIN on a rail separated Letitia from the huge bedroom with many beds, not unlike Threep Cottage Hospital, which she'd often visited with Grandfather. When Letitia went to bed the previous evening, although she was quite slim, she did wonder if the bed would take her weight. She felt the twang of bedsprings every time she moved, and it would take hardly any effort to pick the whole thing up and walk across the room with it.

But with the sun pouring through all the thin curtains, it was lovely waking up in this, her own small space.

The tall windows actually looked in dire need of repair. The frames were rotting and in places, the large panes of glass didn't quite fit. The room must get very chilly in winter. Otherwise, it was a lovely room but barely private. Being used to her own room and never having had any brothers or sisters to share it with, Letitia found the idea of going to bed with lots of other children, all of them much younger than herself, rather odd.

And what strange children they were. The small girl was like an old woman, fussing over her sister. Letitia was sure the injured girl couldn't really be her sister – she didn't look like she was from the colonies at all.

Letitia would actually have loved a sister or a brother; she wouldn't mind which. Perhaps she could adopt one too? And what is it with that girl in the kitchen? Because Letitia was sure that she was a girl, in spite of her being dressed like a boy under her cook's apron and especially in spite of them calling her Brian? Letitia was perfectly aware that she herself was wearing something like boy's athletic shorts under her skirt but there was a good reason for that.

This kitchen person had that condition that she'd read about in one of her grandfather's journals. They referred to it as mongolism in the journal, but the new name was Down's syndrome, so there probably wasn't a good reason for her boys' clothes other than she must like wearing them. Maybe that was good enough?

There was another little curtained area in the diagonally opposite corner, and one spare bed without curtains, near hers. Letitia was pleased that Miss June recognised that she'd need some privacy, although a private bathroom was not on offer. She rummaged for her washbag and followed the sound of splashing and shrieking to the communal bathroom, a long room with a row of sinks with nice bars of soap and knitted flannels for each child. She did her ablutions and spruced herself up in front of the mirror while the younger children jostled and scrubbed each other in one big morning wash.

Miss June appeared at the door of the bathroom. 'Two minutes until breakfast. Ah Letitia, how did you sleep?'

'Very, er ... interestingly,' was the most accurate way Letitia could think of to describe her night.

'Oh good, there's some breakfast for you downstairs, the children have had theirs.'

Miss June then turned her attention to the children. 'All done? Teeth? Hair? Behind your ears? That's a favourite hiding place for dirt.'

'Yes Juuuuuune,' they all said in unison. And, as if Miss June had waved a magic wand, fourteen heads of hair, well-brushed, parted and, in some cases, plaited, filed out of the bathroom under her nose. Amongst them, the under-the-table albino boy from the previous evening was easy to spot. His little white dog was waiting for him. The dog rolled over onto its back as soon as the boy appeared.

'Time to play, Frank!' The boy gave him an enthusiastic rub. The dog righted itself and licked the boy's face as enthusiastically in return, its tail wagging like an aeroplane propeller.

Letitia obviously wasn't needed in this well-ordered and happy establishment. She wasn't needed in this town but she was definitely needed in Southampton, so she really must get going. Who knew when Grandma would take it upon herself to come home again? This was Letitia's opportunity to get some real medical practice.

She knew why she was here – falling asleep, waking up in a panic and getting off the train in Nettlefield rather than Southampton, was why. And it was a lucky mistake. If she was honest, she did have a few flutters about her first adventure. For Letitia, coming from the very small town of Threep, Nettlefield had looked big enough to be Southampton. As the train was crossing a busy road, much busier than Threep anyway, and at quite a height on what she later found out was a viaduct bridge, she'd mistaken Nettlefield Creek for Southampton Docks!

If she had stayed on the train, she'd never have been able to tend to the ratty looking girl with the very messy red hair. Not that the girl was grateful though.

Letitia sat on the bed, pushed her clean underwear to the bottom of the case and made a mental note to not forget her bandages.

She clipped her case shut and followed the children downstairs.

In the living room, Letitia saw a place set for her at the table. She perched on the end of the bench. William, the troublesome young man who worked in the kitchen, placed a bowl of porridge drizzled with honey in front of her.

She hurriedly scraped her bowl as clean as was polite and joined the last of the children at the front door to give her thanks and say her goodbyes.

Miss June was checking shoelaces and tucking in vests before the children went out to play, it being a Saturday morning.

When it was her turn, Letitia shook the matron's hand. 'Thank you very much for having me, Miss June. I'll be on my way now. The ship will soon be here.'

'It's been our pleasure, but are you sure? Is there somebody at home who might like an address for you?'

'No, no one, and thank you, yes, I'm absolutely sure,' said Letitia wondering what Elsie was up to with the house all to herself.

'Well, take some sandwiches for the journey. Brian can whip them up really quickly.'

'I have made some already,' said Brian who happened to be crossing the hall with a pile of dirty bowls, presumably on her way to the kitchen.

Brian soon returned with a parcel of sandwiches wrapped in greaseproof paper. 'They're corned beef, my favourite,' said Brian.

Letitia took them gratefully and noticed how Brian's eyes sparkled with pleasure. Letitia threaded her way through the busy orphanage playground. At the gates, she took one look behind her and gave a final wave to Miss June, who waved back in return.

Letitia crossed the road behind a tram turning out of the shed next door and made her way up to the station. It would have been a lot more fun to run up the bank and maybe balance on the railway bridge parapet wall, but she decided against attracting too much attention.

She assumed she'd have to buy a new ticket, so Letitia joined the queue in the ticket office behind an older woman with a very downturned face wearing a large hat of the type Grandma might wear.

'The Spaniards have got a devil of a lot to answer for,' said the older woman, 'overcrowding our country – first it was two thousand, now its four.' She flapped the morning paper at a man in front of her in the queue.

Letitia bought her ticket with the coins from her purse. She was pleased to see the neatly folded five pound note still there with Grandfather's card. She clipped the purse shut, tucked it inside her jacket pocket, and left the complaining woman in the ticket office. Heads turned to look at Letitia, then turned away. In Threep people would have said hello and smiled, maybe because Grandfather had been mayor and a respected member of the council. But how different was this, not like Threep or even the orphanage at all. Letitia was certainly glad to be going to Southampton.

On the platform, the woman brushed past her without a single excuse or pardon me. Letitia gladly crossed the footbridge to the other platform. She heard distant chuffing and hurried down the steps to the other side. Steam billowed as the train for Southampton came into the station.

A man raised his hat to her in a friendly way, 'After you, miss,' and allowed her to board the train first. This man would do very well in Threep.

'Thank you, very kind of you, sir.'

As Letitia looked up, she caught sight of another man, further down the train, and in spite of his hat pulled low over his face, she recognised his jacket with the sheepskin collar. He must be quite warm in that. It was the man called Harry, who'd come to take Miss June Lovelock out to the dance. Letitia waved, hoping he would look up.

He was carrying a large wooden box. It looked about the size of a typewriter. Those things were very heavy. Perhaps he needed help. She could offer. He was only the next door down; they'd be in the same carriage. She waved at him and called 'yoohoo' as Grandma did sometimes, especially when she couldn't remember a person's name.

But the man pulled his hat lower and moved further down the platform to a different carriage.

Oh well, Letitia got on the train and found a seat. She rubbed the velvet pile back and forth absent-mindedly as the train got up steam and started out of the station. People are certainly strange and confusing here in ... where was she again? She read the name on the sign as they left the station. 'Nettlefield,' oh, yes.

More and more people piled on the train as they neared Southampton Docks. This train went all the way there, how convenient! Are all these people travelling to the docks to greet the Spanish children? Or maybe to help with the rescue effort, like herself. Four thousand, the horrible woman in the ticket office said. Were they all children?

Two women in much more modern cap-style hats were talking about some people they knew from Southampton, who'd gone to Spain to fight for democracy, The fascists were being helped by Mr Hitler in Germany and were actually bombing the Spanish, their own people, women and children. Letitia thought Southampton must be a really kind place if they were prepared to do all this for people they didn't know. And she was going to help too! This is how you make the world a better place, by helping.

The train was slowing down.

'Next stop, Southampton Central!' called the guard, walking down the corridor.

Letitia wasn't going to make that same mistake again. She needed the stop after that for the docks. Feeling the excitement bubble up inside her, she sat on the edge of her seat clutching her father's bag.

Through the steam, on the platform side of the train, Letitia could see a tide of people heading for the doors. But on her other side, she saw another train also waiting at Southampton Central Station. Letitia's train was positioned to give her an almost perfect view into the carriage alongside hers.

That man, Harry, Miss June's gentleman friend, was in a compartment with three other men. She could see the wooden box on the seat. A young man, perhaps a few years younger than Harry, was resting his arm on it. A larger older man had his back towards the window, but an elderly man with a white beard and very impressive white moustache was facing her, talking to the large man. Harry seemed to be resting his eyes.

She only had perhaps a minute to look before both trains started moving, in opposite directions.

The guard was passing outside in the corridor.

Letitia jumped up with her bag and beckoned the guard.

'I've clipped your ticket, miss. We'll be at the docks in a few minutes.'

'Thank you, yes,' said Letitia. 'But what I want to know is, where was that other train going?'

'Oh, that would be the express to London, miss.' The guard checked his watch, then strode along the corridor declaring, 'Next and final stop, Southampton Docks! All change!'

The train pulled in almost to the water. There were lots of people milling about, but she couldn't see any ship loaded with children. 'They won't be off that boat until tomorrow,' said a man in a flat cap marching across the quayside carrying a broom, 'so you all might as well go home for now.'

Home? Letitia couldn't go home. Oh, perhaps she should have stayed with Miss June for a second night. But never mind, she still had her five pound note. She would have to find somewhere to stay.

Outside the docks, near the railway tracks she passed a very elegant building standing proudly on the corner, The South Western Hotel. She must have passed it on the train. The perfect place and so convenient. Grandma would certainly approve.

She straightened her jacket, hitched up her undershorts and smoothed her skirt. She patted her curls into order. If she'd only remembered a hat, her hair wouldn't matter so much. Letitia made a mental note of that for her next adventure. She'd write a more comprehensive list and perhaps not travel quite so lightly.

Under a glass canopy, she marched through the columns either side of the door and across the plush blue carpet up to the reception.

'Yes ... miss,' said the man behind the counter, pursing his lips as he shuffled some papers.

'I'd like a room please.'

'Really. Our tariff starts at five pounds for one night.'

Five pounds! That was all she had. But Letitia figured this wasn't the kind of place to show such dismay.

She took her purse from her pocket.

'The usual practice is to pay when you check out. But I think you'll only be staying the one night.'

Why would he think that? And then she realised this man did not want her to stay more than one night.

Letitia removed the five pound note, unfolded it and slid it across the counter.

The receptionist picked it up in the tips of his thumb and first finger as if it were dirty. His cheeks formed two hollows in his face.

These people were everywhere it seemed. Except in Threep, of course.

Empty now, except for Grandfather's card with the name and address of the person she should contact if she ever needed help, Letitia clipped her purse shut and tucked it back in her jacket pocket. It occurred to her that since she had now spent all her money she might well need the details of the Sir somebody or other on the card.

With long bony fingers, the receptionist swivelled the hotel register round. 'Sign here,' he said and indicated the pen in its holder. He picked some keys off a large board of keys and empty hooks on the wall behind him. A display of clocks beside the keys showed the time in different cities of the world. In London, it was midday.

After signing her name Letitia Zara Ketton, she replaced the pen in its holder and slid the register back across the counter.

'Room 305, fourth floor,' said the receptionist through his pursed lips.

A porter in a jaunty cap and matching bolero jacket scurried up behind Letitia. 'Carry your bags, miss?'

'Er ... bag,' said Letitia 'I'm sure I can manage, thank you.'

'Let me get the lift for you anyway, miss,' said the porter with a kind smile.

Letitia would rather have taken the grand staircase, but she didn't want to discourage the porter's niceness, so she allowed him to usher her inside the lift.

As the porter was pulling the metal grille across, a man in a panama hat slipped inside too. He was a very handsome man, with a narrow line of moustache on his top lip rather like Errol Flynn. 'Third floor,' he said, immediately turning his back on the porter and Letitia.

A strong smell of cologne, such as Grandfather might have used for special mayoral occasions, filled the lift.

As they chuntered up through the hotel floors, Letitia was trying very hard to work out why this man looked so familiar.

5

The Broom Cupboard

Saturday, 22nd May, Nettlefield

IT DIDN'T TAKE LONG for Fingers to get back to her old self. She'd slept all night, not that Baby had. Every half hour, Baby had to wake herself up from the pile of cushions on the floor and lean over Fingers to check that she was still breathing. Though, because Florrie Fingers could snore for England, Baby didn't have to get off her cushion bed every time.

The nest of cushions taken from June's story corner and piled on the sickbay floor had looked very cosy. A year ago, Baby would have been really made up with somewhere like that to sleep. But the cushions slid about, and waking up mostly on the hard floor had given her a crick in the neck. Baby really had gone soft.

The sun shone bright outside when Baby finally got up. She stretched every muscle she could and hoped she hadn't missed breakfast. Fingers, still sprawled over the sickbay bed, muttered through the end of a dream.

At the table in the orphanage living room, Baby tucked in to a bowl of honeyed porridge delivered by Brian. It looked like that goody-goody Letitia had scarpered.

'She went on the train,' said Brian, 'June waved her off. But I expect we'll see her again.'

'What makes you say that?' asked June, who sat down next to Baby at the table.

'She seems like one of us,' said Brian. She pressed her lips together and nodded as if to say there was nothing else to be said on the matter.

Whatever Baby thought about Letitia, Brian just knew these things.

'Brenda, my dear, everything was delicious.' An old man with wispy grey hair, carrying a tray of dirty dishes, appeared at the double doors behind June Lovelock.

'Dad, I was coming to get that.' Brian reached for the tray.

'No trouble at all my dear, it's the least I can do after you've fed me so admirably.' Since being let out of the asylum at Christmas, Brian's dad had been living in the cottage tucked under the railway bridge next to the orphanage. Baby and the other girls had spruced it up for him in the Christmas holidays while The Lillie was getting fixed and June was getting a few more alterations done to the orphanage to try to make the place more homely.

Nobody could remember the last person to live in the cottage before Brian's dad, or what came first – railway bridge or cottage? But who would want to live under a bridge with trains rattling across it all day long? Fortunately, Brian's dad, Mr Alexander Shaw, who was a scientist, seemed to like it.

'I was going to make a cake,' said Brian, 'would you like to help?'

'I most certainly would,' said Brian's dad and followed Brian out to the kitchen, still carrying his tray.

'Well Baby,' said June, 'would you like to do some writing practice now, as everyone's busy and Fingers is still recuperating?'

'Yeah, shall I write to Sophie?'

'Good idea, I'll get some paper and a pencil for your first draft, Baby.' June Lovelock had been helping Baby with her spelling and writing. June agreed with Baby that she and Fingers weren't quite ready for school yet, Fingers even less so than Baby. 'You have to understand how they've had to live for most of their lives,' said June to anyone who disapproved.

Baby had loved Sophie from the moment she dragged Baby out from underneath a horse last October, saving her life. She was like an angel from heaven to Baby. Then Sophie went and got kidnapped by that devil Underwood, Ida's uncle. But it was Ida that had found Sophie, nailed up in one of his coffins ready for shipping out to the Nazis. Perhaps Baby ought to write to Ida too. Though she might be coming home soon to see her little sister, Bonnie. Baby didn't have as much of a chance to miss Ida as she did Sophie. These were strange feelings, different to how she felt about Fingers. Fingers was like another arm to her, or heart ... Baby couldn't quite understand it all.

Would Baby tell Ida about Harry's odd behaviour with the stretcher in the kitchen cupboard? He was Ida's friend first after all. Though she was pretty sure it wasn't the stretcher he was bothered about.

It was funny that it was another kind of wooden box, not coffin-shaped this time thank goodness, that was troubling Baby. And she was sure that Harry had something to do with it.

'Here you are.' June slid a new sheet of paper on to the table with a perfectly sharpened pencil. 'I'll have a look through, if that's all right, after I've sorted Mother out.' She patted Baby on the shoulder as she left the big living room.

Baby started with Dear Sophie, but that was as far as she got because now she couldn't stop thinking about Harry and about that box. If there's one thing that could put a person off writing a letter it would be wondering what's inside a mysterious box at the back of a cupboard.

She left her paper on the table, then tiptoed across the hall and into the kitchen.

Brian and her dad, both in clean orphanage aprons, were looking through recipe books.

'Cooking's only another science,' said Brian's dad.

'Yes, Dad,' said Brian arranging some ingredients on the big old oak table in the middle of the kitchen.

Baby was expecting to ask them for the key, but there it was back in the lock. She turned it, but that only locked the door again, so she turned it back.

'Are you looking for something?' asked Brian.

'Oh, nothing really. Just something I saw when I got the stretcher out yesterday.'

'Ooh, let me see – what was it?'

'A wooden box,' said Baby, 'I was wondering what was inside it.'

'Not Pandora's, I hope!' said Brian's dad, beating some butter and sugar together in a bowl.

But when they'd reached the far end of the cupboard, all Brian and Baby found was the coat that had been on a hook, now in a pile with all the old aprons on the floor. 'Didn't this used to belong to Harry?' said Brian picking up the old coat. 'If he doesn't want it, Dad could have it.' She slung it over her arm and backed out of the cupboard with Baby.

Brian held the grey coat by the shoulders as high as she could for her dad to see. 'Would you like to wear this, Dad?'

He rubbed the lapel between his fingers. 'It's a fine coat with plenty of wear still in it. I wonder where it came from?'

'It was Harry's, from the war when he flew the planes,' said Brian.

'Really? It was his?' He lifted one of the sleeves. 'Look at all these threads. He's unpicked all the badges.'

Baby caught Mr Shaw's eye and was sure he'd had the same thought.

Why would Harry do that?

6

The Arrival of the Habana

Saturday 22nd May – Sunday 23rd May, Southampton

IT WAS ONLY A FEW HOURS AGO that Letitia was waking up in a roomful of poor Nettlefield orphans. Now, here she was on third floor of Southampton's very grand South Western Hotel, trying to amuse herself with her father's old medical handbook.

Letitia had found herself unlocking her bedroom door at the same time as the fragrant man from the lift was unlocking his. He had the very next room. It troubled her that she couldn't place him. Being in such close proximity to a gentleman, perhaps it wasn't quite the done thing to strike up a friendship? But had she been unintentionally rude by not saying hello?

Letitia decided not to worry about it, as tomorrow she would be so busy with the Spanish refugees, a little rudeness would 'pale to insignificance' as Grandma would say. She returned to the chapter on causes of forgetfulness in the elderly. She could only hope. Grandma had the memory of an elephant.

The room's enormous oak-framed bed was the complete opposite to the flimsy metal one Letitia had slept on at the orphanage. She stroked the hotel bed's dusky pink satin bedcovers, lounged on the well-plumped chaise longue and sat on the velvet upholstered stool at the dressing table. She surveyed a collection of glass perfume bottles. She tried each bottle in turn, dabbing behind her ears, on her wrists, even inside her blouse, until she ran out of places. This lavish room had cost all the money she'd brought with her, so Letitia was determined to get good value from it.

Through the window, she saw the docks and the river, which according to the guidebook on the bedside table was called Southampton Water. The guidebook also said the green haze in the distance was the New Forest. Although at almost a thousand years old, it was far from new. Outside the window, she spotted a useful ledge and a handy drainpipe, but the view was so good, she didn't even think about climbing up to the roof.

She was certainly hungry, but money for food was now going to be a problem. Letitia flumped on her belly across the enormous bed and looked for a more interesting chapter. She shouldn't waste this opportunity to apply herself to medical study. Though it would be more fun if Elsie were here too.

Outside her door she heard voices. She knew it was rude to eavesdrop, so she tried to shut them out by concentrating on her book. But the voices were hard to ignore.

'What are you doing here, Rosamund? You're not supposed to be here until tomorrow.'

'But Easton, I have done my best. You have given me very little support. Girls! Girls! Come out of there.'

'Señor Fitzgerald, we want to stay here, we like it here.'

The door banged shut and the voices became more muffled.

Rosamund? Letitia was sure that was Miss Grenville's first name. Was it Miss Grenville? The same Miss Grenville that came to visit Grandma on coronation day? It sounded just like her and she was coming to Southampton after all.

Of course! The man next door was Miss Grenville's fiancé. That was why he looked so familiar. Letitia had seen his photograph. He was certainly very handsome.

She should say hello.

Letitia got up off the bed and reached for the doorknob. But the crash of pottery smashing and the thud of a heavy object falling resounded through the wall between the two rooms. It was followed by shrieking and giggling and what could only have been Miss Grenville's voice calling, 'Easton, no!'

Miss Grenville sounded like she needed help.

That ledge outside the window was just wide enough. Perhaps if she just took a peek to make sure Miss Grenville was all right?

Letitia took off her shoes, a smart new pair of heeled lace-ups, and manoeuvred the dressing table out of the way, taking care with the perfume bottles. She pushed open the window and enjoyed the warm breeze. She climbed through. Crouching on the sill, she realised exactly how high up she was. It was only one more floor than their house in Threep, but the ceilings on each floor were twice if not three times as high. The people walking by on the path below looked the size of tin soldiers. Perhaps this wasn't such a good idea.

Perhaps now was the time to say 'hello.'

She climbed back inside, slipped her feet back into her shoes, retied the laces and brushed herself down.

She heard a door slam in the corridor and a loud wail from the room next door.

Letitia ventured into the corridor – there was no sign of whoever had slammed the door, though she did think she heard the lift grinding. The carpet was so plush it was perfect for creeping, even in one's shoes.

The door to the next door room was not quite shut. Letitia knocked anyway.

Through the gap, Letitia could see Miss Grenville standing in the middle of the room surrounded on the floor by broken glass and a wash basin in pieces. The woman was holding her belly, but failing to control her sobs and sniffing more than ever. Two girls, maybe a bit older than Letitia, were sitting on the bed smirking at each other. The man, Mr Easton Fitzgerald, Miss Grenville's fiancé, was nowhere to be seen.

One of the girls, who were young women really, pointed at Letitia. 'Señora, look!' The young woman tugged on Miss Grenville's arm.

Letitia pushed the door open a little further. 'I just wondered if everyone was all right. Can I help?' But Miss Grenville, standing there in a sniffy, sobby daze wasn't listening.

The young woman who'd pointed, strode over. 'No,' she said quite rudely and pushed the door shut in Letitia's face.

All very strange. And concerning.

But Miss Grenville was strange. Perhaps that was all there was to it. But those girls were Spanish. Where had they come from? Certainly not off the Habana. But then Miss Grenville did say her fiancé was part of an advance party. Perhaps they were too.

What little she saw of them, Letitia didn't like.

Though her belly was horribly empty, Letitia woke up the next morning when the sun was high and bright in the sky. She tore out of bed and flung back the curtains. Hundreds, maybe thousands of people were heading for the docks.

She must run. She had no time to worry about Miss Grenville or her fiancé. They were adults after all. She should look for someone more stable to volunteer with.

Letitia ran. All the way, her bag banged against her leg. She skipped over the railway tracks and pushed through the cheering crowds: 'Mind out, miss!' 'Eeow, that was my toe!' 'Hey! Look everybody, it's nearly 'ere!' Letitia watched the steamship Habana sail into dock, heaving with bodies. She spotted a priest in black robes and maybe a lady teacher. But they were swamped by thousands of children leaning out of the windows on the lower decks, over the rails on the top deck, waving hankies for flags. Some of the boys were even climbing the masts. Though in her experience, boys were less adventurous when it actually came to it. Less to prove, she supposed.

Everybody cheered and waved as rickety ladders were lowered to the quayside. Nurses in crisp white uniforms set up station along the ladders, and the first children were let off under their watchful eyes to be met by official-looking men in suits. The children were quite dishevelled and, when a snaking line of them passed Letitia, the smell of sickness was very strong.

The children clutched younger brothers and sisters or bundles of belongings. Some cried, searching for friendly hands to hold. But they all wore little hexagonal tags, like gift labels. The nurses took them into the back of a lorry and when they came out, they had another label – a flappy rectangular one this time, tied on their wrists – and they smelled strongly of disinfectant. Of course, quarantine checks; this was exactly where Letitia was needed. She ducked under the barrier and strode towards the lorry.

One of the suited men stepped out in front of her. 'Er, miss, where are you going?'

'Over there.' She pointed at the lorry. 'I'm here to help,' she said, and showed him her medical bag.

'I don't think so, miss, back behind the barrier please.'

'But ...'

'No buts, this way.'

Oh dear, she would have to find Miss Grenville now. Miss Grenville would vouch for her.

But with the sun in her eyes and all these people in the way, looking for Miss Grenville was going to be impossible.

After the lorry, the ladies with clipboards took the children to line up at makeshift trestle table desks, where more ladies from the Spanish Relief Committee were sitting with pens at the ready.

A clipboard lady marched in front of Letitia, leading a long line of children across the railway tracks to where double-decker motor coaches were parked by the dock buildings. A small boy struggling to keep up dropped his teddy. Letitia picked it up. 'Here you are, don't lose him,' she said in Spanish, useful at last.

'Oh, per favõr, señorita,' said the boy, who was about seven years old. His face was dirty with dried tears, so he certainly didn't want to lose his teddy, which he clutched even more tightly to his chest. He smiled as best as he could at Letitia.

She so felt for this little boy, labelled like somebody's Christmas present. She read the hexagonal card pinned to his jacket on a string, 'Expedición a Inglaterra' with his number, No 3867. His teddy had one too, No 3868. The boy untied it from around the teddy's neck and gave it to Letitia.

'Oh no, that's yours.' Letitia tried to return it, but the boy was whisked back in line by a lady with a clipboard.

The same lady grabbed the shoulder of Letitia's jacket. 'Come along, young lady. What are you doing over here? That should be pinned to your lapel.' She took the hexagonal label and, with a pin that she produced from her own pocket, fixed the label onto Letitia at the same time as redirecting another snaking line of children.

'But I'm here to help.' Letitia showed off her medical bag.

The clipboard lady was not listening to Letitia's protests. 'I don't expect you understand, but we must get you processed as quickly as we can.' And she pushed Letitia into line before she whisked off to yet another long queue. Letitia was stuck like a sardine in a sandwich.

She caught sight of her hotel neighbour, Miss Grenville's fiancé, what did she call him? Easton? Yes, Easton Fitzgerald. He was standing over his bunch of children, all about eleven years old. Mr Fitzgerald was herding them away from the others. They didn't look well, so that was perhaps why. But wasn't he was supposed to be a teacher?

This was getting Letitia to where she wanted to go, although not as the helper she intended to be. As soon as she arrived at the camp, where things might be a little calmer, she would set the matter straight. With a second label tied to her wrist, Letitia found herself stepping onto the platform of a double-decker motor bus in a queue of motor buses waiting to leave the docks.

The driver from the bus behind them shouted out of his window. 'You off to Nettlefield too?'

'No, it's just you, mate,' said the conductor standing on the platform at the back of Letitia's bus.

The driver on the bus bound for Nettlefield shook his head. 'Nettlefield's well out of my way. I won't be back in time for me dinner. The missus'll be right put out.' He leaned on the steering wheel while Mr Fitzgerald shooed his children on board.

The conductor on Letitia's bus turned his attention to her, 'Come on, young lady. There's more to load, you know,' and he urged her up the steps to the top deck, a tightly packed queue of children following closely behind.

Letitia sat down by a window. Two small boys sat beside her, squashing her up against the glass. She kept a firm grip on the handle of her bag, balanced on her knees.

The bus for Nettlefield with the disgruntled driver pulled up alongside Letitia's bus as they were leaving the docks. All the children on its top deck were sitting quietly, except for the two young women from Miss Grenville's hotel room. They were sitting behind Mr Fitzgerald, squabbling over a magazine.

Letitia noticed that like the two young women, the younger wan-looking children, had no labels, hexagonal or otherwise, pinned to their lapels or tied to their wrists.

7

A Spanish Invasion

Sunday 23rd May, Nettlefield

AFTER BREAKFAST, Baby was sitting at the table in the orphanage living room trying to finish her letter to Sophie that she'd started the previous day, when she heard the telephone ring in the hall.

'Oh, so soon,' said June to the person on the other end of the telephone line. 'But I thought they'd be at the camp for a week or so at least. They'll have to top and toe until we can get some more beds sorted out ... Oh good. So, we'll see you ... I beg your pardon, did you just say two more, so four young people altogether? And they're how old? Oh well, I'm sure we can find some extra beds. But do you really think we're the best place for them ...? Of course, yes, I understand, yes of course we can have them ... Really, you've seen it ... I'm not sure ... Yes, yes, I'll see what I can do ... Certainly, considering the terrible situation at home, I'm sure everyone will be agreeable for a short while. Goodbye, Mr Fitzgerald, see you, er ... shortly.'

Baby felt a few goose pimples pop up on her arms. She wondered what June was agreeing to.

June padded into the living room and leaned over the table. 'We're getting our first group of refugees this afternoon. I can only hope they speak Spanish. I don't have a single word of Basque. I shouldn't be uncharitable, I know, but we're not really ready. I know this is silly of me, but I can't help thinking if Mother had been well enough to go to church this morning, I wouldn't have been here to answer the telephone, then we wouldn't be in this situation. They'd have had to find somewhere else. Not that I'm not absolutely very pleased to help these poor children, but it's the older ones and where he wants to put them.'

Baby knew what June was about to ask. She remembered that man on Friday, Mr Movie Star, checking out The Lillie ... How did he know about it? 'Perhaps you should ask Bri about using The Lillie?' Baby said diplomatically. Though to tell the truth, she didn't want The Lillie taken over any more than she hoped Brian would. But on the other hand, when they, Baby and Fingers, arrived in Nettlefield, they were put up in The Lillie as friendly as anything. She should do the same for these Spanish kids, who, she reckoned, had had a far worse time than her and Fingers. They'd had bombs dropped on them. Baby and Fingers had never had that.

Brian was as hospitable as ever. 'Of course they can stay in The Lillie,' she said, buttering piles of bread on the table in the kitchen, beside a rack of freshly baked biscuits of all different sizes. Brian had a very good explanation for the size thing. 'Some people might not be hungry for a big one,' she said.

As well as Brian's biscuits, the delicious smells of roast meat seeped out of the oven. Cook chopped carrots at the other end of the table. 'Does that mean we have to double up on teatime?' she said.

'It certainly looks that way,' said June.

'Brian, you'll have to slice up another loaf or two at least, my girl,' said Cook. 'They're bound to be hungry.'

Brian's dad and Old Mrs Lovelock had gone for their after-dinner naps when Baby heard the grumbling sound of a motor bus engine outside.

'Hey! Sounds like they're 'ere!' shouted Robert Perkins with his mouth full of a second helping of roast potatoes. Frank the dog popped out from underneath the table.

Though Baby's roast dinner had barely settled in her belly, she jumped onto the bench to look out the window.

Fingers, who was all recovered from her fall off the railway bridge, especially after a good dinner, climbed up too. 'Budge over,' she said squeezing in between Baby and Robert.

Baby could just about see the top deck of the motor bus.

'There's only a few kids on that top deck,' said Fingers, on tiptoes, pressing down on Robert's shoulder for a better look through the window. 'I thought there was meant to be thousands of 'em?'

'They might be all downstairs,' said Robert.

'Let me see, Robit.' Aggie, Robert's particular friend who'd lived her whole ten years at Nettlefield Grange, stood up on the bench too. As knives and forks clattered on clean plates, one by one, all the other kids joined them to see the new arrivals.

Frank took the opportunity to lick up titbits dropped by the children under the table.

'Come on everybody, down you get and let's go and say hello properly.' June pushed open the doors out to the hall and beckoned everybody outside. 'You too, Frank.'

After a final lick, Frank jumped down and trotted after Robert. Baby lagged behind. This Spanish lot arriving meant they were losing The Lillie and the thought of stowing away on that boat to America crossed her mind again. She unhooked her old green silk jacket off the hallstand and joined the others outside in a clump behind June Lovelock.

The children on the bus slowly stepped off the platform, looking around like they expected more bombs to drop on them any minute. Baby counted fourteen of them, exactly the same as the number of regular Nettlefield orphans. The Spanish kids lined up alongside the bus, the oldest no older than herself, maybe eleven years old. They all looked terrified.

A man, putting on his hat, stepped off the bus too. Baby immediately recognised him as her visitor from a couple of days ago. Behind him were two girls who looked about seventeen years old. Brown skin, sunglasses and glossy black curls bouncing just above their shoulders. They carried a smart new suitcase each.

Something about their looks reminded Baby of Letitia, the would-be doctor.

'Hola!' shouted June Lovelock and waved enthusiastically. The orphanage children around her, waved too. But the Spanish children from the bus, who were lined up against it, didn't seem to notice.

June stepped forward with her hand outstretched.

Mr Movie Star didn't seem to notice June's hand. He was sizing up the orphanage, in much the same way as he had The Lillie. The two glamorous girls gripped their cases and peeped over the tops of their sunglasses at the Nettlefield orphans.

And everyone, orphans, refugee kids, big girls and grown-ups more or less stayed put.

Apart from Frank the dog, who wandered off for a wee.

June shrugged as if to say, 'What happens next?'

A lady stepped unsteadily off the bus, still holding onto the conductor's pole. She was about the same age as June Lovelock, wearing a crumpled bottle-green suit and a matching battered felt hat. A boy, also about seventeen years old and looking very pleased with his muscles in a white open-necked short-sleeved shirt, jumped off behind her. He folded his arms across his chest and slowly scanned the orphanage playground.

Baby didn't like the look of that boy. Or the Lady.

A second boy, tall and thin, shy behind a curtain of black hair, jumped down behind him and tried his best to smile as confidently as his friend.

Fingers sauntered out through the large orphanage front door.

June grabbed her and Baby, and practically dragged them over to be inspected by this new untidy woman. 'Miss Grenville, isn't it? Can I introduce Baby and her sister Fing ... um, Florrie. They are refugees too, of sorts.'

Miss Grenville wasn't interested.

Until she was.

Not so much interested in Fingers, but in Baby and especially in her jacket, Baby's much-too-big-for-her green silk jacket.

Miss Grenville plucked at the fabric, leaned over Baby, sniffed and asked, 'Where did you get this?'

Baby felt the woman's eyes studying every bit of her face.

Taking no notice of the strange woman and her interest in Baby's jacket, Mr Movie Star Fitzgerald said, 'Miss Lovelock, I need to use your telephone. In the hall, I assume?'

'Yes, of course,' said June.

But Mr Fitzgerald was already taking his hat off on his way through the big front door.

Baby wriggled out of Miss Grenville's clutches and straightened her jacket as best she could. 'I didn't get it anywhere. It's mine.'

'Manners, Baby.' June put her hand on Baby's shoulder, light and gentle, nothing like the long arm of the law that Baby knew all too well.

But Baby didn't think this rude untidy woman deserved manners.

Mr Fitzgerald reappeared at the door, tapping his hat back on his head. 'It's all arranged. Children back on the bus, we will commence our ... erm, lessons immediately. You've all missed a lot of school. No time to waste chit-chatting here.'

'But it's Sunday?' said June Lovelock.

'I'm quite aware of that.'

And seeming to understand him perfectly, the younger Spanish children silently filed back on the motor bus, leaving the four Spanish teenagers in the playground, their eyes fixed on Miss Grenville.

But Miss Grenville didn't seem at all interested in the four young people or what the handsome Mr Fitzgerald and the younger children were about. She only had eyes for Baby.

The engine of the motor bus grumbled to life again.

Baby tried to hide behind Fingers and was very thankful when Mr Fitzgerald called from the platform of the bus as it was heading out of the orphanage gates. 'For heaven's sakes, Rosamund, attend to your charges.'

Three of the Spanish young people smirked as the strange woman, Miss Grenville, took in her surroundings. One of the glamorous Spanish girls gave Miss Grenville a little wave as if to remind her that they were there.

The three young people were not Baby's idea of people running away from a terrible war. Had they even been in Spain? The fourth, the taller bashful boy, hung back behind the other three. He folded his arms across his chest too. But unlike the one with muscles, he was trying very hard to hide behind the others.

Miss Grenville signalled to June. 'You have somewhere for these young people, I believe?'

'Yes, Baby, Florence and Brenda have vacated their own special ... quarters for your girls. My name's June Lovelock, but all the children call me June.' She offered her hand for Miss Grenville to shake.

Miss Grenville's eyebrows disappeared under the brim of her hat and took June's hand limply. 'Charmed,' she said with a sniff.

'Can we go and play now?' asked Robert.

'Yes, of course, all of you, off you go,' said June.

With whoops and cheers, the orphans ran for the roundabout, the swings, the slide and the see-saw.

With the orphans happily swinging, sliding, bouncing and making themselves dizzy on the roundabout, the two girls introduced themselves.

'My name is Maria,' said one, and the other, almost her twin, said, 'I am Regina.'

'Welcome,' said June, 'Can we help you with your cases?'

But the Spanish girls looked at each other, nodded and firmly gripping their cases, said 'We would like to go to the place where we stay.'

'Of course, of course, you must be so tired,' said June. 'And you, young gentlemen, I'm afraid we haven't quite finished making your room ready ...'

'We will guard these children while you do,' said the boy with the muscles. He marched over to the playground, cleared the roundabout of orphans, climbed on and ordered his shy friend to do the same.

'I will get a key,' Brian ran through the playground and back into the orphanage taking off her apron on the way. She returned in her cap, an old one of her dad's, dangling a key.

Fortunately, the orphans were happy enough with the swings, slide and see-saw. So June led Miss Grenville with Maria and Regina over West Street, up the hill to the station, past the stationmaster's office, the coal heap and through the neatly-clipped tunnel path to the dear old Lillie. Baby, Fingers and Brian followed.

In the little clearing, where the sun always found its way to shine, June stood aside to let Brian unlock the door with her key, but the door was still unlocked from Friday. It reminded Baby of the broom cupboard in the kitchen and the box.

'Welcome!' said Brian. If The Lillie belonged to anyone, it belonged to Brian, as it was where she used to live with her dad.

The Spanish girls pushed their way in front. They kicked off their shoes, dropped their cases inside the door and slammed it shut behind them before anyone, including Miss Grenville, had a chance to follow them in.

Brian's smile faded and her bottom lip trembled.

June put her arm around the girl's shoulder. 'They're probably really tired. You've done a very kind thing, Brian. I'm so proud of you for being hospitable.'

Brian's smile returned but without the sparkle in her eyes. In the sunshine, Baby and Fingers stared blankly at their home. A train whistled, birds chirrupped in the bushes and the girls from Spain laughed and chattered to each other, making themselves very much at home.

Miss Grenville, standing a little way apart, only had eyes for Baby's silk jacket.

'Rightio,' said June, pausing before the tunnel through the bushes, 'do you have everything you need?'

When the orphanage was so well stocked, Baby couldn't think of anything she needed. She could survive on next to nothing anyway.

'I haven't!' said Brian urgently, pointing her finger. 'I need some books.'

'Has your dad finished the others?' asked June.

Baby supposed he didn't take the whole lot with him to the cottage under the railway bridge because he didn't reckon on two Spanish girls taking the place over.

'He's read all his books. But I want some,' said Brian.

'Of course.' June made a little cough and knocked on The Lillie's door.

One of the girls, Maria or Regina, opened it. Her hair that had been pinned in a fashionable style, now cascaded over her face so only one eye was visible. 'Yes,' she said, tapping her toes impatiently.

'Maria?' said June.

'Regina,' said the girl, holding the door only half open.

'Could Brian here come in and get something she's left behind?'

'Very well,' Regina stepped aside, a frown making her face quite ugly.

Baby took a good look at both girls. There was very little to tell Regina and Maria apart. They were both glamourous, and both looked down their noses at Brian in her men's baggy trousers and cap.

Brian ignored the girls' glares as she ran her finger along her dad's library. Books of all shapes and sizes were lined up along the cupboards that ran along the far wall of The Lillie, from the stove to the lav door.

As soon as Brian stepped outside, carrying one very large book, the key turned in the lock.

'What did you choose?' asked June.

'These two,' said Brian, heaving the huge book over to show her.

Two books?

June read the spine, 'Computational Mathematics for Advanced Code and Cypher Decryption. What made you choose this one?'

'It was the biggest,' said Brian triumphantly. From inside the cover of the big book, she pulled out a very thin one with a paper cover, hardly a book at all. 'And this one was the smallest. It was my mum's.'

Baby couldn't quite read the title but on the front cover was a drawing of some mountains.

'May I look?' asked June Lovelock. 'I'd love to visit Scotland, and Glencoe is meant to be so beautiful ... '

Miss Grenville had sidled up to Baby again. She made Baby's skin prickle. The woman was very pale; she looked like she'd hardly ever been out in the sun. Though her nose was red and so were her cheeks in a very unhealthy way. But it wasn't that that made Baby feel uncomfortable ...

'Miss Grenville, when do you expect Mr Fitzgerald back again?' asked June.

'Today or tomorrow,' she said vaguely. 'He's my fiancé actually,' she added, just as vaguely.

'Will he need to stay with us at The Grange? And the children, when will they be back? I'm not sure if we'll have enough rooms ...'

'No, he has accommodation elsewhere. He won't need to stay with you. But I will,' said Miss Grenville, with one long sniff and her gaze firmly fixed on Baby.

8

The Basque Children's Camp

Sunday 23rd May, North Stoneham, Southampton

LETITIA WONDERED WHY the children on the bus for Nettlefield didn't have labels. Had Mr Easton, Miss Grenville's fiancé, removed them because they had already been allocated accommodation?

Of course, given the situation, none of the Spanish children were exactly excited to have come across the sea on a big boat, in very choppy waters by all accounts, but the children heading for Nettlefield seemed to be emotionless. They were ... blank, drained.

Unlike the small whimpering boy sitting next to her on the top deck of the bus. As they motored through the town, he pressed himself to her side.

Letitia recognised the small boy as the same child who'd lost his teddy bear earlier. She felt his hand creep across her lap, searching for hers. It was warm when it squeezed her fingers and her heart squeezed with it.

Where the others had friends, brothers or sisters even, this poor little fellow seemed to be completely alone.

The other boy on their seat, perched right on the edge, was tossing his cap back and forth with a girl a few seats in front, making the best of the situation with a game of pig in the middle. Others copied, chucking caps, berets, apple cores ... anything. Every one of these children had hexagon labels in Spanish pinned to their chests, and parcel labels in English flapping round their wrists.

Over the noise, Letitia said in Spanish to her small friend, 'Don't worry, I'll look after you.'

The conductor popped his head up over the top of the stairs, opened his mouth as if to tell them to be quiet. When an apple core hit his cap, he changed his mind and disappeared downstairs again.

The small boy pressed closer to Letitia. She realised that this must be what it was like to have a little brother. She wriggled her other arm free and put it around his shoulder.

The boy dragged the back of his hand under his nose. 'My name is Ramón,' he said in Spanish.

She replied similarly, 'And I am Letitia.'

He dried his eyes with his sleeve and pushed his teddy out of sight down his jersey.

They motored on through Southampton, around a castle-like arch in the middle of the road while a tram went through it. It looked like the town was busy demolishing the arch; it was rather old-fashioned. They passed a huge brand-new building with a very tall clock tower, and not long after that they were in a tree-lined avenue. Through the trees, Letitia caught glimpses of a game of cricket being played in the afternoon sun. The sight of cricket made her think of tea and her stomach rumble.

The roads got bumpier and the bus joggled practically all the rest of the way. She spotted some gentlemen all togged up in golfing gear in the back of an open top car, motoring down a lane. Then, a moment or two later, some more golfers trudging along on foot in the same direction as the bus. Two boys scurried along, behind them, weighed down by the bags of golf clubs slung over their shoulders.

Finally, the bus arrived at the camp. It stopped at the end of a line of buses on the edge of the farmer's field, where men were digging ditches. In the distance, she could see rows of white tents and children, with armfuls of bedding, going in and out of them.

With Ramón's hand still firmly in hers, Letitia climbed down the stairs and off the bus. Together with the other children, they walked through the gate under a banner that said 'National Joint Committee for Spanish Relief Basque Children's Camp'. A warm breeze carried smells of the earth and things not so pleasant, but pleasanter than the sweatiness of the top deck.

Letitia was beginning to smell less than fragrant herself, so even though she was warm in the sun, she decided to keep her blue jacket on. She wished she'd remembered to put a few more pairs of knickers in her case, though.

Ramón only had his teddy, which was now peeping out of the neck of his olive-green jersey. 'Do you have a bag?' asked Letitia.

'With my brother,' he said.

'Oh, you have a brother, where is he?' Letitia looked all around the busy field for a boy running towards them to claim Ramón. But she could only see clipboard ladies rushing about, more ladies in aprons ladling out broth from big steaming pots, trestle tables of bedding, rows and rows and rows of white tents, and so many queues of children she couldn't begin to count them. Nowhere was there a brother pleased to see Ramón.

'He is gone.' Ramón's belly wobbled with a sob.

Letitia drew him to her and allowed another lady to put them both in one of the shorter queues. 'A drop of beef tea'll do you both the power of good,' said the rosy-cheeked woman in a white apron who ladled them out a mugful each. Letitia sipped the tea. It was hot and weak and the enamel mug burned her lip.

'There, that's much better, isn't it?' said a clipboard lady, scooping up everyone who'd finished into yet another queue for blankets and bedding.

The field was hard, no spring in it at all and littered with stones. Letitia's ankle twisted on one. Her heels were troublesome – she'd have been better off with no shoes at all.

As they shuffled along, the men digging ditches at the edge of the field occasionally leaned on their spades to take off their caps and mop their brows. They waved at the smaller kids, which made the little ones giggle.

A young woman behind a trestle table piled with blankets and pillows gave Letitia a strange bag. The young woman put her hands together as if to pray and then laid her head against them. 'For sleep,' she said.

Letitia felt her brow furrow. 'We sleep in this?' she said in English.

'Oh, you do speak English,' said the girl with the bag.

'I am English,' said Letitia.

'Didn't you come from Spain?' asked the young woman.

Letitia was about to answer no, but then thought that maybe this was how she could stay to help, so she said, 'I was caught up in it all, visiting my aunt in Bilbao.' She rubbed the coarse material between her fingers. 'And is this a sleeping bag?' she added.

'Yes,' said the young woman. She had something of a foreign accent, though not Spanish.

'But it looks like a flag.'

'That is what they were made from. We made them at school. I go to the School of Art in Bournemouth. I am learning how to tailor,' she said, pointing to the stitching. 'This is not tailoring. But it is a good thing we do to help people like me who have been forced from their country. Ten days ago these bags were flags hanging from the walls of our school to celebrate the coronation.'

Letitia felt that she was being sucked into the camp. If she didn't do something she would just become one of these thousands of children and young people. But there was Ramón waving to her from the other end of the table. He was pointing to the tent with the open flap on the end of the front row of white tents. He had attached himself to her and she liked that. Perhaps she'll just get him settled first.

Cries of apúrale, – hurry up, and a new word – mugi, which Letitia guessed meant the same thing in the Basque language, came from the children behind her in the queue. Letitia picked up her flag sleeping bag and joined Ramón.

It appeared they thought that Letitia was Ramón's sister. Of course! The label Ramón gave her must have belonged to his brother. It made her sad and happy at the same time. She really had acquired a little brother.

When they had sorted out their bedding and Letitia had stored her medical case safely under her camp bed, Ramón took her hand and led her outside again.

They were given an enamel bowl and spoon each. Into it another lady in an apron dished up some stew. Letitia could see some meat and vegetables and lots of split peas. Another lady gave them a hunk of bread and told them to go and sit down with a group of children picnicking on the grass.

Some of the children ate their stew hungrily while others looked dazed and confused. Letitia wondered how long she should keep up the pretence of being a Spanish refugee. Was it fair that she was eating food that was really for young people much worse off than herself?

But through a gap in the tent, arranged in such a way that you could see all the way to the fence that surrounded the field, she saw why she shouldn't blow her cover too soon.

That man, Harry, who had not acknowledged her at Nettlefield Station though she was being ever so friendly, was there with his wooden box again. He was now wearing a hat and a smart suit as if he'd been to work at the council. He was handing the box over to Mr Fitzgerald, Miss Grenville's fiancé.

Mr Fitzgerald took the box in both arms but Harry, Miss June's fiancé, she supposed, wasn't letting go. (Do all unmarried ladies have a fiancé? The thought reminded her of Grandma's threat to find someone like that for her). She shook that thought away and, over her soup spoon, watched him whisper into Mr Fitzgerald's ear.

Harry let go of the box and watched while Mr Fitzgerald opened the lid.

A smile slid onto Fitzgerald's face as he closed it again.

Oh, how much Letitia wanted to see inside that box.

Mr Fitzgerald placed the box carefully on the ground behind him, out of sight behind the tent, then reached deep into his trouser pocket. Was he going to pay Miss June's Harry?

Fitzgerald looked left and right and behind, though curiously not spotting Letitia. She supposed that as far as he was concerned, she was just one of several thousand, tired, hungry, traumatised, foreign children who were never going to take any notice of what he was doing. And even if they did notice, they couldn't tell anyone in a language they'd understand.

Mr Fitzgerald had found what he was searching for in his pocket and was handing it to Harry.

It wasn't something Letitia had ever seen in real life before, but she'd seen plenty at Threep's cinema.

The way it nestled neatly in Harry's hand. The way he weighed it for quality. The way he looked round furtively and the way he tucked the object, a revolver, inside his smart jacket, all persuaded Letitia that this man, this Harry, was up to no good.

94

9

Whatever the Plan Was, This Wasn't It

Sunday 23rd May, North Stoneham

LETITIA WATCHED HARRY turn up the collar on his jacket and pull his hat low over his face. She lost him for a moment between the tents. But he had to be heading for the gate, the only way in and out of the field, unless you jumped the fences, which was always an option.

A black van was parked just the outside the gate. Was that for his getaway? Behind it, children spilled out of the motor buses that were still arriving.

Past these tired and dazed children coming in, Miss June's Harry slipped out. He tipped his hat to the men working in the ditch and strode past the van. Wherever he was going, it was on foot.

Letitia thought about running after him. But her curiosity about the box was more pressing. If only she knew what was as dangerous as a gun? What would be its equivalence in value to do a straight swap like that? It was basic maths; an equivalence required equal values.

Over her bowl of stew, which though very welcome was too warm for such a summery evening, Letitia turned her attention back to the handsome Mr Fitzgerald. He now had the box and she'd made up her mind that she was going to find out what was inside it. Of course, it could be something quite innocent like medical supplies, which were indeed very valuable, but you wouldn't swap a gun for medical supplies, would you?

Letitia finished her meal and mopped round the bowl with the hunk of bread she'd been given. Ramón was asleep on the grass beside her, curled round his bowl of half-eaten stew. His mouth was shut and he was breathing deeply through his nose, while his teddy peeped out of his jersey. Letitia could see many kind ladies with clipboards and ladles to take care of him, so she got up and headed towards the spot between the tents where she'd witnessed the exchange between Harry and Mr Fitzgerald and where, as far as she could tell, Mr Fitzgerald remained.

She'd only gone a few steps, when she felt a small hand take hers.

'No Ramón,' she said in Spanish, 'you must go back. This may be dangerous.'

But his hand tightened round her fingers.

'All right,' she said in Spanish again, 'you watch out for me. If anyone follows after me, you distract them by crying.'

Before she could demonstrate what she meant, Ramón let her hand go, made a face and rubbed his eyes with his little fists. 'Si, señorita.'

Letitia was impressed. Had he done this before?

She sat him on the grass a few feet away from the tents, eating what was left of his bowl of stew.

Because men with guns in a children's camp was a very bad thing, Letitia was going to find out what was worth a gun.

In the early evening sun, reflecting golden off the white bell-shaped tents that lined the field in several rows, children with food in their bellies kicked a ball about. Their shadows were long in the grass, and over them, the sky streaked with pink made the whole place look heavenly.

Through this happy scene, Miss Grenville's fiancé, Mr Easton Fitzgerald, was on the move, his arms full of the mysterious wooden box.

Keeping her distance, Letitia followed him.

Mr Fitzgerald had reached the last bell tent when Letitia heard a loud wailing and a crying. She turned to see Ramón clutching his teddy, bawling and rubbing his eyes with his fists.

'There, there, little boy,' said a rather grand lady in a tweed suit and a hat with a feather, as she passed him. 'Yoo-hoo, Mr Fitzgerald! Could I have a word please?' She overtook Letitia, waving at Mr Fitzgerald with a hankie.

'Ah, Dame Janet, is there a problem?' Mr Fitzgerald stepped over ropes and pegs to meet her, carrying the wooden box as if it were as normal as a crate containing hunks of bread.

With no time to worry whether or not it was vacant, Letitia lifted a flap on the tent nearest to her and crept inside. She remembered from girl guides how people forget that tent canvas is no good for having a private conversation. She lifted a small ventilation flap, perfect for spying on Mr Fitzgerald and the grand lady.

The lady eyed Mr Fitzgerald's box. 'What's that you have there?'

'Only an old typewriter,' said Mr Fitzgerald, 'but the owner forgot to give me the key. It's useless, unfortunately, so I'm returning it.'

'What a dashed nuisance and such a bother for you, Mr Fitzgerald.'

It occurred to Letitia that good-looking people can get away with so much more than those not blessed with a handsome face.

The lady continued, 'I was actually going to ask if you think we have everyone now?'

Mr Fitzgerald looked up at the last motor bus pulling away from beside the field. 'Yes, certainly for today.'

'Jolly good,' she said and strode off.

Inside the tent, Letitia felt that small warm hand slip into hers again. She lifted the flap and led Ramón back out into the sunshine.

'Oh well done little boy, you've found your sister!' The grand lady who had been talking to Mr Fitzgerald waved her hankie again and carried on across the field to a group of less grand ladies with clipboards.

Of course, the bit about the key was rubbish. Letitia had watched Harry open the box. She had to stop Mr Fitzgerald taking that box away before she'd had a good chance to look inside it.

Mr Fitzgerald was picking up speed past the kitchen and laundry tents, heading for the gates and the black van.

Letitia whispered to Ramón, who immediately fell to the floor. He clutched his tummy and teddy, rolled on his back and cried louder than ever.

The group of clipboard ladies turned to see. The grand lady in charge beckoned Mr Fitzgerald back. 'Mr Fitzgerald, wait a jiffy! Do come here. Do you know this boy? Is he one of yours?'

'One moment, Dame Janet.' Mr Easton Fitzgerald opened the van's back door and put the wooden box inside.

He jogged back into the field towards the group of ladies surrounding Ramón.

Their expressions changed from concern to coy smiles as Mr Fitzgerald approached and they seemed to forget about the small boy on the grass at their feet. One lady patted her hair in place and squiggled to the front of the group. Another slid her hand into her bag, drew out a powder compact and dabbed her nose. They all fawned round the man with movie star looks, evidently thinking he was Errol Flynn.

Letitia ran through the gate to the van. She could just make out the word 'Underwood' painted over very poorly, in black, on the side. The door wasn't quite shut.

There was the box inside the van and behind the box, a heap of white sheets. She climbed in and lifted the lid of the wooden box. To her disappointment, as far as she could tell, it really was just a typewriter. But she only had time for the quickest of glances because the van door was opening.

Letitia had no choice. She curled up and pulled the white sheets over herself.

Somebody else was climbing inside the van.

She heard the catch quietly click shut.

The van creaked, one of the front doors slammed shut and the motor gurgled into life.

Whatever the plan was, this wasn't it.

10

Miss Grenville's Stare

Sunday 23rd May, Nettlefield

IN THE UPSTAIRS CORRIDOR, Baby waited behind June while she took a pile of old grey blankets down from the top shelf of the West Wing linen cupboard.

'Tell Alfredo and José that these are for sleeping on,' said June as she handed the pile to Baby. 'They'll have to do until we can sort out more beds. I've only got the one spare bedroom for Miss Grenville.'

Baby could just about see over the top of the blankets as she carried them further down the corridor to the Spanish boys' storeroom bedroom.

'And tell them it's nearly time for tea,' called June, tugging at more bed linen on a lower shelf.

The Spanish boys' room was one where the horrible old matron, Mrs Bullar, had stashed her hoard of food ready for the Nazi invasion that she was hoping for.

There was no window, only a single electric light bulb dangling from the ceiling, and the shelves all round the walls were bare. The orphans had polished off the old matron's private stash at Christmas and Alfredo, the Spanish boy with the muscles, was sitting on the only chair in the room, leaning back and his legs outstretched, ordering José, the tall shy one, where to sweep.

'June says these are for you ... to sleep on.' Baby laid her head on her hands to sign what she meant.

'Thank you, put them down there,' said Alfredo.

Baby felt his eyes on her as she laid the blankets on a swept patch of floor. 'She said it's time for tea too.' Baby didn't bother with another sign as it was obvious their English was as good as hers.

Baby caught José glancing at her through his dark fringe.

'You can go now,' said Alfredo and shooed her away. 'Tell your June we will eat here.'

'You can't, there's no table.' Baby actually surprised herself thinking that. Many's the time she'd sat on some old alley cobbles eating chips out of newspaper.

She was glad to go back downstairs and help set the table for tea.

Baby was glad that weird Miss Grenville had gone to sort out those two cocky girls in The Lillie. Though it made Baby sick to think of them in there, doing their hair and goodness knows what else.

From the landing at top of the West Wing stairs, Baby looked out the window across the orphanage grounds.

102

The Spanish children, one behind the other, were being led through the gates by none other than June's old landlady, member of Nettlefield Hands Across the Sea and Blackshirt, Mrs Tatler, in her old-fashioned suffragette hat. What was she doing with them? A worry was creeping onto Baby's shoulders, which she was finding hard to shake off.

Baby ran through the dormitory to the top of the main staircase in time to watch the horrible old lady bring them all in through the front door.

'Oh, Mrs Tatler.' June Lovelock, clutching two armfuls of pillows to her chest, stepped down into the hall to meet them. 'Thank you for bringing our guests back. Is Mr Fitzgerald with you?'

'Oh no, he still has important business to attend to at the church hall,' said Mrs Tatler.

'The church hall? I thought they'd gone to school. I know that would be a bit odd for a Sunday, but all of this is a bit odd isn't it?'

'Well, they did go to school,' said Mrs Tatler puffing herself up, her hat feathers ruffling. 'And it's no business of yours where they go to school.'

'As they are in my care, I rather think it is ...'

But Mrs Tatler was already shooing the children into the living room. 'Tea is ready for them, I assume ...'

'Nearly,' said June, following her old landlady and the silent Spanish children through the double doors.

103

Baby snuck in behind her too.

The only sounds the children made were the soft shuffles of their feet and tiny creaks as they each sat down on the bench in the space made for them by the Nettlefield orphans, bunched up on the other side of the table.

Mrs Tatler, her lips pursed, watched over them all.

Cook and Brian each pushed a trolley loaded with plates of sausage and mash through the doors, nudging Mrs Tatler further into the room.

Baby found a space on the Spanish kids' side of the table next to Fingers, who'd sat down at the end. With her dinner knife, Fingers was mock sword-fighting with orphan Aggie, sitting opposite her.

'Nothing wrong with you now, is there,' said Baby.

'Maybe I am made of rubber,' said Fingers over Aggie's giggles and the tinny clang of metal.

'I have to say,' said Mrs Tatler, standing over the Spanish kids and looking down her nose at Fingers and Aggie, 'our young Spaniards' behaviour is exemplary. Not a peep. As children ought to be, seen and not heard.'

'Thank you for walking them back, Mrs Tatler. Do you need to be getting home now?' said June, spitting a stray pillow feather out of her mouth. 'Florence, Aggie, please could you put your knives on the table.'

Fingers never needed telling twice when it was June that did the telling. Baby climbed over the bench and sat down between her sister and a Spanish boy who was sitting there like a shop dummy. She wanted to prod him, make sure he was actually a living person, but when Brian put his plate of sausages down, the boy tucked in like he hadn't eaten for weeks – maybe he hadn't.

'I'll be here tomorrow morning at eight-thirty to escort the children to their lessons,' said Mrs Tatler, heading for the doors at last.

'What about school? All the children could walk together,' said June.

'They'll be continuing their lessons with Mr Fitzgerald, he's made special arrangements. Much better that their schooling isn't, erm ... confused. '

'Oh. Well, I must take these pillows up to the boys. Do you know what the plans are for Alfredo and José?'

'They'll be needed here,' said Mrs Tatler with one last sniff in Fingers and Baby's direction.

'Needed here? What do you ...?'

'Eight-thirty sharp, Miss Lovelock,' said Mrs Tatler and saw herself out before June could press her for an answer.

Straight after tea, the Spanish kids trooped up to bed as silently and obediently as they'd come in. It was still too early for the orphans, even though it was school the next day.

Baby sat down at the cleared table to finally finish her letter to Sophie, for which June had given her a nice pen.

105

The orphans were either lounging about on the story cushions with books from the orphanage library or playing with some wooden bricks and a trainset on the floor. June was doing a jigsaw puzzle with Robert and Aggie on the other side of the table, while Fingers was getting a tune out of some rubber bands wrapped round an empty biscuit tin.

Miss Grenville staggered through the doors into the happy babble of contented children that filled the living room. A twig was stuck in her hair, so she looked like she really had been dragged through a hedge backwards. Perhaps she couldn't find the tunnel from The Lillie back to the station? It was getting dark.

'Ah Miss Grenville, you're back. Would you like to join us?' said June.

Miss Grenville waved her away with a sniff and sat down at the table anyway, only a little way down the bench from Baby.

Baby slid as far away from her as she could and continued with her letter, trying to ignore the woman. But Baby couldn't settle. Whenever she looked up, Miss Grenville was watching her, scanning her. Miss Grenville's face, rosy in the wrong places, was otherwise drawn and pale, but her expression determined and unblinking. Baby wanted to hide inside her jacket, but her jacket was hung up on one of the coat stands in the hall. She wanted to get it, but what if the woman followed her?

With nearly an hour to go before June sent the kids to bed, Baby blew the ink dry on her best copy and put the cap on the pen. She slid the letter and pen across the table to June for safe keeping. 'I'm a bit tired. I think I'll turn in,' she said.

June looked up from the puzzle where Robert was slotting in the last piece. 'Are you feeling all right, Baby?'

'Yeah, I'm alright.' But with a tiny glance sideways towards Miss Grenville, Baby tried to signal how uneasy she felt. Baby had had stares, of course she had, but this was weird. It was like someone had come along and glued all the stares and strange looks she'd ever had in her whole life, into one really hard one.

'Miss Grenville,' said June, 'I've made up a room for you downstairs, but perhaps you'd like a cup of tea in my office later, when the children are in bed? I'm really interested in the work of The Spanish Relief Committee.'

'If you would like,' said Miss Grenville followed by three joined-up sniffs.

While the woman was distracted, Baby slipped out through the living room doors. She unhooked her green silk jacket from underneath June's outdoor coat and hurried with it to the stairs.

Behind her the living room doors swung open and Miss Grenville lurched out into the hall.

Baby ran to the top of the stairs, feeling the weird woman's stare in her back as if it were a gun aimed to shoot.

11

A Bumpy Ride with a Mysterious Box

Sunday 23rd May, on the road

LETITIA COULDN'T HOLD her breath any longer and, after a gasp, caught a lungful of a damp musty smell. At least these sheets hadn't been used for some time.

The other person in the back of the van was moving closer and she felt a small familiar hand reaching under the cloth for hers.

She peeled the cloths away and there was Ramón crouching by the wooden box, smiling at her.

Letitia put her fingers to her lips and together they sat with their backs to the partition that separated them from Mr Easton Fitzgerald in the driver's seat. If she twisted and looked up, she could see the top of his well-oiled head through the partition window.

The time on her wristwatch said a few minutes past seven. She hoped they weren't going far. She felt every bump and rut in the road. Ramón snuggled into her and let the motion of the van lull him off to sleep.

Trying not to worry about where they were headed, Letitia had some time to think. Did that girl, Baby, know about Harry? Was she taken in by him too? Of all the young people that she met at that orphanage, the one called Baby seemed to be the most astute or at least the most suspicious. Of course, there was that girl, Fingers, that Letitia tried to help, but she was just plain grumpy. It then occurred to Letitia, perhaps they were suspicious of her, Letitia Zara Ketton?

She really ought to tell somebody in authority about the gun. But who to tell? These people at the camp were in authority, sort of. If she ever did go back to the orphanage, she would try to tell Miss June Lovelock. But she was walking out with the man! Would Miss Lovelock believe Letitia? She would definitely not be telling Miss Grenville – the woman was deranged, far from the right sort of person to be looking after children from a war zone.

Thinking back though, was it a typewriter? Remembering her glance inside the box, she had a feeling the typewriter was missing something. The keys were there, but there should also be a ribbon of ink and she was pretty sure that was missing. She was tempted to take another proper look inside the wooden box, but if

Fitzgerald did look back she would be in full view, and besides, that would wake Ramón.

But Letitia wanted to know. She gently laid Ramón on the sheets, and on her hands and knees reached for the lid of the box.

The car stopped and the driver's door opened.

Letitia sat back against the partition.

The back door clicked.

She was sure Mr Fitzgerald could hear her heart beating. She tensed every muscle in her body. He would look inside and find them and she'd be in such trouble.

At least he no longer had his gun. Miss June's suspicious gentleman friend had that.

But she heard some familiar voices, speaking in English but with a Spanish accent. 'Oh Easton, before you get that old thing out, come and see what we've done ...'

Letitia peeped up through the window in the partition and saw those girls, those label-less Spanish girls, drag Mr Fitzgerald through some bushes.

Letitia took Ramón's hand, opened the back door a little way and jumped out.

What a relief it was to get out of that horrible van.

It was still light, but her watch said it was nearly nine o'clock. They'd been in that van only forty minutes, not even an hour, but it felt a lot longer.

In Spanish, Ramón asked, 'Where are we?'

111

Letitia could see a coal heap, a large shrubbery and the railway station buildings!

They were back in Nettlefield. If she remembered rightly, the orphanage was only down a slope (or if feeling more adventurous, a roll through some long grass down a bank) and across the main road. Would they be pleased to see her back?

She brushed some of the wrinkles out of her skirt and combed Ramón's hair out of his eyes so they both looked a bit more presentable.

When Letitia looked up, she was surprised to see Harry, the man with the gun and now, with somebody in overalls on his arm that certainly wasn't that lovely Miss June Lovelock. Harry and this other person were walking out of the station buildings. A train was at that moment heading out of the station too, across the railway bridge.

In spite of the blue overalls that this new person was wearing, Letitia was pretty sure it was a girl, about her own age, white, and though tall, a bit on the scrawny side.

Letitia watched the two of them saunter together down the slope to the main road.

Letitia ran with Ramón to the top of the bank and yes, they were going through the orphanage gates, across the playground and into the orphanage through the front door.

She was aware of Ramón gripping her hand. She'd accidentally swapped her father's medical bag for this child. As she didn't know her father at all, she didn't know what he would have thought about that, but she was certain Grandfather would have approved. She was going to take much more care of Ramón than she had her bag.

'What are we going to do?' Ramón asked in Spanish.

The truth was, at that moment, Letitia didn't know.

How could she tell Miss June what she knew about this Harry? If she challenged him about the gun, what would he do? She really ought to say something, but she would have to find the right time. In the meantime, she'd have to keep watch. She believed the correct term was surveillance, which sounded a lot better.

As well as that, a memory from home was stirring about the 'typewriter' that wasn't quite a typewriter. Letitia was certain that somebody trustworthy should know about it.

Ah well, out of the frying pan and into the fire ... 'I think, we'll go over there,' she said, pointing towards the warm light coming from the large open door of Nettlefield Grange Orphanage.

12

Letitia's Surveillance

Later Sunday 23rd May, Nettlefield

TO LETITIA, the gunman Harry, this new girl and everyone at the orphanage all seemed like one big happy family. You hear of these lawless families. Letitia felt awkward and out of place with this one. But she'd made a decision to keep watch and she was going to stick to it.

Miss June Lovelock waved in the warm light from the front door. 'Letitia – you've come back! Come in and join us. It's lovely to have you back. And who have you brought with you?'

'This is Ramón,' said Letitia. 'He only speaks Spanish.'

'Oh well, that's to be expected,' said Miss June, scooping the two of them inside. 'Hola, Ramón,' she said, taking his other hand, 'you must teach me some more Spanish words.'

In the orphanage living room, the new girl, who had a faintly oily smell about her, was trying to put her bags down, but the white-haired boy (the biscuit thief) and the scrawny girl with trailing laces were fussing over her too much.

'Oh children, I know you're pleased to have Ida back, but let her put her bags down first,' said Miss June Lovelock, 'and Aggie, let me tie up those laces.'

'Where's Baby?' said the girl in overalls, called Ida.

'Oh, she's having an early night,' said Miss June.

'Really?' said Ida. 'Here, not in The Lillie?'

'No. I mean yes. Baby's upstairs,' said Miss June, 'Can we catch up about that in the morning? Look here's Bonnie.' She turned to the orphan girl with the golden blonde hair waiting patiently behind Ida. 'You've been so looking forward to Ida coming home, haven't you?'

'Yes,' said Bonnie, and immediately wrapped her arms around Ida's waist.

'And Letitia,' said Miss June. 'You will be staying again? You can have the same bed and we'll find a space for Ramón, is it? Where's your bag?'

'I forgot it.'

'And did Ramón forget his too?'

'Yes,' said Letitia, not able to look Miss June Lovelock in the eye.

Miss June mmmed and nodded her head. It was clear she could read as well between the lines as on them.

Miss June led Ramón, and Ramón led Letitia to the pile of cushions in the corner. 'Perhaps you'd like to share a bedtime story with Ramón?' Miss June handed Letitia a picture book, Folk Tales from Around the World. 'There are some lovely pictures in this one.'

Ramón snuggled in her lap and stared at the pictures of lush green forests, candy-coloured towns and characters in bright peasant clothes. Letitia was glad of the book, she could look over the top and keep watch, especially on Harry who was helping the white-haired boy with his jigsaw puzzle at the table.

Miss June then gathered all the children together for a bedtime story. They each had their own cushion to sit on around her chair. Letitia could see no sign of the small brown girl called Baby. The red-headed girl called Fingers took her cushion as far away from Letitia as she could.

Harry got up from the table. 'Well, I'd better be going. You know what Mrs Tatler's like, don't you, June?'

'Yes, she certainly expects her tenants to be back at what she thinks is a "reasonable" hour. Do tell her that that we haven't heard a peep from her charges.'

'Will do, Junie,' said Harry, blowing her a kiss.

Miss June blushed but her smile sparkled as she waved to Harry on his way out through the living room doors.

As Harry left, two much older boys entered – one, short and muscular, the other behind him, taller but stooping.

'Ah boys, did you enjoy your sausages?' said Miss June.

'The dinner was acceptable,' said the smaller muscular one, 'although in Spain, our meat is of a much higher quality.'

'Hopefully, Alfredo, you won't go hungry here in England. I apologise that your beds are so makeshift.'

'They are adequate for tonight,' Alfredo sat down on the bench, leaned back against the table and stretched out his legs.

The children had started larking about with their cushions and were making a bit of a racket around Miss June's story chair.

The taller boy behind Alfredo was staring intently at Ramón. He looked rigid with fear.

Letitia curled her arm around Ramón, who was gazing at the pictures in their book.

Miss June was scanning the small bookcase. 'Now which one shall we have tonight, children?'

The children called out various story titles: The Princess and the Pea! Three Billy Goats! The Singing Ringing Tree!

At this, Ramón looked up from his book and, as soon as he saw José standing behind Alfredo, he cried 'Zé!' and tried to wriggle out of Letitia's lap.

But the taller José, still standing behind the muscular Alfredo on the bench, was now shaking his head and holding the back of his hand to his face in a stop, be quiet sign.

Letitia gently but firmly held the small boy down. There was only one sort of person that would have got that sort of reaction from her new small friend. And this tall Spanish boy, 'Zé – short for José, was too young to be his father.

José had to be the rightful owner of the hexagonal label Ramón's teddy was wearing at Southampton docks. He had to be Ramón's brother.

Letitia whispered in Ramón's ear in Spanish. 'The other boy will hurt him. It must be secret.' Letitia could only guess at that, but it satisfied Ramón.

'Settle down now, children. Let's have his one.' Miss June pulled a book off the shelf, settled into her story chair, opened the book and announced, 'The Singing Ringing Tree.'

There were cheers and a few sighs from the children, but they all quietened down at last for the story.

While Miss June read, Ramón felt lighter in Letitia's lap. Fortunately, Miss June had many other children to watch over. Letitia hoped Miss June hadn't noticed the

118

change in Ramón's demeanour or that fact that he couldn't take his eyes off José. Had Alfredo, the shorter muscular boy, noticed that? During the story he was scanning each child – what was he looking for? José behind him continued to look very nervous.

The story paused and the children groaned.

'Come on now, children, we'll have the rest tomorrow evening,' said Miss June. 'It's getting dark – so easy to forget how late it is this time of year. It must be gone eight o'clock by now and that means it's well past your bedtime!' She shooed them towards the door in the corner of the room that led to a staircase, an alternative route to the large dormitory directly above the living room that Letitia had used when she first arrived in Nettlefield.

'Oh June, do we have to?' said the children together like a well-rehearsed chorus, but obediently they all got up and started filing through the door.

Alfredo stood up too and beckoned to his companion. Letitia did not suppose the two young men were friends. In Spanish, Alfredo said, 'We have work to do. It will be trouble for you if you don't do as Señor Fitzgerald said.'

What work could they have to do?

'But I am hungry, Alfredo. I can't learn English when I am hungry,' replied the taller boy also in Spanish. 'I'll get food from the kitchen. Do you want anything?'

Alfredo grunted, shrugged his shoulders and barged past the last few children on their way to bed.

When everyone else had gone, Ramón wrestled his arm away from Letitia and ran to the tall boy and wrapped his arms around his middle. 'Zé! Where did you go? I lost you!' he said in Spanish.

'Oh, these children,' said the tall boy, in English, 'they are homesick, they are happy to see any person from home. Shall I ask the child if he came with a brother or a sister?'

Letitia was about to say it's all right, I understand, I speak Spanish, when she realised that them not knowing that fact could be quite useful. Instead, she said, 'Oh yes please, do,' in her nicest English.

José turned to Ramón and said in Spanish, 'You should have stayed at the camp. You were safe there. Say nothing, you hear? We must keep quiet. Do not tell the girl you are my brother. If the senõr finds out, it will be bad, very bad for both of us, you hear?'

Ramón nodded but when he caught Letitia's eye fear flashed across his face. Ramón knew Letitia could understand Spanish. Letitia smiled as kindly as she could at Ramón to let him know that it was all right, she wasn't going to tell. But it was impossible to convey all of that in a look. She decided to take a risk.

'I understand,' said Letitia, in Spanish. 'I know what you have said, and I promise, it is all right. I will not give you and Ramón away. If you are talking about your teacher, I don't think he's a good person.'

In Spanish, with his fist clenched, José replied, 'I know he isn't.'

A gruff, muscular voice called 'José!' from the other side of the door to the West Wing stairs.

José's eyes opened wide at the sound of Alfredo's summons. José trembled as he gave Ramón, his brother, a very hasty hug.

The door opened and Alfredo leaned in. 'Come on,' he said in English, 'What is the matter with you? You will not wake in the morning if you don't sleep.'

Letitia wondered what did they have to wake up for? They didn't have to go to school, did they? And why did they have to concentrate so much on their English, if they were going home again in a month or so? Letitia remembered Miss Grenville saying on her visit to Grandma that coming to England was only a temporary measure to keep the children safe.

'There you are Ramón,' said Miss June, 'I've found you a bed all to yourself, can I show you? Letitia, you know where you're going, don't you? Perhaps if you sleep in your undies tonight, I'll find you some things to wear tomorrow. I hope you're stopping this time?'

'Thank you, yes,' said Letitia and watched Ramón happily follow Miss June and, a little further ahead, his brother too, up the stairs.

Letitia did feel a bit hungry, so José's idea of going to the kitchen for food was a good one.

The girl, who curiously called herself Brian, was sitting at the kitchen table poring over a huge book. Letitia supposed that, with her Down's syndrome, the girl was pretending to read and was merely turning the pages of the book she had open in front of her for fun.

Letitia stood behind the girl and said, 'Well done! Aren't you clever?' as if the girl were five years old and had only just learned to tie her shoelaces.

The book was in fact a maths book – lots of equations, some of them were quite interesting – to do with the concept of relativity that Mr Einstein had been talking about. As much as she tried not to, Letitia did love maths, it was so easy to read, unlike the medical journals.

'Yes, I am clever. I am reading my father's book,' said Brian. 'I am trying to learn too.' Brian pointed out the name on the spine, Alexander F. Shaw. 'My dad likes books but he left this one behind, so I rescued it,' said Brian proudly, with a smile that made her eyes twinkle. 'I am on the next chapter now,' said Brian as if asking for permission to turn the page.

'Oh, of course,' said Letitia.

And there it was.

A photograph and a diagram to explain the photo filled the next page. It was a very early version, it had to be, and but the principle was the same.

The title of the chapter to which Brian turned was Codes, Ciphers and the Principles of Probability in their Computation, and the photograph was of the not a typewriter. Very similar if not almost identical to the not a typewriter in the wooden box.

Brian traced her finger round the picture of the machine. 'This is a very interesting machine, it's called ...'

'Enigma,' they said together.

'Most people say they were invented by the Germans at the end of the war,' said Brian. 'But my Dad says two Dutchmen were the very first inventors.'

Letitia completely revised her opinion of the girl.

13

Baby's Early Night

Sunday Night 23rd May, Nettlefield

UPSTAIRS IN THE DORMITORY, Baby slung her jacket over the curtain pole of the cubicle that June had rigged up for her and Fingers. The weather had got too warm to keep her clothes on in bed so, she took off her summer jersey, her skirt, boots and socks, which she was only just getting used to wearing. And in her vest and pants she slid between the cool sheets.

The dormitory was quiet except for the sleeping breaths of the Spanish kids lying top to toe in the seven beds lined up under the windows. Fingers was still downstairs with the others. She'd quickly recovered from her fall and was oddly excited to be stopping over at the orphanage in the dormitory, like a real orphan. But Baby was tired of the odd day they'd been having and, though it was still light outside, she wanted to go to sleep.

But she was wide awake.

She and Fingers had their own beds inside the curtain, but they were rickety metal things and it was nowhere near as cosy as being in the huge room-bed at The Lillie. She really had gone soft.

Baby tried pretending to go to sleep to see if that would work.

It didn't.

Later, Baby heard the other kids come in with hushed giggles and whispers. She heard the rustle and flap of sheets and blankets, and Fingers swishing back their curtain and leaning over Baby to see if she was awake. Baby snored to put her sister off. Then she heard Florrie Fingers swish the curtain closed again, climb into her own bed and snuggle down with the creak of bedsprings. Within a few minutes, Fingers was snoring for real.

Baby tossed and turned but she couldn't fall asleep, not properly. She had half-awake dreams about Moll, where she knew Moll was dead and gone but Baby saw her anyway. They were more sad memories than dreams.

In the end, she turned back her sheets and carefully pulled the curtain open. It rattled a bit on its rail, but no one woke up. She thought maybe if she could see the moonlight shining through cracks in the curtains at the window, it would trick her into believing that she and Fingers were back in their barrel at the docks with Moll on guard outside.

She soaked up the silvery moonlight but she couldn't forget where she was. There was still an empty bed for Ida next to Bonnie's, just in case, as well as that other curtained-off one that June put that Letitia in. Baby felt good that Ida's hadn't been given over to the bossy boys or giggling girls or even these strange silent children. Though, of course, the giggling girls were in The Lillie. It was a good thing that two other Wonder Girls, Gin and Sophie, weren't due home to The Lillie any time soon. Gin was with her dad, who was now out of prison and visiting family overseas. She promised faithfully she'd be back but also said, 'How could I give up the chance to dance in Berlin, darling?' And Sophie was learning tailoring at the Art School, further west along the coast in Bournemouth.

Baby slipped back in between the sheets. Because of the heat, there was only one blanket and no eiderdown. She pulled the sheet up to her shoulders and shut her eyes to have another go at falling asleep.

But the quiet night sounds had become too loud and annoying to Baby. The creak of bed springs, children's snuffles and turnings in bed, and the faint click, click, click of a door being opened.

Baby heard a sniff sniff outside her cubicle curtain.

It was her, Miss Grenville, sneaking into the dormitory.

What did she want?

Baby had a horrible thought – what if she was up to the same game as Ida's bad Uncle Arthur last Christmas? What if she was looking for blonde kids to parcel up and send to Hitler too?

Baby slipped out of bed with barely a creak from the springs and crept to the gap in the cubicle curtain.

Miss Grenville in her stockinged feet was creeping round the dormitory checking every bed. She leaned too close over one of them and the kid rolled over in their sleep, which gave Miss Grenville a bit of a fright. It wasn't that one she was looking for.

Baby knew who she was looking for but didn't want to imagine why.

A breeze blew the curtain away from the window and in the moonlight Baby saw something proper weird.

Miss Grenville was wearing her – Baby's – green silk jacket. Miss Grenville must have pulled it off the outside of the cubicle curtain pole without Baby noticing. It wasn't so much the colour that was difficult to see in the moonlight, but the shape of it. The two big square pockets that sagged on the fronts. One of them contained the evidence of a life Baby had before she came to London, a life she'd had in India, the country that Moll said she came from.

But Baby's silk jacket was still over the curtain pole.

There were two.

Baby pulled her own jacket off the rail and felt in the pocket for the note that she never ever took out. She could never ever forget what it said, though ... Look after Baby, with a lipsticky kiss. The note was still there. She slung the jacket back over the rail.

Baby felt sick in her belly. What did this mean? Was this woman coming for her, to take her away? But why? The Blackshirts wanted to get rid of people like Baby. Maybe that was what the woman was helping them do?

Miss Grenville was more than halfway through her inspection of the sleeping children.

Baby pulled the curtains closer together. The rail above her scraped with a tinny metallic sound. Then she couldn't help it: her nose was too close to the curtain, which had a musty old mothbally smell. Baby felt the tickle. She couldn't hold it in. And out it came, not very loud, but loud enough. Baby sneezed.

Fingers turned over.

Miss Grenville stopped three beds away. She looked up from the two sleeping orphans and her eyes locked with Baby's.

With a delight that she couldn't hide, Miss Grenville strode towards Baby and Fingers's cubicle with a purpose, the complete opposite to her usual vague waffliness. She'd found what she was looking for. She'd found Baby.

Baby drew back from the curtain and jumped on her bed. The springs creaked.

Fingers snuffled and turned over.

Miss Grenville flung open the cubicle curtain with a rattle of rings.

'There you are, Baby,' whispered Miss Grenville triumphantly.

Baby pulled up her blankets, covering her vest and pants and lack of pyjamas.

Miss Grenville sat on the bed.

The bedsprings groaned and Baby felt the bed dip with the weight of the woman.

Miss Grenville turned to Baby. 'You are my baby,' she said.

Baby shuddered.

Miss Grenville then leaned in far closer than Baby was comfortable with and said, 'Baby, I am your mother.'

14

Miss Grenville's Story

Sunday Night, 23rd May, Nettlefield

THE MOONLIGHT SEEPED through the orphanage curtains and into the cubicle, where the strange Miss Grenville, her eyes like puddles, was sitting on the edge of Baby's bed.

The woman really was mad. Was she actually one of those weird, wicked people that go after kids? There was no way she could be Baby's mother. Baby was Indian, or was when she was born, not that she remembered of course. This woman came from a village in England.

Baby slid up the bed as far she could to get away.

Fingers snuffled and, with the creak of bedsprings, turned over in her sleep again.

Baby's bed creaked even more worryingly as Miss Grenville edged closer still.

Baby pulled the sheets up to her neck. 'You can't be my mum. I haven't got one.'

'Oh, Baby,' said Miss Grenville in her breathy voice, 'you have, or did. You were my baby.' Miss Grenville looked down at her hands clasped neatly together in her lap. 'You are right, though. I didn't actually give birth to you. The woman who did was unable to care for you. She wanted me to have you. I know she did.'

'How do you know that?' asked Baby.

But Miss Grenville was already lost in her memories. 'I was young,' she said. 'I was lonely and I wanted something to love. My family was so cold. How strange it was to be in the heat of Bombay only to feel so cold, inside. But I always did. I wanted, needed something of my own to love.'

'Should have got a dog or a cat ... or a doll, then,' said Baby.

'Oh, you were like a little doll, a little brown doll.'

Baby stiffened at the thought of being a doll or a pet.

'Your real mother was very poor. I think she lived at the side of the road. It was where I always saw her with her other children running around in the dust and the heat. You were at her breast. You were tiny. She fed you constantly herself. It was the only way she had to keep you alive, I suppose.

'I saw her with you every day on my way to the club. I wasn't supposed to walk out on the street, but I defied my father's orders and I did – just to see you.'

Baby had seen people like this before, posh folk who mostly walked by stepping well out of their way when the three of them, her Moll and Fingers, were huddled on the pavement up West near the theatres. But once in a while you got someone who'd look at her and Fingers, with an aah and an ooh, like they were kittens or puppies. She knew this sort of woman.

Miss Grenville went on with her story. 'One day your mother looked up at me. She was asking me to help her, I'm sure of it. The only way I could think of was to take you, to relieve her of you. So, I bent over her, stretched out my arms and let her put you in them.

'And you smiled. With those big dark eyes, you looked straight back at me and smiled. I never saw the woman again. Was she relieved at one less mouth to feed? Was she glad to be rid of you? I have no idea and at that moment I didn't care. I didn't even mind the smell and the dirt, because I had you, a real live baby.

'I hailed a rickshaw. I knew everyone would be at the club so I ordered the rickshaw cyclist to take us both home. Our house was much bigger than our home here in England. It was how we lived in Bombay. It was easy to hide you.

'My Ayah bathed you and found some of my own baby clothes. I grew up in India, so they were just the thing, perfect for the climate. My Ayah helped me to keep you secret.

132

'We lived like that for months. We even celebrated your first birthday together.'

Baby desperately looked for clues that the woman was talking rubbish. 'How did you know it was my birthday?'

'I guessed your age. I wanted to celebrate. It was about this time of year. I suppose you'd be nearly twelve years of age now.'

Twelve? Baby wanted to stay eleven forever and she certainly didn't want to think of herself being dressed up like a doll.

Miss Grenville was trying to catch Baby's eye again. Her hand, like a spider, crept closer to Baby across the covers.

In the dim moonlight, Baby could make out more of Miss Grenville's face. Her eyes really were like puddles – big and brown and sort of empty.

'But then my father told us – my mother, my brother and I – that we were returning home to England. I was determined to bring you too. How could I leave you? I was your mother. He said all our servants would be dismissed but I pleaded with him to keep Ayah. She had to come. How else would I have fed you? Of course, he didn't know why I wanted Ayah to come but he let me have my way.'

Baby was trying her best to listen to this story, but it wasn't a story. It was her. Was Miss Grenville telling the truth? How did Baby feel about the woman who gave her up, her real ma? Did she really give Baby up? Would Baby do that to someone? No. Baby was confused. She didn't know if she was angry with her real ma on the road for giving her away or sad, so very sad that her baby had been taken from her.

Whatever Baby's feelings were inside, Miss Grenville's words settled on Baby's skin like the lightest silk – clingy and fine. Though she could remember none of what Miss Grenville was describing, the words fitted with the little she knew and, at that moment, Baby found herself believing them.

Miss Grenville continued, 'My father is dead now, so you can come home with me to Threep and we can be mother and daughter again. Perhaps you can go to school. You will live how I always intended you to live, how your mother would have wanted if she had ever known.'

Fingers turned again in her sleep and Baby heard a grunt. Was her sister waking up?

'What happened, then?' Baby whispered. 'How did you lose me?' Up till then the only thing Baby knew was that Moll found her in her green silk jacket, with the card that said Look after Baby next to a lipstick kiss. Moll never said where she found her though.

'Well,' said Miss Grenville, 'It was impossible to hide you getting off the boat. I begged father to let me keep you, but he was adamant. He dismissed Ayah there and then ordered her to take you too. I barely had time to wrap you in my spare jacket and pop a little card in the pocket with instructions for who might find you.

'Oh, I did look for you from time to time, on our trips to town. But with our father dead, my brother was so protective. Though there was one time. It was outside the theatre. I could have sworn it was you with an old woman but Cecil, my brother, told me it couldn't be because you'd probably be dead by now. But look, he was wrong. Here you are!' Miss Grenville's face lit up with a smile and in her voice, Baby heard a squeak of excitement. 'I'll leave you now to sleep. I have a few things to organise.' She stood up with the twang of bedsprings. 'Don't worry, there'll be time to say goodbye to your friends before we leave for Threep.'

Questions jabbed at Baby's thoughts like a fork pricking sausages, but one thing she was certain of, she wasn't going anywhere with this woman.

Miss Grenville wafted out into the moonlit dormitory. Baby heard the dormitory door click open then shut. She looked across at her sister. Under her blanket, Fingers let out a snore. Maybe she hadn't woken after all?

Baby pulled the cubicle curtains carefully together and got back into bed.

But it was impossible to go to sleep after that.

135

Until now, Baby had hardly given a thought to her ma.

Her real ma, the woman Miss Grenville stole her from.

Baby threw back the covers and pulled her silk jacket off the rail again. She reached inside the pocket and took out the card, Miss Grenville's card.

Baby read it one last time. 'Look after Baby,' she whispered to herself. Then with all her might, she tore the card up until the bits were too small to tear any more.

15

Where's Fingers?

Monday 24th May, Nettlefield

BABY TOSSED AND TURNED for ages, all night it seemed. When she did wake, the sun streamed through the cubicle curtains. She got out of bed and peeked out at the rest of the dormitory. Both the orphans' beds and the Spanish kids' beds were empty. The pillows were plumped and the blankets drawn back to air the sheets.

Fingers's bed was empty too, though her sheets and blankets were all rucked in a heap. Baby's jacket and the torn scraps of card were on the floor just inside the curtain. Baby kicked them under the bed.

Not Miss Grenville but the thought of her real ma, sitting by the road, miles and miles away in India, got confused with her memories of Moll. Baby still missed Moll enough to bring a tear to her eye. Miss Grenville though – Baby didn't like her one bit. But if it weren't for her she'd never have had Moll, or Fingers? But then again, if it weren't for Miss Grenville, she'd have grown

137

up where she should have grown up, with her own family and people. Would Baby have loved them as much?

But how would her life have been that different? Perhaps Baby just grew up in the wrong place, a street kid in London instead of one in … where did the woman say? Bombay, that was it. But Baby wasn't a street kid any more, was she?

And the bad people in the world, Blackshirts and Nazis and the like, would Baby have felt the same about them if she'd just been a kid with a family, in India? Would she even have known about them?

All these questions made her head hurt with the thinking and wondering. But perhaps, what she felt most awful about was that the thought of her real ma didn't bring a tear to Baby's eye, and the fact that some small part of her wished that her real ma didn't exist at all.

But it was all too much to think about, especially when the Grenville woman was lurking about. So Baby opened an imaginary box inside her head and for the time being put it all inside.

Breakfast was over by the time Baby went downstairs. But there was still a bowl of porridge with a mug of tea set out for her on the table.

There was no sign of any of the kids, neither weird Spanish ones nor regular Nettlefield orphans. It must be past school time.

There was no sign of Fingers either.

Fingers wasn't tidying up the reading corner and she wasn't helping Brian collect dirty cups and bowls. She wasn't even in the kitchen, teasing the kitchen boy, William.

Miss Grenville had disappeared too. Was it all a dream?

But at the far end of the kitchen corridor, Baby did see Leonard Cook. Leonard wasn't a cook but the young man from the laundry who had helped them out last Christmas with his very useful laundry van.

'Oh, hello Baby, you look a bit lost?' Leonard had one hand on the door handle while the other clutched a big sack of dirty sheets.

'It's Fingers who's lost,' said Baby.

'Oh, again. She's a right one, isn't she?'

'You haven't seen her?'

'No sorry. Look, I've got to get on. Got loads of extra hours with all these Spanish nippers. I'm 'ere, there and everywhere this week.' He heaved the sack over the door step and out to his waiting van.

Fingers must have gone out burgling. Even though she wasn't meant to do that anymore, Fingers couldn't resist every now and again. June didn't know of course. Fingers told Baby it was just to keep her hand in, and she only did filthy Blackshirt places anyway. Baby knew June would say that was no excuse.

139

Baby decided to wait in the empty playground, on one of the new swings. Backwards and forwards, swinging in the morning sun was really soothing when you had problems. It put them out of your head for a bit.

Baby was wondering what school would be like, when a familiar figure strode through the orphanage gates and across the grounds on Harry's arm.

'Look who I found on the train, last evening,' said Harry.

With a burst of joy, Baby jumped off her swing and met them halfway. 'Ida, you're 'ome!' Baby wrapped herself round Ida Barnes's middle and felt the lovely drape of Ida's arms over her shoulders.

'I took Bonnie to school and look who I met on the way back!' said Ida.

'Is June in her office?' asked Harry.

'I expect so,' said Baby.

Harry strode across the playground and disappeared through the orphanage front door.

'I've got lots to tell you,' said Ida, pushing her arm through Baby's.

'But it'll all be about engines, won't it?' said Baby. Ida was training to be a mechanic in Southampton.

'It won't all be about engines,' said Ida.

Baby had lots she could tell Ida after last night, but she didn't want to talk to anyone about that yet.

The orphanage front door opened behind them.

140

'Where did that girl come from? She was there last evening.' Ida pointed at the open door where that goody-goody Letitia had just stepped out.

Letitia was looking about her like she was checking the coast was clear, which, to Baby, from her time on the streets of London, was a very familiar look. 'Bri said she'd be back. Her name's Letitia and she's a bit like you, Ida,' said Baby.

A small boy appeared from behind Letitia.

'Oh. Is that her brother?' asked Ida.

'I dunno. But it looks like Bri was right about something else, too.'

'What's that?'

'Brian said that she looked like one of us.'

'I suppose she does,' said Ida.

Because picking up stray kids was what they did.

Harry appeared at the front door again.

'But,' said Ida, 'I don't like the way she's looking at Harry.'

As Harry passed Letitia on his way out of the orphanage, Letitia stepped away from him and drew the little boy closer to her as if Harry, of all people, might hurt him.

'I think I'll go and see Mr Rogers,' said Ida. 'Do you want to come?'

Baby thought about it but Mr Rogers was Ida's friend, and his garage was her sort of place much more than Baby's.

'See you later, Wonders!' said Harry, sauntering past Baby and Ida across the grounds and out through the gates.

'No,' said Baby, answering Ida's invitation. 'I think I should check up on little Florrie Fingers. She's scarpered again.'

'You don't think she's ... you know, burgling?'

'Wherever she is, and whatever's she's doin', it's probably trouble.'

Baby waved Ida off up West Street as Ida ran to catch up with Harry. Then, with a shrug of her shoulders, Baby resigned herself to another frustrating hunt for her sister.

She crossed the street and climbed up the bank to the station and the spot they'd slept in when they first arrived in Nettlefield. But there was no Fingers curled up in the grass today.

Satisfied that Fingers wasn't dicing with death on the railway bridge again, Baby stepped on to the path that led to the ticket hall and brushed herself down. With all the sunshine of the last week or so, the grass on the bank had grown well past her knees.

Baby headed towards the station buildings.

Footsteps tap-tapped behind her. It was long past the busy rushing-to-work time of day for a Monday morning, but folk were still going into the station to catch trains to here there and everywhere.

Baby passed the ticket hall and the stationmaster's office, where the stationmaster was sitting at his desk. He waved to Baby from over his cup of tea. 'All tickety-boo, Baby my dear?'

Baby didn't want to tell him that she'd lost her sister again just yet, in case the little tyke was up to mischief, so she only slowed down enough to wave back with a 'just about,' and what she hoped was a cheery smile.

There were those footsteps again, the same crisp tap-tap-tap. Baby turned to look but no one was there.

16

Not So Goody-Goody After All

Monday morning 24th May, Nettlefield

BABY WAS PRETTY SURE what had happened. Fingers had heard that woman, who wasn't Baby's ma, trying to tell Baby that she was. Baby didn't need a ma and she didn't want a ma and she certainly didn't want one like Miss Grenville. And she knew for certain that Fingers felt the same. They were independent young people and June Lovelock respected that.

So here Baby was again, looking for Fingers, hoping her sister hadn't got herself locked in a coal bunker, nabbed by the long arm of the law or, worst of all, snagged by one of Nettlefield's Blackshirts.

Baby carried on to the coal heap and the engine shed. A few motor cars were parked in the station grounds. She passed some folk running back towards the ticket hall. Where were they going, she wondered, Hamwell?

Southampton? And from the other side of the fence she watched the ten-thirty train for Portsmouth arrive in a cloud of steam, suck up the passengers off the platform, and chuff off over the bridge towards the viaduct over the town creek, a smelly, muddy old place when the tide was out.

There was only one likely place left to look.

The obvious place really.

It wasn't exactly forbidden to go there, but Baby didn't want to announce her arrival. So she crept through the tunnel that led to the clearing outside The Lillie.

There was a rustle in the bushes behind her. Baby glanced back through the leafy tunnel. But there was nothing between her and the sunshine warming the station grounds at the other end.

The Lillie's door and windows were open. Music was playing, modern big jazz band stuff. One of the Spanish girls was painting her toes in the sunny spot by the door.

Where was Fingers?

Baby pressed herself into the bushes.

A voice from inside The Lillie said something Baby didn't understand, in Spanish she supposed.

The girl painting her toes replied, 'In English. Easton said we must speak English.'

'You like him!' said the first voice in English, in a sing-song way. Which then changed to downright bossy, 'Come inside. I need you here. Help me!'

145

'Oh, can't you wait until this polish dries?' The girl screwed the top on the bottle then leaned back in the doorway and lifted her face to the sun.

'Do you want me to tell him what you have been doing instead of learning how to operate this thing?' said the first voice from inside The Lillie.

'All right, all right.' The girl by the door stood up and walking awkwardly on her heels went inside. 'I'm coming!' Both girls now talked in English with hardly any Spanish accent.

On her hands and knees, Baby crawled across the clearing. She loved the mossy, earthy smell. It made her ache to be back to normal, living in The Lillie with the other Wonder Girls instead of those girls, who Baby seriously doubted would ever be Wonders.

The inside girl was sitting at the table in Brian's place by the window. Baby only caught a glimpse, but she was sure the thing with knobs and dials in front of the Spanish girl was a wireless.

The music stopped and was replaced by crackling screechy noises.

Baby crouched underneath the open window and listened.

'Maria, what have you done? We're not supposed to be using it for dance tunes.'

Something stung Baby's head. She felt through her hair. A small fir cone was stuck in the tangles. Baby looked up to see where it had come from.

Another cone stung her forehead.

She heard a 'psssst' from above her.

Baby looked up at the tall evergreen trees that grew round The Lillie. It was hard to see anything through the thick mass of feathery green leaves. She crawled close to the trunk and peered up through the branches.

Fingers was clinging to a branch as near to the top of the tree as you could go without being on a very bendy twig.

Baby stretched her mouth silently round the words – What are you doing? She very much felt she wasn't going to let Florrie Fingers out of her sight ever again. She'd keep her on a lead if needs be.

Fingers pointed downwards to a broken branch below her.

The Spanish girl poked her head out through the window. A pair of headphones was hooked round her neck.

Baby's heart beat even harder. When the girl was looking the other way, Baby scrambled behind the tree trunk trying to imagine what she'd say if the Spanish girls saw her. Oh, just come for a look at the old place – keep it simple.

The soft clank of the window being pulled shut was a relief but then, above her, the branches creaked.

Baby was wondering how on earth she was going to get Fingers down when, from nowhere, a girl in blue joined her at the bottom of the tree.

But the girl wasn't there for long.

Baby felt her mouth drop open in amazement. Not just any girl, goody-goody Letitia was shimmying up that tree as easy as if she were climbing into bed. In a smart blue suit and tip-tappy heeled shoes, too! As far as Baby could see, Letitia had no fear in her at all.

With her skirt hitched up, showing off a pair of shorts a bit like Jesse Owens wore last year at the Olympics and her legs clinging to the trunk, Letitia reached out for Fingers. 'Let go, I will catch you,' she said in a whisper, loud enough for Baby to hear.

'Not on your nelly,' said Fingers, a bit too loudly and very definitely.

And to be fair, having seen Letitia's bandaging, Baby would have said the same thing.

But unless Fingers wanted to stay in that tree sharing a nest with the birds, she didn't have much of a choice. The trunk was thick and Fingers's arms and legs weren't long enough to grip it and climb down it like it was a drainpipe.

The spindly branch that Fingers was clinging on to made a huge creak and snapped.

Baby's heart yo-yoed from her throat to her belly. Not again!

But Letitia grabbed Fingers's arm, like she was a dolly. 'I've got you,' she said.

And all Fingers could do was dangle in the Letitia's grip as Letitia climbed down the tree as easily as she'd climbed up.

Baby's mouth stuck open in amazement.

When Letitia and Fingers were both on solid ground, Letitia let Fingers go, who then crumpled into a heap at Letitia's feet.

Letitia blew a stray lock of hair off her face, unhitched her skirt and brushed bits of bark from her jacket.

Finding that her mouth could still actually work, Baby said, 'Where did you come from?'

'Oh, just over there somewhere.' Letitia pointed vaguely in the direction of the station 'Shall we just get out of earshot from those girls? Which way is it again?'

'Oh, yeah, course.' The last thing Baby wanted at that moment was to think up excuses for spying on the Spanish girls. So she led Letitia and the dazed but completely unharmed Fingers away from The Lillie through the other tunnel that, before Christmas, had been so useful for Ida's house in Camellia Lane.

The allotments were bright green with new leaves and budding fruit and veg. A few older men, shirt sleeves

149

rolled up, were busy with their spades and hoes and rakes. One, sitting in the sun with a knotted hankie on his head, gave Baby and Fingers a friendly wave.

'Were you following me?' asked Baby of Letitia. 'I mean, I'm really glad you came along, but why were you there?'

It was Letitia's turn to shrug her shoulders. 'I don't know. Sometimes you want to do one thing, but the universe is telling you to do something else, and this morning it was telling me to follow you.'

Baby wondered what it was that Letitia wanted to do. But topmost in Baby's mind was what on earth was Fingers doing up that tree?

'I just wanted to see what they were doing, make sure they were looking after the place,' she said. 'And it was a good place to hide, 'til the branch broke.' Fingers opened the allotment gate onto Camellia Lane.

'How could you see inside from up there?' said Baby. 'They didn't put a window in the roof, did they?'

'No, but I did get a look inside when they weren't looking, and you should see the mess they're making.' Fingers's forehead wrinkled and she jutted her bottom lip out. 'They haven't been in there five minutes. And another thing.' Fingers stopped dead on the pavement as a man in a cap wobbled past on his bike. Fingers faced Baby with her hands on her hips. 'I don't want her,' she said very definitely, pointing at Baby with a forefinger that meant business.

Letitia, who was now a few steps ahead, looked round.

'Not you,' said Fingers, 'not now you rescued me good and proper this time. I mean 'er with the silly voice, telling you a pack of lies last night. We ain't got ma's. Never had, never will.'

Baby thought it was impossible for them never to have had ma's but she decided not to argue. 'Don't worry about her. I'm not going anywhere.'

The frown on her sister's face faded. 'All right then.'

'Did you see the wireless?' asked Baby.

'Yeah, and they had summat else too, as well as that wireless. It looked like ...'

'Like something Miss June Lovelock uses in her office?' piped up Letitia. 'Like a typewriter?'

'Yeah.' Fingers caught up with Letitia, who happened to be right outside number seven, Ida's old place, where a frazzled woman was balancing a crying baby on her hip. 'But it didn't have any paper,' said Fingers, 'so it ain't a typewriter, is it?'

'No, it isn't,' said Letitia. As they turned into Trinity Street, Letitia explained about the Enigma machine, how it was used to create and decipher coded messages, and what she'd seen pass between Miss Grenville's Mr Fitzgerald and Miss June's Harry. 'Those Spanish

151

children,' she said, 'I'm positive they didn't come with all the others on the boat.' Letitia explained about the children not having labels. She said, 'I don't know for sure but I feel they are in danger, from Mr Fitzgerald, those girls and definitely one of the big boys at the orphanage.'

Baby had had prickles about Mr Movie Star Fitzgerald since he invited himself into The Lillie the other day.

But Harry? Hadn't they'd been through all that before Christmas? He started off being a Blackshirt, then he wasn't, then he was, then he wasn't ... was he back to being a Blackshirt again? Was he being truthful with June Lovelock? Baby hated to think of someone taking advantage of June's kindness.

There was nothing for it, they were going to have to find out once and for all. 'This way,' said Baby. 'Fingers, it's time for a bit of burgling, and this time I'm coming too.'

'Burgling?' Letitia's face lit up.

'Afraid so,' said Baby looking her up and down. 'And I'm afraid you're a bit big for it.'

'Oh.' Letitia drooped with disappointment.

Not so goody-goody after all.

17

Letitia's Concern

Monday 24th May, Nettlefield

LETITIA WAS DISAPPOINTED not to go burgling, which sounded terribly exciting, but mostly she was very concerned for Baby and Fingers's safety. She had tried to impress upon them that the man, Harry, was dangerous. What if he pulled the gun on them? But Baby and Fingers assured her that they knew him, he wouldn't, not on them. Letitia had no need to worry at all because, for a start, they wouldn't be climbing trees.

They were experienced, they said, and hardly ever got nabbed. Letitia had a feeling she could do with some of that experience but perhaps now was not the time. Besides, she needed to check on Ramón. She had left him with his brother, José, while that bullyboy watchdog, Alfredo, was elsewhere. What if Alfredo had returned?

Letitia parted company with Baby and Fingers on the pavement by the churchyard. Baby pointed Letitia in the right direction for the orphanage. 'It's that way. Keep going past the tram shed and it's the other side just before the bridge.'

Letitia trudged away from the church, along the street, past houses, a pillar box and the occasional shop. She was getting hungry too. Maybe there was some luncheon at the orphanage or sandwiches, perhaps? Brian, the apprentice cook, seemed to love making sandwiches.

Letitia stopped for a tram coming out of the shed and found the orphanage just as Baby had said, beyond the tall hedge.

The gates were open and the playground empty. The front door was shut but not locked. She let herself in. 'Hello, it's me. Letitia! I'm back!'

Squinting in the sunshine that came in with Letitia was Brian, with an old man who was indeed carrying a tray of sandwiches.

'You're just in time!' said Brian in a clean white apron. 'Me and Dad have been experimenting.'

'Corned beef and banana in a honey vinegar dressing. Rather good, if I may say so,' said the old man, Brian's father. 'Best eaten today though, the bananas were already on the turn.'

The old man had the same glint in his eye as Brian. 'About a hundred years in the future, they'll be mad for this sort of thing,' he said.

'Dad's always saying things like that,' said Brian.

'You mark my words Brenda, my dear.'

'How old will I be then?' Her brow furrowed as she thought. 'One hundred and fifteen years old. I don't think anyone gets to be that old, do they.'

'Probably not my dear,' he said sadly and carried the tray of sandwiches through the double doors, which had been wedged open, into the living room.

Letitia was just about to follow the father and daughter, when Ramón appeared at the top of the stairs. José was standing behind him. Ramón started down the stairs and beckoned to José to follow. But José shooed his brother down and remained at the top. Letitia took the small boy's hand and led him into the living room.

The sandwiches were surprisingly tasty. Letitia, Brian and her father hardly made any dent at all in the mountainous pile. Brian covered what was left with a damp tea towel to keep them nice for the orphans after school.

To take her mind off worrying about Baby and Fingers, Letitia settled herself and Ramón in the story corner with some picture books.

It was about half past three when she heard the soft shuffle of feet in the entrance hall, accompanied by a harsh unfriendly voice. 'They've been worked very hard today, so I'm sending them up for a nap.'

The label-less Spanish children trooped past the open living room doors.

155

'Of course, Mrs Tatler,' said Miss June, who'd also just come in weighed down with two full shopping bags. 'The poor dears must be so disorientated.'

The soft shuffle of feet continued upstairs. It occurred to Letitia that saying the children had been 'worked' was a very strange way to talk about them.

Not long after Mrs Tatler had left and Miss June had had a chance to put down her shopping and take off her hat, the English orphans came home from school with whoops and cries. Quite the opposite to the Spanish children. That little white dog appeared from some hidden corner and dashed through the living room at top speed.

'Aw, Frank, I'm pleased to see you too!' The boy with the white hair was being extensively licked in the doorway. After a quick change into play clothes, they were all allowed to let off steam outside.

While Ramón was getting to know the English orphans in the playground, Letitia hovered by the gates to look out for Baby and Fingers. She should have gone with them – the morning's rescue proved that they needed her.

Miss June wasn't worried about Baby and Fingers's non-appearance at all – not at teatime, nor later at storytime. Letitia was beginning to worry that they had indeed been 'nabbed'.

She waited until Miss June had seen all the English children into bed before she raised her concern again. Apart from Ramón, the Spanish didn't mix at all. By this time, it almost dark outside.

'They're independent young people who need a certain level of freedom,' said Miss June, rather brusquely, as she went into her office and closed the door.

Perhaps Letitia should have set her worries about Baby and Fingers to one side. Excepting railway bridges and tree-climbing, they certainly looked as though they could look after themselves.

Letitia wondered if something was on Miss June's mind. Much was tumbling around hers. Where to start? Grandma would say at the bottom, then the only way was up.

So Letitia knocked on Miss June's office door. 'Miss June? It's me, Letitia.'

'Come on in, dear,' said Miss Lovelock with a weary sigh, any hint of impatience gone.

Letitia gently pushed the door open. Miss June was sitting behind her desk cradling a cup of warm milk in her hands. An old lady dozed in a wheelchair beside her. A small desk lamp was the only light on in the room.

The old lady woke up as Letitia entered and reached for Letitia's hand. 'Oh, hello dear, how lovely to see you.' She smiled sweetly before nodding off again. The lady's hands were soft and cool. Her skin felt as delicate as tissue paper.

Letitia gently laid the old lady's hand back in her lap.

'We always have a little catch up about the day before Mother goes to bed,' said Miss June. 'It helps her memory. This is a peculiar time, though isn't it? I'm just so pleased Mother is oblivious. One war was enough for her. Sometimes it's hard to know what to believe.'

On Miss June's desk sat her own typewriter, a large heavy object. Beside it, a piece of paper, printed rather than typewritten and lined with creases where it had been folded. It was a handbill such as Grandfather might have given out at election time, but the picture was of that man in Germany, Adolf Hitler. Letitia recognised it for what it was, propaganda. Why would Miss Lovelock have that? Letitia's thoughts were getting more jumbled than ever. All was certainly not as it at first seemed.

'Yes.' Miss June tapped the handbill with her forefinger. 'I know.' She could obviously see Letitia's look of concern. 'Baby found this and gave it to me not long after I became matron here. There was some trouble to do with the Blackshirts – you've heard of them? And I've just come across this again. It feels like there's a loose end somewhere, something not quite tied up. But why am I telling you, Letitia dear? We've only just met and you're here to help those poor Spanish children.' Miss June's forehead wrinkled. 'Was there a reason you brought Ramón back? Did he get left behind? Was he meant to come with others? I've had so little information – I'm sure there's a ton of paperwork somewhere. If I had it, I'd understand.'

Letitia wasn't sure how to answer. Was this the time to tell Miss June her suspicions about Harry? Should she also tell her about the Spanish boys, about how José was in danger? And those girls, were they really refugees? But it was clear that Miss June's questions weren't really directed at her.

'Was there something I could help you with, Letitia?'

This question, however, Letitia could answer quite easily. 'Could I possibly have some paper and a pen, please? I need to write a letter.'

'Of course, here you are.' She opened the desk drawer and drew out two sheets of stiff cartridge paper. 'Those new ball point pens are even messier than normal ones. Use my spare pen and here's a bottle of ink.' Miss June opened another drawer on the other side of the desk. 'And here are envelopes and stamps too. I'm glad you're writing home, Letitia.' She indicated a 'post out' tray on her desk. 'Just put it in there when you've finished.'

'Thank you.' Letitia tucked the envelopes and stamps in her jacket pocket and picked up the ink, pen and paper, but paused at the door.

'Was there something else?' asked Miss June.

'I can speak Spanish. I just wanted to let you know that.'

'Oh, that is useful, thank you. I can see how that would make you a very important asset to the whole operation.'

'But please don't let the shorter Spanish boy know yet.'

'You mean Alfredo? No, I won't if you think that would be best. I can see he's a little more ... forceful than José ...'

'José knows about my Spanish and I think he's in trouble,' said Letitia.

'Really? How? Oh dear, this is all getting so out of hand. How is he in trouble?'

'I'm not sure yet but he's certainly quite worried,' said Letitia.

'Right. I think I probably need to sleep on this and make some decisions in the morning. Don't stay up too late, will you? I have a feeling that very soon we'll need our wits about us.'

'Thank you,' said Letitia.

Letitia left Miss June thoughtfully sucking the end of a pencil, while the elderly Mrs Lovelock dozed in the little pool of light from the desk lamp.

The moon shone through the window, giving Miss June a silvery halo. For a woman with no children of her own, she really was the perfect mother.

160

Letitia returned to the orphanage living room with all her letter writing materials and, under one electric light, she sat down at the table to write.

From her pocket she took the envelopes, the stamps and her purse – empty apart from Grandfather's card. Dear Grandfather, how Letitia wished she was writing to him and not this Sir … Hugh … Sinclair … she read, with just an ordinary London address, not a hospital or any authority that should know about people with guns and suspicious teachers in orphanages. But Grandfather gave her the card and perhaps, having lost everything useful in her father's medical case, she should use this card before she lost that too. She'd just say hello, make contact.

When Letitia had finished, there was the second sheet. She wasn't sure why Miss June had over-supplied her with writing materials; perhaps she didn't want to be disturbed again?

She might as well use it; there were a few things she could do with from home.

Dear Elsie, she began …

Letitia was nearly done with a few instructions and what she thought was a modest list of necessary items, when the new girl, the big sister of golden-haired Bonnie, wandered in wearing an old satin dressing gown and carrying a cup of warm milk.

'Hello,' she said, 'I couldn't sleep. It's so nice to be back here. I'm Ida, and you're Letitia? Right?' She offered her cup. 'Would you like some? I'd make you your own cup, of course. It's only warm milk. After all the goings-on at Christmas, I lost the taste for Ovaltine. Oh, I see you've already got a cup!' Ida pointed to an empty cup left on the table.

It wasn't Letitia's cup, and she didn't want milk. Letitia was trying to work out what to say to the girl, who appeared to answer her own questions.

But again, Ida jumped in. 'I'll let you finish your writing, don't mind me.'

Fortunately, Letitia only had to sign her name and address the envelope. She put the cap on the pen and turned to Ida, who was sitting on the bench with her back to the table and her legs crossed.

To Letitia, Ida looked quite grown-up in one way – the way she sat and behaved belonged to someone at least seventeen. Her dressing gown was very elegant, which was a surprise.

'Oh, you like this? It belongs to my friend Gin, who is much better at clothes than I am. I really prefer overalls.'

Letitia knew that Ida was an orphan. Strictly speaking, Letitia was an orphan too, though she didn't feel like one because she had Grandma and she had never really known her actual parents. And thinking about it, she was pretty independent as well, like Baby and Fingers and all these girls.

Letitia decided to launch straight in with what was going around and around in her brain. 'How much do you know about Harry, Miss June's young man? Do you trust him?'

'What do you mean?' said Ida, sitting up.

'Oh, just, how much do you know about him?'

'I know that he rescued my sister and saved my life,' said Ida, and turned to Letitia with a much harder stare than before. 'So, of course I trust him!'

'Oh,' said Letitia, and made a mental note to be very careful when speaking about Harry in Ida's hearing.

In that awkward moment, Letitia heard the big front door slam shut and the distant rumble of engine. Was that Baby and Fingers coming back, at last? Maybe they'd have something to convince Ida that Harry wasn't all he seemed? She folded her letter, put it in the envelope and addressed it to Elsie at The Manor, Threep, Norfolk. 'I'm just going to put this in Miss June's post out tray,' she said.

But Ida had her back to Letitia and was now sitting grumpily at the table, resting her chin on her hand.

Oh dear, Letitia really had offended her.

Miss June's light was still on, but neither Miss June nor Mrs Lovelock were there. Letitia placed her letter on

163

top of the little pile of letters already in the tray, to go out with the morning's post.

She heard footsteps in the hall. That had to be Baby and Fingers, which was good as Ida was still up and the orphanage being quiet made it the perfect time to talk. Letitia was turning to go when she noticed that Miss June's swivel chair had fallen over. She picked it up and tucked it back underneath the desk.

Her skin prickled. The room didn't feel quite so cosy any more.

The pile of letters to be posted was already quite large. Perhaps she shouldn't add to Miss June's responsibilities? So Letitia retrieved her letters from the post out tray. Perhaps she'll put them in the post.

More footsteps in the hall, rather heavy for Baby, but she did wear those boots, didn't she?

On her way out of Miss June's office, Letitia walked straight into Alfredo carrying a pile of bedding. 'The matron has permitted us to move to a better room,' he said by way of explanation.

'Oh, that's nice,' said Letitia, her uneasiness growing. She told herself not to be silly.

She decided to post her letters straightaway. She'd spotted a pillar box earlier, soon after she left Baby and Fingers. It would only take a minute or two.

In the orphanage playground, a swing seat was hooked round its struts and the gates were open. Letitia ran to the box a little way up the main street, posted her letters and on her way back, closed the gates and unhooked the swing.

The run had done her good. But Letitia still struggled to fall asleep. She couldn't work out where Alfredo and José could be moving to. The only rooms suitable for sleeping in, that she knew of downstairs in the orphanage, were the sickbay, Miss June's room and Mrs Lovelock's room.

18

The Truth about Harry Miller

Monday 24th May, Nettlefield

BABY WATCHED LETITIA disappear along West Street back to the orphanage. Maybe they should have let her tag along? She'd make a brilliant cat burglar. But Fingers said it wasn't so much getting in or out or up or down as being small enough to hide once you were in or out or up or down.

Pleased to give the Blackshirt greengrocers on the corner of Trinity Street a wide berth, Baby and Fingers ran full pelt past the shops towards Doswells' Alley.

Doswells' department store on the corner of West Street and High Street was closest to the Town Hall and took up the space of half a dozen shops. The alley cut Doswells' off from its smaller neighbours, and it was where Harry Miller lodged with Mrs Tatler.

Even in the bright May sunshine the alley was darker than usual since the pet shop had been closed. And the folks in the Baker's Bonnet Pub were making too much noise at the far end to be bothered about two small girls taking off their boots, tying the laces together and slinging them across their shoulders.

Outside Mrs Tatler's front door, Fingers reached in her skirt, a new one with loads of pockets, that Sophie had made before she went to the art school in Bournemouth. Fingers pulled out a bit of bent wire and wriggled it about in the lock, until a clunk confirmed that she'd unlocked it.

She pushed the door open and crept inside. Baby followed and carefully pushed it shut again behind them. Baby could smell old stew coming from the kitchen at the back. Once upon a time that would have made them hungry, but not anymore. 'Might mean she's coming back for dinner. We'll have to be quick,' said Baby.

Baby followed Fingers up the stairs one, two, three flights to the top where the ceiling sloped.

There was one door at the top. Before Harry, this was where June Lovelock lived while her ma lived in the asylum. The asylum was where they wanted to put all the folks who were too much trouble.

The door to Harry Miller's flat had a lock but there was no key. When Fingers pushed it, the door opened with a tiny squeak.

'Are you sure 'e lives 'ere?' said Fingers.

The room was bare, as if Harry had cleared out and just left Mrs Tatler's old furniture.

A threadbare grey blanket covered the bed, next to a bare chest of drawers. All Baby could find inside them was a few old socks and a baggy pair of men's undershorts.

A kettle sat on the gas ring next to a white sink with a wooden draining board. Fingers tugged on the little curtain underneath it.

'Careful!' said Baby.

Fingers took out a nearly full bottle of amber liquid and two glasses. 'Whisky,' she said and put them back. A little table by the window was bare too, nothing underneath it just space for feet. The chair hadn't been tucked in either.

On the other side of the room was a wardrobe with wonky doors that didn't quite meet in the middle.

'What are we actually lookin' for?' asked Fingers, heading for the wardrobe.

'Evidence,' said Baby. 'We're looking for evidence that Harry Miller, once and for all, is good or … bad.'

'Well, that won't take long. He hasn't got anything worth pinching.' Fingers pulled on the wardrobe door. But with the creak of splitting wood it came away from its top hinge and the door clunked skew-whiff onto the floorboards.

'What have you done?' said Baby.

'I only opened it. It was already broke!'

'Not that broke it wasn't!'

168

From downstairs came the sound of the front door slamming shut.

'Someone's come home,' said Fingers.

'And I hope they're not coming up here. Help me with this door.'

Together they tried to prop it back in place, but it wouldn't stay and the thud, thud, thud of at least two pairs of feet on the stairs was getting louder.

Muffled voices joined the footsteps on the stairs, one was Harry Miller's.

Fingers dived under the bed. 'It's too late, hide!' she whispered.

Baby recognised the oily tones of Easton Fitzgerald as the other voice, yes you're right, it is safer to meet here …

'But we can't leave it like this!' whispered Baby.

With the ratchet sound of the door to Harry Miller's room opening, Baby dashed in the wardrobe and pulled on the door. It scraped the boards. Her heart in her throat, she lifted the door and propped it on the wardrobe ledge.

As Harry and Fitzgerald were entering the room, Baby pulled her hand out of sight and with her thumb and forefinger pinched the butterfly screws that fixed the handle to the outside, holding the door shut.

Baby smelt Fitzgerald's man perfume come in with him

Through the gap between the doors, Baby could see the draining board with its little curtain, the table in the window and the chair with Easton Fitzgerald lounging on it, his panama hat on the table, his back to the window and his legs stretched out into the room.

'What did you say the matter with it was?' said Harry reaching behind the curtain under the draining board. He took out the bottle and the two small glasses. 'Too early?'

'No,' said Fitzgerald.

Harry poured a small measure of the drink into each glass.

'The girls are struggling. They say that the Enigma's lights are not working correctly.' He gulped his whole measure of whisky in one swallow.

'They do know how to use the code book, the one I gave you at the camp? It was in the box,' said Harry.

'Are you suggesting they don't understand the importance of this mission, Miller?'

'Not at all.' Harry leaned against the draining board, cradling his own full glass in his hands. 'How are they doing with the radio? Not just trying to find the latest tunes on the BBC, are they?'

Fitzgerald took a breath to speak. It came out as a hiss, 'These young women, these agents, are vital to the subjugation of the British Isles. It will not be as messy as in Spain. If it transpires that handling the Enigma and operating the radio are beyond them, I will reassess their abilities and assign them a role more suited to their talents, as I see them.'

'Yes, as you see fit,' said Harry. 'And your boy on the boat, did he identify any more suitable children for the main arm of the operation? Because without your little spies, the agents will have no information to send anyway.'

'No, he didn't and I haven't yet decided what to do with the boy. But those silly women at the camp are only too eager to help. I have them eating out of my hands.'

Fitzgerald studied his empty glass.

Harry was ready with the bottle. 'Another one?'

But Fitzgerald shook his head and put the glass next to his hat on the table. He was staring at the wardrobe.

With her fingers tight round the screw, Baby leaned back into the musty darkness. The wardrobe was empty apart from Harry's flying jacket. She felt the sheepskin collar brush her forehead.

'What's wrong with your cupboard, Miller?' Fitzgerald leaned forward on the chair, his gaze shifting to the floor. 'And those marks on the floor?'

Baby could feel her fingers getting sweaty and the screw slipping out of them.

'Oh, that old thing,' said Harry. 'If Mrs T knew I was working with you, she might give me a better room.'

Baby pulled on the door screw for a better grip.

171

The door juddered.

'I think you have a rat, Miller.'

Baby held tight on to the screw, willing her fingers dry, Fitzgerald to have another drink and to stop bothering about the wardrobe.

But he was getting up.

Baby's breathing got shallower as she ran through her options. Had Harry locked the door behind him? Could she run for it? Was Fingers still under the bed?

Fitzgerald was reaching for the handle on the wardrobe door. 'It's broken, isn't it?'

'Yes,' said Harry, putting himself between the wardrobe and Fitzgerald. 'Now about the camp ... The women have no idea what we're doing?'

Baby felt a little wave of calm wash over her. But her thumb and finger were beginning to ache; she didn't know how much longer she could hold on.

'Of course not! Do you take me for an idiot?' Fitzgerald grabbed his glass off the table. 'Yes, I will have another one.'

Harry left his own untouched glass on the draining board and obligingly poured Fitzgerald another drink.

Fitzgerald swallowed the lot in one go again. 'And you can help. I need you at the camp now. If we can recruit fourteen suitable children, then they can form the next cohort. I already have placements for them and hopefully the next group will not need this level of organisation. If we can get the children on our side without as much persuasion, shall we say, it will make the whole operation that much more efficient and will certainly appease my contact in Berlin.'

'You haven't told me who that is or exactly where the children are going.' Harry had left his position by the draining board and was crossing the room towards the wardrobe.

Baby couldn't take much more of this. Perhaps they just ought to run for it?

'No,' said Fitzgerald, his eyes narrowing as he put on his hat. 'Time to go, Miller. I have a vehicle. Do you have everything you need?'

'Yes, everything,' replied Harry, his back to the wardrobe door. Everything went dark.

Baby heard the door to the attic room open.

Harry moved away from the wardrobe; Baby could only see Fitzgerald's used glass on the table. The attic door closed with a clunk and a grinding of the latch, followed by two pairs of feet retreating down the stairs. As soon as she heard the front door slam, Baby blew out a sigh of relief and let go of the screw. The wardrobe door slipped off its ledge and toppled over against the bed.

'Watch it!' said Fingers, crawling out from underneath the bed.

Baby stepped round the door and turned on Fingers. 'If you hadn't broken it!'

'What you bothered about?' said Fingers, nose to nose with Baby. 'We didn't get caught, but more to the point we haven't found anything,'

Sometimes Baby could happily fling Florrie Fingers off the railway bridge herself. Baby was sure that they had just found out a lot. If only she knew what it all meant. 'These are dangerous people!' she said, and made do with gripping her sister's shoulders and giving her a shake instead.

Harry's flying jacket slipped off the hanger and landed with a thud on the wardrobe floor.

'Well, there's no doubt he's up to something with the Blackshirts hereabouts. Come on let's go.' Baby turned the knob on the attic door.

But it was stuck.

'Has 'e locked it?' Fingers fished around in her skirt for her lock-picking wire and set to work.

After at least half an hour of trying and a lot of bad words about locks, doors, and Harry Miller, Fingers slumped to the floor and said, 'It's no good, 'e's rammed that key in good and proper. I can't get it out.'

'Well, that's a first,' said Baby.

Fingers got up and let the door have a kick that would have won the FA Cup.

But it still didn't budge.

They tried shoving, pushing and rattling but after a few hours of this, and Fingers trying again and again with her lock-picking wire, they heard a wireless downstairs in the house. Baby was all out of ideas but, one thing for sure, they didn't want the old woman, Tatler, to find them, least of all with her wardrobe in bits.

She checked the window. They were three floors up. If they tried climbing out of Harry's window it was a drop straight down with nothing, not even a twig, to break their fall.

The springs creaked as Baby sat on the bed.

They creaked again as Fingers flumped next to her. 'I'm hungry an' all.'

Baby tried all the drawers in the chest and under the sink again.

But there was only that bottle and the glasses. Baby knew how bad that was for you. Moll never touched it.

Baby tipped the drink from the glass and the bottle down the sink before she joined her sister on the bed again. 'I'll have to think.'

'I'm still hungry,' said Fingers with a sleepy whimper from her side of the bed, having abandoned Harry's jacket as too warm for the weather they were having.

After the disturbed and disturbing night that she'd had previously, Baby was tired. And hungry too.

But sleep was all they could do until someone unlocked that door and they could make a run for it.

175

When they finally woke up it was still light outside, but instead of that orange evening glow over the Nettlefield roofs, the light was the harder, whiter morning light of the next day.

Baby rubbed sleep dust out of her eyes.

Fingers was still asleep next to her on the bed.

Baby shook her sister. 'Wake up, it's morning!' she said, and spotted Harry's jacket strewn across the broken wardrobe door on the floor on the other side of the bed. 'You did go through his pockets, didn't you?'

Fingers sat bolt upright, then leaned over and grabbed Harry Miller's flying jacket.

'I thought you would have done this, what's wrong with you?' Baby snatched the jacket off her. It was heavy, the sheepskin collar was soft and the leather creaky and, like Fingers's skirt, it had lots of pockets, inside and out.

Most of them only gave up bits of matted fluff.

But in one, on the inside of the jacket, fastened with two buttons, was something hard with sharp points.

Baby fumbled as she undid the buttons. They were stiff.

The thing inside felt cold like metal, and from the pocket she took out a gold cross.

'Worth a bob or two, that,' said Fingers, looking on over Baby's shoulder.

The cross, shaped like four arrowheads pointing to the middle, was decorated in blue and was fixed to a black and white striped ribbon. Between the arrowheads were golden eagles, and on the cross some words written in a language Baby couldn't understand.

There was something else in the pocket too. A small bundle of badges – stripes, wings, some metal, some cloth, things with scraps of thread all round them like they'd been sewn on somewhere once upon a time.

'It might not be dinner or breakfast, but this is evidence, hard evidence,' said Baby.

And like a window opening to the truth inside her head, she worked out in an instant what the matter with Harry was.

Baby put the cross and the badges into one of her own skirt pockets as footsteps and a clanking noise were coming up the stairs.

Baby and Fingers hid behind the bed.

A snooty voice on the other side of the locked door said, 'What has that man been doing to my property?'

Baby heard the key rattle and grind in the lock.

The door opened and Mrs Tatler bustled in with a mop, broom and bucket.

'Run for it!' shouted Fingers, who leapt across the bed and barged between Mrs Tatler and the door frame.

'What the dickens!' said Mrs Tatler, dropping her bucket and losing her balance.

Before the lady could set herself aright, Baby threw Harry's jacket over the woman's head and followed Fingers hurtling down the three flights of stairs, out the front door and into the alley.

They sped away from West Street to the back streets and Camellia Lane.

In Dahlia Road, when she was sure no one was coming after them, Baby shooed Fingers into the passageway between the houses. Catching her breath, Baby said, 'Harry Miller might well have been a brave pilot in the war, but it wasn't for Britain.'

19
'We Really Need to Talk'
Tuesday 25th May, Nettlefield

LETITIA PEEPED OUT through her curtains. The sun was streaming through the dormitory windows onto the Spanish children's beds, all neatly made with a pillow and turned sheets at both ends. On the other side of the room, the regular orphans' beds were messy and not entirely empty of orphans. A few, including Ramón, were still asleep while others were playing in their pyjamas.

Ida sat up in her sister Bonnie's bed. Bonnie, with orphans Aggie and Robert, was playing with a wooden train set on a pretty floral rug in the middle of the dormitory floor.

'What time is it?' asked Ida. 'Shouldn't you be getting ready for school?'

'I don't know,' said Bonnie, pushing a train around its track.

'We can't find June.' Aggie looked up. Her hair was a messy tangle round her face.

'Cook ain't in the kitchen, either,' said Robert.

Frank the dog was happily stretched out in a sunny patch of floor alongside him.

'Is anyone making your breakfasts?' asked Letitia.

'Brian's downstairs,' said Robert, 'but she says she needs some help because William's only good for washing up.'

'I'll go,' said Ida, with an unfriendly frown at Letitia. Putting on that elegant but old satin dressing gown, she dashed through the dormitory.

Letitia pulled on her shorts under her skirt. She had a feeling the day could be one of action and followed Ida out through the doors to the main stairs.

But as soon as she was through the doors, Letitia turned back. Something about the Spanish children's beds was shouting to her and she'd missed it.

Oblivious, the orphan children carried on playing with the train set, though Frank, in his sunny spot on the floor, did stretch and lift his head briefly as Letitia came back into the dormitory.

On each Spanish child's pillow there was a photograph, neatly placed in the middle.

Letitia picked up the nearest. The picture of a father and mother carrying a baby looked recently printed. The edges were quite sharp and the corners hardly bent at all.

180

But it wasn't exactly a happy picture. The mother and father weren't smiling. Keeping a smile on your face while a photographer sorts themselves out was tricky. Letitia knew that from experience. But these people looked more scared than bored.

Letitia picked up the photograph on the pillow at the other end of the bed – a different family, but the same sort of picture.

And it was the same for each of the seven beds – fourteen pictures, fourteen families. Each huddled in a frightened group. And another thing, each photo had the same whitewashed wall background. Was it the same wall? How could you tell? And were these people dead or alive? The newness of the photographs suggested that they were alive, or were until very recently at least.

On her way down the stairs, Letitia tried to work out what this meant. The children who were not allowed to talk were trying to tell her something. But what exactly?

In the kitchen, Brian was stirring a huge pot of porridge. 'It's nearly ready,' she said. 'Ida's setting the table. Please can you take that?' Brian indicated a wobbly stack of thick white slices of bread on the kitchen table.

'Do you think they'll have time for marmalade sandwiches?' asked Letitia. 'Aren't the children already late for school?'

'There's always time for sandwiches!' said Brian.

Letitia balanced the stack of slices on a big plate with some butter and marmalade and wobbled across the hall and through the double doors to the living room, where Ida was placing bowls around the table.

'You took your time. Have you got the spoons?' said Ida in a rather unfriendly way. She was obviously still upset that Letitia was casting aspersions on Harry's character.

'No, I haven't, sorry. I'll get them,' said Letitia, setting her plate of bread slices down on the table before heading back to the kitchen.

'I'll need a knife too, for spreading that lot,' called Ida after her, with a tut of impatience. Ida was definitely not going to forgive Letitia in a hurry.

Letitia quickly fetched a butter knife and a handful of spoons from the kitchen, but on her way out she collided with Alfredo who was on his way out of Mrs Lovelock's room. 'What were you doing in there?' she asked.

But any answer Alfredo was going to give was interrupted by Brian coming out of the kitchen behind them with her huge pot of porridge. 'Out of the way!' she said, 'Hungry children to feed!'

Ida appeared and snatched the cutlery off Letitia. 'They're already late!' she said, and marched back to the living room with Brian and the porridge.

'This room is now mine,' said Alfredo, much too importantly for a guest in the house.

'But it's Mrs Lovelock's room.' Letitia tried to peer over his shoulder to see if the old lady was in still there.

But she could only see José skulking behind Alfredo.

'Where's Mrs Lovelock ... and Miss June?' asked Letitia.

'They have been called away,' said Alfredo.

'Where have they been called away to? And why?' The air around Letitia suddenly cooled and she shivered at the thought of this lovely place without Miss June.

'That is not your concern.' Alfredo pushed past Letitia. 'We have preparations to make. Come, José.'

'I will get a broom to sweep with,' said José, looking intently at Letitia.

'Be quick, they will soon be here.' Alfredo barged through the orphans, who were leaving the living room with porridge smeared around their mouths and slopped on their school jerseys.

In the middle of the toing and froing, Ramón had appeared and was watching his brother.

José shook his head at Ramón to say not now. José then leaned over and whispered in Letitia's ear. 'Believe me, I am not part of this.' He pressed into her hand a tightly folded piece of paper.

Letitia recognised the feel of it as the same paper Miss June gave her for her letter to Elsie.

Alfredo barked his orders from the stairs. 'José! Come!'

'I must go,' said José. 'Please take care of Ramón for me.'

'Wait, you forgot the broom.' Letitia quickly fetched one from the kitchen.

'Thank you.' José took the broom. Then, careful of the children but ignoring his own brother, he joined Alfredo on the stairs.

At that moment, the outside door at the far end of the kitchen corridor burst open and Baby and Fingers ran in.

'You're back!' said Letitia, rushing back along the corridor to meet them. 'I was getting worried. Where have you been?'

But before Baby and Fingers could explain, Letitia heard a ripple of orphans' laughter come from the hall at the other end of the kitchen corridor, where Ida and Brian were trying to get the children packed off to school.

Miss Grenville, her arms loaded with boxes and packages, was joining the chaos, where Ida was doing a good impression of Miss June Lovelock. 'Shh, children! That's not very kind.'

Miss Grenville didn't notice that the laughter was aimed at her. 'Oh, we're going to have such a wonderful party!' she said to the general muddle of children and teenagers as Ida was trying to send the orphans, one by one, out to school. They were at least half an hour late.

'Oh Gawd, hide me,' said Baby from behind Letitia's back.

Miss Grenville caught orphan Aggie's sleeve as she was passing. 'Find Baby for me. I have to tell her about her party.' Miss Grenville's hair was as messy as Aggie's, her cheeks bright red and her expression wide-eyed yet intense. A few brightly coloured scarves were swathed round her neck and she was wearing that green silk jacket again, the same one that Letitia had seen Baby wearing, though Miss Grenville's was a lot cleaner.

'Oi ain't seen her, miss,' said Aggie, spitting breadcrumbs and heading for the front door.

'No matter, I'll tell her later,' said Miss Grenville breathily, before she wafted up the stairs, an escaped party streamer trailing behind her.

'What's happening?' asked Baby. 'Where's June?'

'I don't know,' said Ida, scraping sweaty strands of hair off her face as the last orphan, waving a chunky marmalade sandwich, ran out the front door.

Ida addressed Baby and Fingers, ignoring Letitia. It was only Ramón's hand slipping into hers that made Letitia feel a little less beastly.

Brian, in a porridge-splattered apron but otherwise clean, cool and calm, returned to the kitchen with the empty pot.

Clutching José's folded letter, Letitia took a deep breath and decided to be brave. 'Can we all go into the kitchen for a moment?'

William, the kitchen boy, hunched over the sink, his arms plunged to his elbows in washing up, looked up as they went in, but glares from Baby and Ida persuaded him to return to his job.

When Baby, Fingers, Brian, Ida and Ramón were inside and the kitchen door closed, Letitia swallowed and said, 'I think we really need to talk about what's happening here, and that includes Miss June's gentleman friend.'

'Too right,' said Fingers.

'What are you saying about Harry?' said Ida. 'Have you forgotten what he did for us? If it hadn't been for him ...'

'I know,' said Baby. 'But what do you make of these?'

Fingers rummaged in her skirts and produced an assortment of badges strewn with stray threads, and a cross on a black and white ribbon.

Letitia immediately knew what it was, though she never thought she'd see one in real life.

Ida gingerly picked up the cross. She tried to read the words, 'Po ... Po ... I can't read it. It's not English, is it?' Ida looked up, her face full of fear.

'May I?' said Letitia, holding her hand open.

'The words translate as Order of Merit,' she said. 'It is in French, but the medal is actually German. Prussian if you want to be absolutely accurate. I learned about it at school. In the war it was nicknamed the Blue Max, and Germany awarded it to their bravest pilots.'

Ida looked up, her eyes brimming with tears. 'He wasn't one of ours at all then, was he?'

'No, it doesn't look like he was,' said Letitia as kindly as she could.

Ida pulled out a chair, sprawled her top half over the kitchen table and cried into her arms.

'I knew all along he wasn't to be trusted,' said Fingers.

Baby gave her sister a shove. 'Not a time for that.'

Ida raised her head, sniffed and dragged the back of her hand under her nose. 'What does all this mean?'

'It means,' said Letitia, 'that something very dangerous is going on and those poor mute Spanish children are right in the middle of it.'

Letitia explained about the photographs on their pillows. 'I don't know how or why these children came here. They certainly didn't come on the boat with all the others. He has a purpose for those children, and we need to find out what it is.'

Baby remembered what she overheard in Harry's flat. 'He's making 'em into spies,' she said.

'Into what?' asked Ida.

'Spies,' said Baby. 'For Hitler. It's what that thing in the box and that wireless those girls have got in The Lillie are for. The other word for a wireless is radio, ain't it?'

'But spies – how?' said Ida, her face screwed up with the puzzle. 'That makes no sense. They're children.'

'Children grow up,' said Brian enigmatically.

That undisputable fact felt very important to Letitia.

William, his hands still wet from the sink, had joined them around the German medal.

Baby grabbed William's shirt, pulled him down to her level and, nose to nose, looked him hard in the eye. 'Not a word to anyone, you hear? If I get to hear you've blabbed that we're onto 'em, you'll wish you was in the clink with that devil Underwood.'

William stiffened and nodded his head so violently you could imagine it nodding off.

'Now go and finish that washing up,' ordered Baby.

'José gave me this just now.' Letitia unfolded the paper she'd been clutching. She explained in whispers how Ramón and José were brothers. José's letter was in Spanish, Letitia translated it as she read:

Letitia, I am sorry to write in Spanish, but I must write quickly.

I promised my mother that I would bring Ramón to safety in England. They took Ramón on the boat but they said I was too old for it. I asked our teacher – Fitzgerald – to help. I overheard him talk to the Englishman about taking children to England on the Englishman's plane. Fitzgerald said there was no room for me on the plane but he would get me on the boat if I helped him. He gave me instructions in an envelope and told me not to open it until we were at sea.

The instructions told me to find children who support Franco and would like to help Franco's friend, and friend of Spain, Hitler. I AM NOT FASCIST. But it was too late to say I would not help. I panicked and threw the letter in the sea. I told Ramón he must go to the camp where he will be safe. I told Fitzgerald the instructions had blown away before I could read them. If Fitzgerald finds out that Ramón is my brother, he will do to him what he is doing to the children who came on the plane ...

'Why didn't he just go to the camp too? It would be easy to hide amongst thousands of kids,' said Baby.

'Perhaps he wants to rescue those children?' said Letitia.

'There's more writing on the other side,' said Brian.

Letitia turned the paper over to just a few more sentences and a scrawled line across the page. She read:

When we reached England, I discovered where those children came from. They do not support Franco either ...

'That's all, it looks like he had to stop writing,' said Letitia.

'Where are their families, then?' said Fingers.

'In danger!' said Ida and thumped her fist on the table. 'We're all in danger from these people.'

William dropped the bowl he was drying.

'I trusted Harry,' said Ida.

'Blackshirts, Hitler, Franco fascists ... they're all the same,' said Baby, as orphans Aggie and Robert burst into the kitchen followed by Frank the dog.

'What are you doing here, why aren't you at school?' asked Ida.

'We saw 'er',' said Robert.

'Me an' Robit run back as soon as we saw 'er getting in 'er car and everything,' said Aggie, clinging onto Robert.

A car was pulling up outside the orphanage front door.

'Who? Miss June?' Letitia, with Ramón gripping her hand, went to look.

But the woman who met them in the hall was not Miss June Lovelock.

The woman who met them in the hall was as far from Miss June Lovelock as you could possibly imagine. A tight black blouse, bulbous calves, blood-red lips and a large bag over one arm. 'Robert Perkins, are you still here?' boomed Mrs Hilda Bullar, Blackshirt and former matron of Nettlefield Grange.

Letitia heard Ida gasp before she whispered into Letitia's ear, 'Get out quick!'

Letitia heard running footsteps and a door bang. When she looked around, Baby, Fingers, Ida and Brian had gone. The door at the far end of the corridor, where Baby and Fingers had only a short while before had burst in, now swung open.

Through the other door, the large front door to the orphanage, Letitia could see the car, a dark red Austin with its engine running. Miss Grenville's fiancé, the teacher, the kidnapper, the spymaster, Mr Easton Fitzgerald sat in the driver's seat, and in the back sat José, his palm pressed flat against the window.

As if it had been tattooed into his hand, Letitia knew exactly what José was trying to say.

HELP!

20

The Nettlefield Resistance

Tuesday 25th May, Nettlefield

NEXT DOOR TO Nettlefield Grange Orphanage, the cottage under the railway bridge was tucked so well out of sight most folk forgot it was there. Not on purpose, like they did for the asylum and like they used to for the orphanage before June Lovelock took over. They just didn't notice it. And over time, the cottage became more or less invisible behind its scraggly hedges and bramble-covered garden, snug where the bridge met the embankment.

It was the obvious place to hide and work out a plan of action: the perfect HQ for what Baby was now thinking of as The Nettlefield Resistance.

Brian's dad put a full kettle on the kitchen range. 'This is when we know we're British, when in times of crisis the top priority is a cup of tea,' he said.

'But I have to get Bonnie before that woman does,' said Ida, her hand already on the door handle.

Before Christmas, Ida's sister Bonnie had come so close to being stolen away forever by former orphanage matron and filthy Blackshirt, Mrs Bullar, that Baby could perfectly understand Ida's panic. 'But Ida,' said Baby, 'she's got a different evil scheme this time. She's in with Fitzgerald, ain't she?'

'Yes, I know. But they're Blackshirts, Fascists, Nazis – her coming back proves they're still here and in power somehow; how else did she get out of jail? And they won't stop until they get what they want, or somebody stops them. Just 'cause we stopped Uncle Arthur doesn't mean they've stopped wanting blonde children like Bonnie. I can't leave Bonnie there with that woman in charge again. Whatever else she's up to now, I can't risk it.'

What Ida said was right. The Blackshirts could easily have more than one evil scheme on at the same time. The thought was overwhelming. But worrying about what else the Blackshirts might be up to wasn't going to help the orphans, English or Spanish.

Ida was still wearing Gin's old satin dressing gown over her pyjamas. 'I should get dressed first. Oh …' Ida took her hand off the door handle. 'my overalls are still next door.'

'You need a disguise,' said Brian, climbing the ladder to the room under the thatch where her Dad slept and where Brian too was bunking down while The Lillie was otherwise occupied.

'I think, my dear,' said Brian's dad, 'that we'll all need disguises if that woman has truly taken Mein Kampf to heart. We'll all be prey to her machinations.'

Baby wasn't entirely sure what Brian's Dad meant, but when she looked around the room at Brian, Fingers, the long grey-bearded Mr Shaw and herself, she agreed from experience that those Blackshirts – Nazis – didn't like anyone who was a bit 'different'.

Ida started pacing backwards and forwards in the small space between the kitchen table and the door. 'Bri, what are you doing up there?'

The ladder creaked again as Brian climbed down with a bundle of clothes over her shoulder and some ladies' shoes hooked on her fingers. 'These will fit you. They're from Gin's case of 'Aunt Constance' clothes. You can wear them too and fetch Bonnie!'

'You're a Wonder, Bri!' said Ida, grabbing the clothes.

'I know.'

Brian's dad covered his eyes as Ida shed the gown and her pyjamas down to her undies and then dressed in a skirt, a lady's blouse, a jacket and high-heeled shoes.

Brian plonked a hat on Ida's head and pulled it low, over her eyes. 'You're Aunt Constance, now.'

Straightaway, Ida looked about ten years older than her fourteen years.

'What shall we do about Letitia?' said Brian.

'We'll figure that out,' said Baby. Letitia was pretty good at looking after herself and besides, they needed someone on the inside to look out for all the kids. It occurred to Baby that Letitia was their spy. With that thought, a plan was forming in Baby's mind.

'I'm going now.' Ida opened the door.

'Wait!' shouted Baby. But the ten o'clock Portsmouth train thundering across the railway bridge above them drowned out her voice. Baby grabbed Ida and waited for it to pass.

'Have we got a plan?' asked Brian.

'Yes, we have,' said Baby. 'Bri, you are going to keep yer head down and carry on at the orphanage as normal. Letitia's in there to help. If you keep her away from the first aid box, she's really good in an emergency. Let 'er do the runnin' around in there.'

Baby could feel Ida pulling away. 'Ida, Bonnie is safe at school for the day. Before you get her, me and Fingers could use you all dressed up like that.'

Ida relaxed her arm. 'All right, what do you want me to do?'

'Come with us, we're going to the Town Hall.'

'Good,' said Ida, opening the door. 'I know exactly what to do.'

196

Baby, Fingers and Ida left Brian in the little shaded kitchen with her dad and a fresh pot of tea.

The three of them strode past the orphanage, and headed up West Street towards the Town Hall. As Ida's legs must have grown at least six inches in as many months, Baby and Fingers had to run to keep up with her.

They ran under stripy shop awnings, past lady shoppers in cotton dresses and little straw hats, and pavement displays of everything thing from rosy red apples and freshly baked buns to backyard brooms.

Ida's heels click-clacked, business-like up the Town Hall steps. She pushed the huge door open, to the surprise of the doorman who was inside in the shade, mopping his sweaty forehead. Ida made straight for the sign that said Children's Department, pointing up the sweeping marble staircase. Baby had never been inside the Town Hall. It was ten times grander than Nettlefield Grange. A smooth marble floor, a wide curving staircase, lamps strung with diamond bits of glass that reminded Baby of one of Brian's dad's contraptions, and carvings all around the walls. It was how she imagined a palace to be.

Bold as brass, Ida strode down a corridor and hammered with her fist on an office door. Baby of course knew who she was looking for: Mr Wimpole, the council official who used to be June Lovelock's boss and who'd promoted her to orphanage matron at Christmas-time when he changed sides. He used to be a Blackshirt.

Was he one again?

Ida straightened her skirt and tucked her hair inside her hat. Baby and Fingers stood behind her.

'Come,' said a deep official voice from the other side of the door.

Ida opened the door.

'Who are you?' she said to the large man with a bald head, except for a short fringe of hair above his ears. The man, who was not Mr Wimpole, sat behind the desk, a fat wad of papers in front of him and a pen in his hand.

'How impertinent!' He screwed the cap on the pen. 'My name is Moles, Mr Moles,' He tapped it on the shiny new nameplate on the desk in front of him. 'And who do you think you are, madam?'

'My name is Barnes, Miss Barnes, and I'm here to see Mr Wimpole.'

Ida Barnes still couldn't tell a fib to save her life. What happened to Aunt Constance?

'Mr Wimpole has moved on,' said the man.

'Or been moved on,' whispered Baby to Fingers.

The large man called Moles shuffled his papers then pointed at Baby and Fingers. 'Who are these ... er, persons? Are they with you?' His top lip curled into a sneer.

'I am concerned about the welfare of the orphanage children,' said Ida. 'I'm sure you are unaware that the orphanage has been taken over by an escaped convict and known Blackshirt.'

'On the contrary, I'm fully aware that Miss June Lovelock has been replaced with someone much more suitable for the role.'

As Ida spluttered some noises that were meant to be English, Baby pushed in front of her and leaned over the desk. 'So, what are you saying?'

Fingers joined Baby at the desk and in her most threatening voice said, 'Yeah, what are you saying?'

'I should think that's quite clear,' said Moles. 'If you continue to refer to the returning matron as you just did, I shall call the police and have you arrested for slander. Having been found innocent of all charges, Mrs Hilda Bullar has been released, her record expunged and a full compensation awarded. Mistakes were made in orphanage accounting. Now if that is all, I have a very busy day. Goodbye.' He stood up from his desk, strode to the front it, and with his bulk, as good as pushed all three of them out the door.

In the corridor, Ida was heaving to catch her breath, her chest rising and falling persuading Baby that at any moment fire could spurt from her nostrils. Ida raised her fists to bang on the door.

But Baby pulled her away. 'It's no good, it's as I thought. He's one of 'em. They're all over the place.'

'I know, I just didn't want to believe it ...' Ida looked hopelessly up at the Town Hall's high ceiling, decorated with fancy plasterwork. 'But we mustn't give in to them.'

'We're not giving in to them,' said Baby, grabbing Ida's arms, looking her in the eye. 'We're going to fight and we're going to win and we're going to do it by being clever, much cleverer than them.'

Furniture scraping and footsteps came from the other side of the office door.

'We gotta get out of here.' Baby dragged Ida away, down the stairs, across the echoing hall and out into the sunshine warming the Town Hall steps.

'You go and get Bonnie out of school,' said Baby.

'And keep 'er safe,' added Fingers.

'All right,' said Ida. 'I suppose we've beaten them once, we'll just have to do it again.'

'That's the spirit,' said Baby.

Ida pulled her shoulders back and stood up straight. 'I'm going there now.' She ran down the last few steps, crossed the end of High Street and marched past Doswells' shop windows, where mannequins in bathing costumes lounged under frilly sunshades.

Baby and Fingers ran after her. They watched Ida turn up Doswells' Alley, dark, compared to the bright sunshine in West Street, and the quickest way to Nettlefield School.

'Take her back to the cottage! He'll keep her safe,' shouted Fingers.

'Don't tell the whole of Nettlefield,' said Baby. 'You don't know who's listening.'

But Ida was already out the other end.

At least one of the orphans would be safe from Mrs Bullar. When Baby thought of the others, sitting at their desks with no idea of the horrible surprise in store for them, it was as if she'd been given a giant sack of potatoes to carry, old mouldy ones too.

But Baby wasn't one to be weighed down for long when there was a job to be done. 'Right,' she whispered to Fingers, steeling herself for action, 'we're going to find out exactly what those Blackshirts are up to and then we're going to find June.'

'And her ma?' asked Fingers, who wasn't generally a fan of mothers.

'Too right, we are,' said Baby. 'But first things first. What on earth could those Spanish kids be learning in the church hall with Fitzgerald and Mrs Doris Tatler?'

21

The Church Hall School

Tuesday 25th May, Nettlefield

BABY WAITED FOR A TRAM to pass and crossed over the road.

Fingers dashed after her.

They turned off West Street just before the travel agent's shop, where Fingers used to stare at the pictures of the cruise liners in the window.

They were soon outside the wooden gates to Arthur Underwood's old yard. Arthur Underwood, the undertaker and Ida's uncle, was now locked up in prison for kidnapping, thanks to the girls.

'You don't think he's been let out an' all, do you?' Baby locked her fingers together to make a step for her sister.

'Well if 'e 'as then that's us for it.' Fingers stepped up and stretched for the top of the gates.

Baby strained under Fingers's weight. 'S'pose so,' said Baby. She had never let that Nazi devil scare her off before and she wasn't going to start now. Plus, Fingers had always said she could burgle a police station full of coppers and be in and out before they were any the wiser.

Fingers clambered up. The new soles on her boots felt like bricks on Baby's shoulders.

Fingers hitched herself over the gates. With the clump of her boots on the other side, the clank of bolts being slid open and the scrape of the gate across the cobbles, they were both inside.

A window was broken, a fresh crop of weeds grew between the stones but there was still a patch of oil where the undertaker used to park his van. The stable door hung skew-whiff on one hinge. Ida had said that Queenie, Underwood's horse that used to pull the funeral cart, had been taken out to pasture somewhere near Swan Bay.

Fingers moved a plank of wood, leaning it against the fence, to reveal another gate. She opened the latch and led Baby along a sunny overgrown alley, to the back of the church hall. 'This was where 'e came in secret to pick out the blonde kids, when she brought 'em all to church. 'E dragged 'em back along this 'ere alley and boxed 'em up in 'is workshop,' said Fingers.

Baby shuddered at the memory of all the goings-on last year.

Standing under an open window, Fingers whispered, 'D'you wanna look first, or shall I?'

'You can look first.' Baby got down onto her hands and knees under the window. A long blade of grass tickled Baby's nose as Fingers climbed onto her back.

'Can you see anything?' asked Baby.

'Enough,' said Fingers, her boots pressing into Baby's back as she craned to see. 'They're all there.' She stepped down off Baby's back.

'Who?'

'Them. All of 'em. 'er and 'im and 'er and all of 'em sitting and watching those kids 'stead of their apples and buns.'

Sometimes, Fingers's refusing to use most folks' names, especially folks she didn't like, got very frustrating.

'Can you see June or her ma?' asked Baby.

'Nope.'

'Right, it's my turn ...' said Baby.

The curtains at the window were drawn but not closed. So Baby had just enough of a view of the church hall-cum-classroom to see what was going on. She felt the sun warm the back of head.

They were all there. Mrs Tatler, Harry Miller's landlady and minder for the Spanish children was there with Mr Fitzgerald and the rest of the town's Blackshirts. The whole lot of them belonged to the Hands Across the

Sea group, who organised the coronation kids' tea party the other week.

It was the Spanish kids now sitting round that tea party table, their heads bent low over old writing slates. Fitzgerald paced around them, peering over their shoulders, a stick tucked under his arm. Baby hated sticks like that. They hurt.

At the front of the church hall, near the stage, a blackboard was propped on an easel and a cloth was draped over it.

The door to the hall opened and in walked Moles from the council. 'Just to let you know, Fitzgerald... ' he announced, 'Hilda Bullar has reported that Nettlefield Grange is ready for you now.'

'Very well,' said Fitzgerald. 'Mrs Tatler, you must take these children back after drill.'

Moles joined the other Blackshirts at the back of the room, some of whom Baby didn't recognise.

Mrs Tatler marched past the cowering Spanish kids to the front. She coughed a little dry cough into her hand.

'Pencils down,' said Fitzgerald. 'Mrs Tatler will now drill you in sentence practice. Do this badly and you will fail us, and then you know what will happen.' He tapped the covered blackboard with his stick.

Gasps and nods to say 'we understand' went around the kids' table. Every one of them sat up straight to attention.

205

'Thank you, Mr Fitzgerald,' said Mrs Tatler, giving him a sickly smile.

Fitzgerald's hair shone with oil. The sun shone through the gap in the curtains like a spotlight, making him look especially like a movie star.

Baby hoped her shadow wouldn't give her away.

'He-hem ... Repeat after me: I saw my friend today. Who did you see?'

The kids chanted the sentence back, giving it the same pretend jolly expression that Mrs Tatler had.

These kids sounded like they'd done this a hundred times before.

Baby couldn't risk it any longer: any moment one of them could turn and see her at the window. She climbed down off Fingers's back as the Tatler woman was squeaking out another sentence.

Baby grabbed Fingers's jersey and pulled her along the overgrown alley and through the gate into Underwood's yard again. 'They're bullying those kids into being nosey,' she said.

'Ain't that what spies do?' said Fingers.

'Yeah, but who are they meant to be talking to?'

'Can't we go and find June now?' asked Fingers.

'Yeah.' Baby was about to push the yard gate open when she realised where she was. Wasn't it here that Underwood kept their friends hidden all that time?

Baby pushed up her sleeve and reached through a broken window into the workshop. She unhooked the catch and climbed through ... only to meet Fingers already inside.

'Door was open,' she said.

The place stank, a strange mixture of chemicals and rot, but it was as dead as the graves in the churchyard. No sign of the wicked Arthur Underwood. But no sign of anyone else either, not upstairs where he'd hidden Bonnie or down in the cellar where he'd kept their friend Sophie.

Maybe it was something about the horrible smell, but Baby's brain was working. 'What did Fitzgerald say about the women at the camp?'

Fingers shrugged. 'What camp?'

'The children's camp at Southampton where those Spanish kids oughta be!'

'Er ... I can't remember.'

'He said he had 'em eating out of 'is hand. He thinks he can do anything there, whatever 'e likes – pinching more children for instance? How about hiding June Lovelock too?'

'And her ma!' said Fingers. 'What are we going to do, then?'

'Go there and find 'em of course!' said Baby, unbolting the yard gate.

'What, you mean we're going to go camping in Southampton?'

'More or less ...' said Baby. '... on the train, the old way.'

Fingers whooped, punched the air with her fist and led the sprint up West Street. Baby followed, dodging prams covered by sunshades with trailing fringes, old ladies with baskets of fruit, and the postman with his early afternoon delivery.

The 'old way' was without tickets.

22

The Orphanage has become the Opposite of Itself

Tuesday 25th May, Nettlefield

Standing with Ramón in the entrance hall of Nettlefield Grange Orphanage, Letitia felt the large woman's gaze fall on her like a cold shower at school. It was only since leaving Threep that she had experienced this sort of thing – the receptionist at the hotel, the woman in the queue for tickets at the station. But the look from Mrs Bullar was ten, twenty, a hundred times more than their distaste. It was hatred.

What had Letitia done to inspire such a feeling? But then she realised it wasn't what she had done. It was who she was. She was different. But was she really that different? Hadn't they mistaken her for a Spanish person at the docks? But it wasn't just about looks. And perhaps that said something about the good people of

Southampton who were helping with the boat and the camp. They welcomed the differences.

She dashed back into the kitchen with Ramón, who was muttering José's name over and over with something that sounded like praying. The temptation was to escape with Ramón through the same door that Baby, Fingers, Brian and Ida had. But Letitia wasn't going to do that. She had to find out where the Spanish children had come from. According to José's letter this was very important. It was what he was about to tell them before he had to stop writing. And he wanted her help.

She had to make those Spanish children talk to her, tell her exactly what danger they were in.

She sat Ramón down at the kitchen table.

'My brother! Help!' he said in English; he was learning – but what a way to learn!

'Don't worry,' said Letitia. 'We shall find him.' She poured a glass of milk for the small, trembling boy. 'Drink this while I think.' Hoping the Bullar woman wouldn't invade, she pulled out the chair next to Ramón while he drank. How on earth was she was going to rescue José, make the Spanish children talk and stop Fitzgerald without putting anyone in any more danger?

She also had to admit that she was a little annoyed with the others leaving her high and dry. But she'd have come back anyway. She couldn't have abandoned Ramón.

Bumps, bangs and crashes echoed through the building along with bellowed orders to 'Remove this rubbish!' 'Strip those useless fripperies!' 'Out! Out with all of this junk!'

And what about all the English orphans too – what a terrible shock they were going to have! They would be coming home from school in just a few hours.

The latch on the kitchen door clicked. Letitia sat up, straightened her back and steeled herself for resistance.

A person in an oversized homburg and swamped by an ankle-length coat, tatty with stray threads, walked in. The person, who was too short for Mrs Bullar, closed the door quietly behind themselves.

They removed the hat and put it on the table. 'Hello,' said Brian flinching at another crash which sounded like it came from the hall.

'Brian! I am very pleased to see you, but is it safe for you here?' asked Letitia.

'Yes. Dad has given me a disguise. I wanted to make sure you were all right. Mrs Bullar is horrible.'

The door crashed open again and Cook lumbered in with two full bags of groceries. She heaved them onto the table. 'I came to work this morning and that whatnot Alfredo sent me 'ome and told me to come back later. Well, I knew something was up when I saw her in her motor car. Goodness knows how she got out the clink, but I thought if there's one thing I'm doing, it's going to help those poor little nippers out – all of 'em. So, I bought a few extra supplies on the way. That Bullar woman's none too generous with the housekeeping.'

'Oh, did you buy this out of your own pocket?' said Letitia.

'More the jar on the mantelpiece for a little trip to Bournemouth with me sister come the August bank holiday, but that will sort itself out, don't you worry about that.' She began emptying her bags on to the table. 'Get your apron on Brian my dear, and let's get a nice hot pot on with his scrag-end of lamb the butcher let me have cheap when I said it was for the Grange kids.'

'Can I help?' asked Letitia.

'Course you can, my dear. The more the merrier,' said Cook, rolling up her sleeves. 'Here, does that little one want a jam sandwich? Brian!'

And that was how the Letitia spent the morning, amongst the delicious smells of cooking, listening to the blunderbuss destruction going on in the rest of the building. It was strange, but the simple tasks she and Ramón were given – peeling potatoes, stirring the mixture for sponge pudding and putting the kettle on for a pot of tea – allowed her to think.

As Letitia was clearing the teacups she heard the horrible little woman who had been chaperoning the Spanish children. Letitia opened the door a little way to listen. She needed all the intelligence she could gather.

Mrs Tatler was in the entrance hall. Was that the soft shuffling of Spanish feet coming in with her? It wasn't far off midday. Had they finished school early?

'Here they are, Hilda. Are we ready?' said Mrs Tatler.

'We certainly are, Doris,' said Mrs Bullar in a voice that reminded Letitia of cod liver oil.

'I think they'll need to eat before they recommence their education this afternoon. Easton's very certain that there should be no suspicion that these children have not been well fed, is he not?' said Mrs Tatler.

'Yes,' said Mrs Bullar, the word seemed to hiss reluctantly from her lips, as if the only person who should be well fed was herself. 'Cook!' she bellowed.

At which command, Cook left the kitchen to receive her orders.

Half a minute later, Cook was back shaking her head. 'Ooh, I don't know. I hope there's some justice down the track for that woman and her like. You can see those foreign nippers are terrified out of their boots.' She gathered together a small leaning tower of dishes and a bundle of spoons. 'Brian, you stay in here with the littl'un while me and the miss sort this out. Most likely you'll have to make another pot for our lot.'

Cook carried the pot while Letitia followed with the bowls and spoons.

In the living room, the Spanish children sat to attention, rigid with what had to be a mortal fear of stepping out of line – the orphanage really had become the opposite of itself. The children sat seven to a table facing the bare, black hole of the fireplace at the far end of the room, where a blackboard on an easel was set up. Above the fireplace, fixed to the wall where the children's paintings used to be, was now a horrible old portrait of an elderly man with giant mutton chop whiskers. Below the portrait, the blackboard was mostly covered with an old linen cloth. Letitia could see the corner of something pinned to the board. It clearly wasn't being used in the normal way.

Letitia and Cook served the lamb hotpot and were immediately shooed out by Alfredo as the children ate in silence.

It was only when she went back to collect the dirty dishes and spoons that Letitia could see what was going on.

Alfredo marched to the front with a stick under his arm. He paced in front of the covered blackboard, declaring phrases that could have come from Grandma's book of etiquette, but in a manner that was so false they could only have been uttered by that character Mr Charles Dickens wrote about in David Copperfield, Uriah Heep.

The children repeated these phrases in the same false way – 'Thank you for having me. May I leave the table?' When they didn't do it well enough to satisfy Alfredo he lifted the edge of the cloth covering the blackboard with his stick.

Whatever the Spanish children were frightened of, it was under that cloth.

The children whimpered and repeated the phrase more enthusiastically – 'Thank you very much for having me! Can I stay forever?'

Alfredo removed his stick from under the cloth and gave the children another phrase for them to copy after him. He had repeated this exercise several times before he noticed that Letitia was still in the room. 'What are you doing still here? Out, out with you!'

'More to the point,' said Letitia, 'What are you doing? Your teaching methods are Victorian.'

'What is that you're saying? You should be back in the kitchen with the rest of the staff.' He waved his stick angrily. It caught the cloth, which hooked onto the stick and waved like a flag over the small class of Spanish children.

It was quite funny.

But no one was laughing.

The images on the board were so far from a laughing matter they made Letitia feel sick to her stomach.

Each photograph, pinned to the board, had in its background an ancient building, large and ornate with many windows. In front of the building, in each photograph, were some gallows and on each set of gallows was a person, hanging from them. Dead.

The children whimpered and hid their faces in their arms. They had seen them before.

Alfredo struggled to unhook the cloth and replace it over the board of photographs. While his back was turned, Letitia crouched by a child with their face in their hands. In Spanish, Letitia said, 'Will you talk to me? Will you tell me how I can help you?'

The child was too upset to answer. But the boy behind the child, who looked a little older, though none of them could be any more than ten years old, whispered in English through his fingers. 'Meet us before the sun rises. Tomorrow. Upstairs.'

23

Baby & Fingers at the Camp

Tuesday 25th May, Southampton

THE LAST TIME BABY and Fingers had got on a train was to come to Nettlefield from London, before they knew any of the girls. It was strange to think that was less than a year ago, how quickly they'd become a family.

On that train trip, unusually, they had a ticket each.

But it was much more fun without.

Together, they ran up the slope to the station and dashed past the stationmaster's office to the gap in the fence. Fingers pushed her way through and held the slat open for Baby. Brushing themselves down, they joined the ticket holders making their way over the footbridge.

On platform two, Baby and Fingers slipped into the small crowd waiting for the train to Southampton. Perhaps if this was how it was going to be at the orphanage from now on – Bullar in charge and Spanish girls taking over The Lillie – maybe they could just get on a train, go to Southampton Docks and get on the boat to America, or even go back to London and catch a boat there? It would be easy.

What was Baby thinking? They couldn't abandon everyone. They were fighting, weren't they? They were The Nettlefield Resistance and they were going to win. Somehow. But at that moment, Baby couldn't help feeling it was all going to rack and ruin.

The train chuffed over the railway bridge and into the station.

Whatever was going on, Baby was going to enjoy the ride anyway.

They found an empty compartment without a corridor. That was a relief – no climbing into luggage racks to hide from the guard.

Baby stroked the velvet seats and made herself comfortable while Fingers looked out the window. They both enjoyed the ride through the countryside and across rivers with sailing boats. It was like going on holiday.

Outside Southampton Railway Station, a modern building with curves and lines for decoration, Fingers marched up to a boy selling newspapers on the step.

'What d'you want?' said the boy, holding his wad of papers close to his chest.

'Where are all the kids?' asked Fingers, looking up at him.

He looked down his nose at her. 'What kids?'

'The ones from the boat,' said Baby.

'Oh, you mean the Spanish nippers,' he said, backing away. 'They're up at North Stoneham.'

'Where's that, then?' asked Baby.

The boy smirked. 'It's a bit of a walk, right up past the old golf course.' He pointed up the hill towards the town. 'Go that way, take the London road.'

How far could a 'bit of a walk' be? She still had her old boots on, but they'd been mended and it wasn't raining and they couldn't be going *all* the way to London, could they?

Baby and Fingers walked on up the hill away from the station. They passed a little park with lots of flowers and a fountain in the middle, and on the other side of the road, a great big new building with a tower. Bells were chiming out an old hymn. The time on the clock at the top of the tower said four o'clock.

'How far is it?' asked Fingers.

'I don't know,' said Baby, 'but there's plenty to look at. Didn't get much of a chance the last time we were 'ere.'

Fingers slumped and pushed out her bottom lip. 'Walking's boring,' she said.

Baby ignored her and trudged on. They walked up a street of shops with awnings, like Nettlefield's West Street. Baby checked they were going the right way. 'Just keep going, missy,' said a man pushing a barrowload of spuds across the street.

219

They reached a wide tree-lined road. After some big houses, a few old churches and a pub, the road cut through a common where people were playing cricket and football. The common was big enough for a few games to be played at the same time.

The road seemed to go on forever.

'I'm hot,' said Fingers. Her jersey was already tied round her middle and her ginger curls were stuck with sweat to her forehead. 'And thirsty ...'

'The sooner we get there, the sooner you can have a drink,' said Baby.

'I can have a drink back there.' Fingers pointed at the pub behind them, on the edge of the common.

'They won't let you in.' As soon as Baby said it, she realised how stupid that was, Fingers could get in anywhere. But Baby still kept on walking. At least under the trees they were shaded from the sun.

Eventually they came to a crossroads, a road sign pointing to London straight ahead. 'We're not going all the way back there, are we?' Fingers huffed and sat down in the grass at the side of the road with her back up against the road sign.

Baby studied the sign, trying to remember the name of the place the newspaper boy had said. It sounded a bit like Southampton, but that was where they were. She read 'Uni - ver – sity Coll - ege, East - leigh and Stone -

ham. That was it, Stoneham! Come on, it's straight ahead. We're nearly there.'

Fingers pulled herself up. Bits of twig and grass stuck to her skirt, which she didn't bother to brush off. Baby strode on up the road listening to Fingers's boots scuffing the path behind her.

It turned into a long, hot walk with a few wrong turns and lots of complaining especially when they turned down the road for the wrong golf course. Turned out, there were two of them. But eventually, they found the camp. The rows of bright white tents and hundreds and hundreds of children were unmistakable as the camp that Letitia had talked about.

The sun was going down and the orange evening light made the field glow and the kids' faces shine. Big pans of whatever it was they'd had for their tea were being hauled away. Baby grabbed Fingers's jersey. She was half asleep on her feet. 'We gotta be quick, else there'll be nothing left.' Baby dragged her sister down a table where a lady in a pinny was still ladling out the grub.

Baby picked up a couple of bowls abandoned in the long grass and stood with Fingers behind a Spanish kid who was queuing up for seconds. The old lady scraped the pot and filled all three of their bowls with a carroty stew. 'Waste not want not,' she said as she heaved the huge pot off the table and carried it away. The Spanish kid went back to his friends picnicking on the grass.

221

Baby and Fingers sat where they were by the table, too tired to do anything else.

As they were tucking in to the stew, the sun dipped out of the sky, lighting the few clouds near the horizon with a red-orange glow. Children were being shooed to their tents, games of football ended, and tables cleared by the camp ladies with children to help them. A lady with a big pile of blankets bustled by, telling Baby and Fingers: 'Hurry up, it's bedtime.' But she was too busy to check up on them.

Baby looked over her bowl to see if she could catch a glimpse of June Lovelock or her ma or Fitzgerald or Harry. But there were too many people to pick out anyone she knew, good or bad. She felt her eyelids getting heavier and heavier. All really she wanted to do was sleep. As soon as she'd scraped the bowl clean, Baby crawled with Fingers under the table and curled up behind the cloth, among fresh stacks of clean bowls and pots and pans.

As she drifted off to sleep with the earthy smell of the fields in her nose and her sister curled beside her, already snoring, Baby's last thought was: 'How on earth are we going to find June Lovelock and her ma amongst this lot?'

24

The Spanish Children Speak

Sunrise, Wednesday 26th May, Nettlefield

AT THE END OF THAT LONG DAY, Letitia slipped into bed with the curtains to her little cubicle tied open. All the children, Spanish and English, were asleep. She could see the albino boy, Robert, and his friend, Aggie, top to toe in the same bed. Frank the dog's tail stuck out from underneath it. After Robert and Aggie's announcement about the return of the Bullar woman, they'd run back to school to warn the others, so the orphans' homecoming wasn't quite as traumatic as Letitia feared.

Letitia hardly dared fall asleep herself, but she was so tired after keeping up with the kitchen work and worrying whether at any moment Mrs Bullar would burst in, she found her eyelids getting heavier and heavier.

Alfredo was pacing up and down outside the dormitory doors. He didn't stay there on guard all night, did he? She hadn't noticed him there before, but seeing his head through the windows in the doors pass back and forth was a little like counting sheep. She prayed that the dawn would wake her in time.

The next thing she knew was a gentle tapping on her shoulder.

She rubbed the sleep from her eyes and in the first light of day, she counted nine, ten, eleven, twelve, thirteen, all fourteen Spanish faces, wide-eyed and hopeful around her bed. Each child held a photograph of a family, their family she could only assume.

Letitia sat up, trying to peer past the children through the gap in the fabric. 'Alfredo, he is gone?' she said in Spanish.

'Si,' replied the boy.

Letitia recognised him as the one who spoke to her downstairs.

'Alfredo goes when he thinks we are all sleeping. We are good at pretending now,' said the boy. The photograph he held to his chest was of a mother and two little girls clinging to her legs.

Letitia looked closely at it. She estimated that the wall behind the boy's family was at least a foot taller than the mother. It almost formed the entire background of the picture. At the top of the picture, where it was marked with a faint spiral of spiky lines, there was only a thin strip of sky. Letitia wondered if it was blue. It seemed wrong to have a sunny day for such a sad picture. 'You showed me these before. You left them on your pillows. These are your families, right?'

The boy nodded, his eyes shiny with tears. 'What is left of them,' he said.

What is left? Of course, the war. Letitia then realised what she had been looking at. She felt so stupid – it was obvious where these people were. 'May I have a closer look at your picture?'

The boy let her take it.

The spiral of spiky lines wasn't a mistake in the developing or a dirty mark. It was in the picture as much as the people and the wall. It was barbed wire.

'Are they in prison?' said Letitia.

The children nodded vigorously. 'Yes,' said the boy.

A girl at the foot of Letitia's bed said, 'Franco does not like us, so he puts us in prison.' She was proudly holding a picture of two women with short hair, wearing long trousers, their chins jutting out in defiance.

Another boy, the tallest child, said, 'The teacher, Fitzgerald, started a prison school.' The tall boy was holding a picture of a man and an old woman. The man wore a black beret, and the woman was dressed in black from head to toe. 'Our parents liked the school at first – we were learning English and about Britain. They liked it until they realised what the school was for.'

'... to turn you into spies,' said Letitia.

'Yes,' said the first boy, 'for Franco's friend, Hitler.'

225

'He gives us the pictures to remind us who else will die if we fail,' said the tall boy.

Letitia still couldn't quite understand how it would work. They were children. But didn't Brian say something that felt important? She said children grow up.

Letitia knew that people caught spying could be sentenced to death. Not only could their families die, these children could too.

'Are you sure that your families are still alive?'

'We think they are,' said the tall boy, pointing to his photograph.

'So, who are the people in those other pictures, the ones I saw on the board downstairs?' asked Letitia gently.

The boy looked down. He took a breath but it was like the answer was stuck in his throat.

'My brother,' said the girl holding the picture of the two women in trousers. She had the same defiance, the same jutting out chin, as her mothers.

Another child said, 'My father.' Another, 'my big sister' and another 'my mother.' Around the group each child named the family member they had lost – the family member that the fascists had hanged.

Letitia's heart was breaking and tears stung her own eyes.

The girl with the two mothers said, 'They killed them and they made us watch.'

'Oh my word!' Letitia clasped her hand over her mouth. The awfulness of it made her feel sick.

A motor car engine rumbled and the orphanage front door slammed.

The children stiffened.

They all heard the matron bellow: 'Teasdale! I have missed you!' in a voice that sounded like if she had missed the kitchen boy, it was for all the wrong reasons. The Spanish children darted back into bed, slipping their pictures under their pillows.

'Wait!' whispered Letitia. 'You haven't told me your names or how I can help?'

But the Spanish children were not to be disturbed from their pretend sleep.

And Letitia did know how she could help. It was very clear what she had to do.

She was going to discover exactly what Fitzgerald and his nasty gang of fascists were planning to do next, expose the gang and save those children.

It would probably be a good idea to get the others in on the action too.

If they weren't already.

25

So Many Tents to Hide One Old Lady

Wednesday 26th May, North Stoneham

IN THE MORNING, it took Baby a few moments to remember where she was. Waking up on damp grass reminded her of when she and Fingers first arrived in Nettlefield, well before she knew June Lovelock or any of the girls that she'd come to love like sisters. But the chinking sounds of spoons on crockery reminded her that she'd spent the night under a table at the camp for the poor Spanish kids.

Baby peeked under the cloth to see lots of kids' legs, lined up for their breakfast. Peeping the other way, she saw pairs of adult legs, not so crammed together, sturdy legs. Except those nearest to her wore torn stockings, and the legs in them were grazed and scabbed with dried blood. The babble of an unknown language surrounded her, but she could guess pretty well that it was Spanish, or perhaps that Basque language June talked about.

The Spanish was interrupted by a few words of English, 'Would you like some breakfast?'

The English voice sounded very familiar. Baby looked out from under the cloth.

There she was.

Of all the people helping out at the camp, it was June Lovelock!

Luck was definitely on their side.

But another pair of legs came along – legs in trousers with sharp creases, legs ending in shiny shoes. And with them came the hushed, oily voice of Mr Movie Star, Easton Fitzgerald: 'Do that again and your mother will no longer be under the impression you've brought her on a 'lovely camping holiday in Dorset.' Believe me Miss Lovelock, I need very little persuasion to eliminate your mother entirely from our arrangement.'

'I've learned my lesson, Mr Fitzgerald. I can see that was a mistake now,' said June.

The slop of bread soaked in milk and the shuffle of kids' feet continued only interrupted by 'Ooh, hello Mr Fitzgerald, how lovely to see you.' 'Have you come for breakfast?' 'We could set you a special table …' The ladies' voices getting fainter as he carried on down the table.

Baby suddenly remembered Fingers. Where was she? But from somewhere not too far away, she heard her sister's voice. It was yelling, 'GOAL!'

Baby peeked through the legs in the breakfast queue and there was Fingers doing a victory dance in the middle of a football game! It seemed 'goal' was the same in any language. A yellow cloth was tied round her arm. All the kids playing football had one.

Fingers was blending in all right. But they couldn't forget what they came here for.

Baby peeked out from under the cloth. 'Psst, June.'

'Baby! Well I never ...! What are you ...? How did you?' said June Lovelock.

'We've come to get you and your ma. Where is she?'

June crouched down. 'It's too dangerous. They're both armed. I've seen their guns. If I don't go along with it, they're going to do something dreadful to Mother ...'

'Both?' said Baby.

'You know, don't you? I can't believe I trusted him. It's all my fault. I've already heard them arguing about her, about me, about us ...' she said in a tearful whisper.

'We all trusted him. For a while,' said Baby, knowing of course that June Lovelock was talking about that turncoat Harry Miller. 'But it ain't your fault. Do you know where they're keeping 'er, your ma, that is?' asked Baby.

'They've moved her. I don't know where she is now.'

An older lady's voice came from above the table. 'What are you doing down there, miss? We have children here that need their breakfast.'

June stood up.

'Me 'n' Fingers'll find her,' whispered Baby.

'Oh, Baby, you must be careful ...'

The breakfast queue had finished. Baby crawled out from under the table. June spooned Baby out an extra large bowl of milk-soaked bread, which Baby sat down to eat, on the grass, at the edge of the football match.

Another lady in a pinny rushed out from the far end of the table and tied a yellow cloth around Baby's arm too. 'It's so we know who's been fed, dear. Eat up now.'

Baby watched Fingers pick up the ball and run with it. Baby was sure that wasn't supposed to happen. The other players, nearly all boys, flung up their arms and shouted in Spanish, or Basque or something that sounded really cross. One snatched the ball off Fingers, dropped it and kicked it high up in the air. All the other kids ran after it. Fingers ran too and caught them up easily. Baby didn't think Fingers had a clue about the rules, but it was giving Baby the beginnings of an idea. If they could only find June Lovelock's ma first.

Baby looked out across the fields, the games of football and hundreds and hundreds of tents. She couldn't begin to count all the kids and the helpers, there were so many! There must have been a lucky star in the sky to make her and Fingers fall asleep under June's table. Could they be that lucky again and find her ma?

Luck, it turned out, was sort of on Baby's side.

Because rather than June's poor old ma, Baby spotted somebody a lot more useful, dragging a big sack across the field.

26

Leonard

Wednesday 26th May, Stoneham

BABY LEFT HER BOWL and spoon with some kids who were splashing each other with soapy water at a washing up table, and ran after a young man in baggy brown cords and shirt sleeves rolled up to his elbows.

Leonard Cook was dragging a big sack, overflowing with dirty sheets and smelling a bit like an old toilet.

'Leonard! Am I glad to see you!'

'Hello Baby! What are you doing 'ere? Want a lift back to Nettlefield?'

'Er yeah ... but not yet,' said Baby.

'Well, I'm back 'ere tomorrow about elevenish with this lot.' He nodded towards sacks of dirty laundry.

'Can we, er, talk a minute?'

Leonard's eyes widened and the creases on his forehead deepened as Baby described all the latest Blackshirt goings on. Then he leaned in to listen to Baby explain what she wanted him to do.

'Can we count on you, then, Leonard?'

'Too right!' he said, and climbed into the driver's seat. 'I'll see you tomorrow, then.' He closed the door and waved through the window as he started the engine.

To the sound of grinding gears and racing car revs, Baby watched him turn out through the gate and drive down the lane. Leonard Cook loved any excuse for a high-speed chase.

The thought of Leonard's driving always made Baby feel just a little bit sick.

But she had no choice.

She beckoned Fingers away from the football and explained the plan, such as it was.

Fingers was pleased that mostly what she had to do was keep playing football. 'But you mustn't upset 'em, not yet,' said Baby, 'and look out for my signal.' She waved her arm in the air like she was a city gent hailing a cab.

'When do I do the other thing?'

'Tomorrow.'

'Can I go now, then?'

Baby grabbed Fingers's arm. 'All right, but play nice.'

Fingers ran off and rejoined the footballers who were waiting for her in the middle of the field, while Baby started on the search for June's ma. Perhaps she should have got Fingers to help, but when had her sister ever

234

had a chance to play like that? And besides, luck was on Baby's side.

Figuring they'd have stashed the old lady well out of the way, Baby headed for the far end of the field, carefully lifting tent flaps and peeking inside as she went. For Leonard's sake, she hoped June's ma wasn't too far away. That old van had conked out the last time it had to go off the road.

But soon, because there were so many tents and they all looked the same and weren't all in straight lines, it became a very confusing task. Baby couldn't always be sure that she wasn't looking in a tent she'd already checked.

Baby spent the whole day looking for June's ma, and Fingers spent it on the football pitch of sorts. Baby looked till it got dark, but by that time she really was going round in circles. It made her realise how extraordinarily lucky they were to find June so quickly.

Her head full of worry, Baby curled up with Fingers for one more night amongst the clean bowls under the table.

'What if we don't find her?' said Fingers.

'I dunno,' said Baby.

'Do you want me to look for 'er too?'

'No, you play football. That's very important,' said Baby.

27

Fingers Plays Football

Thursday 27th May, Stoneham

BABY WOKE UP on Thursday morning with the dread that they still hadn't found Mrs Lovelock. Was she even still there to be found? And then the dread of what was going on with the Bullar woman at the orphanage. Everything seemed to be falling apart, and in such a short time.

She didn't actually know what time it was. She crawled out from under the table. Her clothes were damp in spite of the blanket June had sneaked under the table for her and Fingers to lay on.

A dewy brightness lay over the camp. Baby shielded her eyes against the sun peeping over the tents.

The first tent flap opened and gradually the rest followed. Children burst out all over the place, and the hustle and bustle of the camp getting up was like the orphanage but times a hundred or more.

Fingers crawled out too as the ladies in aprons were setting up the big pots of the milky bread and putting all

236

the bowls on the tables ready for breakfast. Fingers ran off for a kick about with the football. As soon as breakfast was ready, Fingers joined Baby in a long snaking queue. They ate sitting together on the grass and in no time were scraping their bowls clean.

'You found her yet?' asked Fingers.

'No, but there's still plenty of time.'

Baby was sure there actually wasn't.

Fingers returned to kicking the ball about with the other kids, leaving Baby heavy with responsibility. She had to have more of a plan if she was going to find June's old ma in time. Baby trudged over to a little clump of trees at the edge of the field for a think. She settled herself under the fence and she saw June Lovelock hurrying towards her, nervously looking from side to side.

'I only have a minute,' said June, leaning on the nearest tree trunk. 'Look, Baby, none of this is your fault. I'm going to be brave, and stay here with Mother, wherever she is. I want you and Fingers to go …'

But at that moment a black Morris van drove through the gate and parked by the kitchen tents.

June Lovelock smartly joined a group of ladies in aprons.

Baby tucked herself behind a tree. The name on the side of the van was painted over, but she could still make out the words 'Underwood and Son'.

Fitzgerald got out of the driver's seat, barged between two ladies with empty breakfast pots, and strode across the field.

Now, that was a clue to Mrs Lovelock's whereabouts if ever Baby saw one.

She followed Easton Fitzgerald across the field, passing the activities being set up by camp helpers on the tables that had just been cleared after breakfast.

More of the Spanish kids had joined Fingers's kickabout, which was fast turning into a full-blown game of football.

Fingers stopped and with her foot on the ball, shouted, 'Now?'

Were there enough kids? Was it the right time? She couldn't lose him now. Without taking her eyes off Fitzgerald, Baby shook her head. 'Not yet,' she mouthed.

Fitzgerald lifted the flap on a white tent in a long row of white tents, one row back from the front. All the tents were the same. Fitzgerald bent to go inside. Baby took a deep breath, fixed her eyes on the spot where she saw him disappear and as she'd seen him do, strode purposefully towards it.

She slipped between the tent and its neighbour, and through the canvas heard a high quavery voice sing, 'Oh, I do like to be beside the seaside ...'

Baby's skin tingled on her arms. That had to be Mrs Lovelock. How could Baby have missed her?

The singing stopped and Baby heard the voice ask, 'Are you one of the camp entertainers, dear? I do love a sing-song.'

'Be quiet, old woman,' said Fitzgerald.

'Is that a box of costumes you've got there? Are you going to put on a play?' said Mrs Lovelock.

'Didn't I just tell you to be quiet? Or do you want this again?'

'I won't be quiet until I'm in my grave, young man, you can be sure of that.'

The tone of Mrs Lovelock's voice changed. It made Baby wonder if Mrs Lovelock knew exactly what was going on.

'You asked for it, old woman.'

Baby felt her heart leap to her throat. What was he doing to her?

A few minutes later, Fitzgerald came out of the tent carrying an old cardboard box. A trouser leg flapped out the top of it as he marched swiftly through the camp and back to Underwood's van. Why didn't anyone stop him? But Baby couldn't worry about that because one way or another, she and the other girls were going to have a jolly good go at it. But right then, she had to check Mrs Lovelock was all right.

Baby cautiously opened a flap on the tent.

In front of her was the basket-woven back of a wheelchair. A knitted blanket flopped over the chair's arms and Baby could see the wispy grey hair on top of old Mrs Lovelock's head. She was surrounded by boxes of junk, as far as Baby could see. Or disguises, perhaps – there was a thought. The opposite flap on the tent was open too, through which Baby could see snatches of Fingers's game and a table of kids doing some writing with a young woman.

At the back of Mrs Lovelock's head were the two ends of a gag.

Mrs Lovelock's head had lolled on to her chin.

Baby felt another jolt to her chest at the thought of what he might have done. But then she realised he wouldn't bother gagging a dead person.

The gag cut into Mrs Lovelock's mouth. Baby put her ear close to the old lady's chest to make sure though. Mrs Lovelock smelled like a garden, not like an old lady at all, and thankfully let out a little snore.

Baby undid the gag, trying not to wake her. It would be hours before Leonard was back with his van. Letting her sleep was the best thing.

All Baby could do now was wait.

She watched Underwood's van drive away and joined the table of kids who were writing. The young teacher put a piece of paper in front of her. 'Write a little story about home, dear. Best handwriting, now.'

The paper was nice and thick. It would fold up nicely.

So Baby wrote.

240

As she set to work, she caught another glimpse of Fingers kicking the ball and running after it. Four boys were chasing after her. More kids had joined the game and were jostling for their chance to have a kick too.

Could Fingers keep that up for another three hours on top of all the playing yesterday?

What was Baby thinking? Of course, she could.

The game turned out to be a lot longer than three hours. Though the players changed and Fingers had breaks for drinks of water, while she looked out for any sign from Baby, it was still a marathon match. A camp lady brought Mrs Lovelock a cup of tea and a sandwich. Where did they come from? Was Fitzgerald threatening them too? Baby felt nervous and goosepimply about who else might be in on Fitzgerald's plot. And considering the stuff that was in the tent with Mrs Lovelock, who was in disguise?

Baby kept her head down and stayed conveniently close at the table with the little class of kids. Between her worries, she quite enjoyed it.

But as the day wore on, she became more and more concerned about Leonard. What was he doing? She see-sawed between worrying that something awful had happened to him and getting cross that he wasn't there. Hadn't she explained what was at stake?

Shortly after two o'clock, a cream-coloured car drove through the gate and stopped by the gates where Underwood's old van had been parked. Moles, the Blackshirt from the council, got out of the driver's seat, and Fitzgerald from the passenger side.

Why was he back? And with reinforcements. If only Leonard had been on time.

But a few minutes later, the laundry van finally appeared. Leonard parked it between the cream-coloured car and the large utility tent from where all the breakfast pots had appeared earlier. He jumped out and pulled two full sacks of laundry out through the back doors and dragged them over the grass to some ladies waiting by another large tent. Shading his eyes with his hand, Leonard scanned the field and, when he spotted Baby waving her arm like she was hailing half a dozen black cabs, he waved back.

Fingers spotted Baby too.

Fingers picked up the football and ran with it.

The Spanish footballers were furious. They shook their fists and shouted what could only be rude words at Fingers in Spanish or Basque as she led them across the field around the serving tables, school tables, everything tables. Picnic plates and schoolbooks tumbled into the grass as more kids joined the chase. Tables went over as Fingers gave them a mighty heave on her way. She ran

242

through big tents and little tents, more and more chairs upturned, blocking the path and collapsing tent poles.

Fingers outran all the kids and all the adults, causing havoc behind her. Never once letting that ball go.

Fitzgerald burst out of Mrs Lovelock's tent. Baby had been distracted. She hadn't seen him go in. How she hoped he hadn't done anything else to June's old ma ... She hadn't heard a gun go off, had she? She'd definitely have heard that.

She slipped through the other flap at the back of the tent that she used before. Inside the canvas, the noise outside was muffled. Mrs Lovelock was still there, hair a bit more ruffled, but ungagged as her high-pitched trembly voice started up again, 'Oh, I do like to be beside the seaside ...'

With Fingers running a riot outside, Baby took hold of the wheelchair handles. 'Time to take you out for a little walk, Mrs L,' she said and released the brakes on the back wheels. With all the effort Baby could muster, she pushed ...

But instead of Mrs Lovelock's quavering old voice, a man's voice said, 'You'll need some help with that.'

Kneeling in front of Mrs Lovelock, was Harry, Harry turncoat Miller.

He stood up, his hand on the gun, tucked in the waistband of his trousers.

28

Glencoe

Thursday 27th May, Nettlefield

AFTER TWO DAYS of the oppressive Bullar regime, Letitia, while pretending to dust, listened to and snatched glimpses of the chanting through the windows in the living room doors. Mrs Bullar, Mrs Tatler and Alfredo were leading the class, sharing the old-fashioned rote learning in either etiquette or sentences specifically designed to elicit information. The blackboard and easel remained covered by the cloth.

At ten o'clock, Mrs Bullar beckoned to Mrs Tatler, and together they headed for the doors.

Letitia buried herself in the coats on the hatstands.

'What do you think, Hilda? Are they ready?' Mrs Tatler looked up at the larger woman as they came through the double doors into the hall.

'Yes, I think so Doris, I'll tell Easton.'

'Well, I'll be going, then,' said Mrs Tatler.

'Very well,' said Mrs Bullar. With none of the niceties of saying goodbye, she retreated to the office while the drilling in the hall continued.

The children being 'ready' did not sound good to Letitia.

Miss Grenville had also retreated. Whenever Letitia did spot her, she was either blowing up balloons or trailing party streamers. She seemed to have forgotten about her fiancé, Mr Fitzgerald, as thoroughly as he had of her.

In Miss June's office, Mrs Bullar was talking on the telephone, which had been moved in there for her private use.

Cook was carrying an enormous pile of wet washing outside to hang up on the lines at the back of the orphanage. 'She's stopped the laundry coming. Can you believe it? I don't know how I'll be able to keep up.'

Cook's hands were too full to close the door behind her so, by the sink full of dirty breakfast bowls, Letitia heard snatches of the new matron's telephone conversation. Mrs Bullar laughed through most of it, with the occasional, 'Oh, you are so amusing, Easton!'

Mr Fitzgerald being 'so amusing' was very hard to believe. Letitia hadn't once heard him make a joke and his smiles were all so ... oily.

Mrs Bullar was still on the telephone. 'Yes, four o'clock would be perfect. Yes, yes they'll be ready.' The woman's voice was sickly-syrupy and booming at the same time. It drowned out the drilling of the Spanish children with Alfredo, which was one thing, but it all made Letitia feel sick with worry. What was the place coming to, and where were Miss June and her mother and Baby and Fingers? She was no closer to a plan to rescue them and bring that sham Nazi teacher to justice. And now it sounded like something important was going to happen at four o'clock.

Time was running out.

She took a deep breath and attended to the washing up, which was really that boy William's job. He had disappeared too, but that only irritated Letitia. With her hands plunged to her elbows in a sink full of lukewarm water, Letitia prayed for a good idea.

Brian came in with a tray of yet more washing up. 'Here's Dad's,' she said.

Ramón peeped out from behind Brian. As soon as he saw Letitia, he ran and wrapped his arms around her middle. Brian put her tray on the draining board and gave Letitia a towel. 'Here you are. He needs you. I'll do this.'

Letitia dried her arms and sat down at the table with Ramón on her lap. He was so light he reminded her of a dolly she used to have. She used to dream of that dolly coming alive. But Ramón was a real person who, in his short life, had had a terrible time. For a few days he'd known the joy of finding his brother alive, but with José's disappearance he was once again a forlorn little soul on Letitia's knee.

The kitchen door opened.

Ramón slid off Letitia's lap and hid under the table.

The grey-bearded head of Brian's father, Mr Alexander Shaw, looked in. 'Is the coast clear? Can I sneak in here with you? She's still talking on the telephone and the door is shut.' He pointed over his shoulder, across the kitchen corridor, towards Miss June's office.

'Dad, you must stay in the cottage. This is dangerous. She mustn't know about you and Bonnie ...' Brian was clearly the most grown up of the two of them.

'No, I know my dear. Don't worry. I wanted to make sure you were all right over here and I've also run out of reading material.'

'It's all right, Ramón. You can come out,' said Letitia.

'Hola, young man,' said Mr Shaw.

Ramón looked up at Letitia, at the same time trying to hide in Letitia's pinny, as if to ask Have I been found out?

'This is my dad, Ramón,' said Brian, hooking her arm through Mr Shaw's.

Which brought a smile to Ramón's face. 'Papa?' he said.

'I've got a book you can read,' said Brian, and went to the broom cupboard where she'd been hiding the books she rescued from The Lillie.

'Aah, that old thing,' said Mr Shaw.

In that moment, it dawned on Letitia that the Alexander F. Shaw on the spine of the book must be the very same Mr Shaw sitting with them in the kitchen. 'Gosh,' said Letitia, 'you're that Mr Shaw?'

'I am,' he said, taking the book from Brian.

A much slimmer book, a pamphlet really, fell out from between its pages.

Mr Shaw picked it up. 'Oh, I remember Eileen buying this on our honeymoon shortly after the war. Glencoe is a place of great beauty but also great sadness. I always wondered if the sadness of Glencoe influenced the course of mine and Brenda's lives. Brenda's dear mother died giving birth to her. Here you are Brenda, my dear.' Mr Shaw handed the pamphlet to his daughter before he fumbled for a handkerchief from his trouser pocket.

'I have read all of this book,' said Brian. 'It has a story about some soldiers who pretended to be nice to stay with some families, but then they were ordered to kill the people they were staying with, and they did!'

'Oh, my!' said Letitia standing up as if to make a pronouncement. 'Of course!'

But she didn't have time to explain her revelation, because a door slammed shut along the kitchen corridor, followed immediately by the unmistakably heavy footsteps of Mrs Bullar approaching.

'Quick, in here, Dad.' Brian pushed her father into the broom cupboard.

Letitia gently pushed Ramón in after him.

The kitchen door opened with the stench of body odour poorly masked by Yardley's Lavender. 'Coffee! I need coffee, for three! And be quick about it.'

Letitia heard the giggles of the Spanish girls, Regina and Maria, behind Mrs Bullar.

'Did someone say coffee?' Miss Grenville, still swathed in a colourful collection of scarves over the silk jacket that was very similar to Baby's, squeezed through the small gap left by Mrs Bullar, into the kitchen. 'I'd love a cup,' she said. Miss Grenville was apparently unaware of the dramatic changes that had been taking place at the orphanage. She now appeared to have her own agenda, her fiancé, Mr Fitzgerald, seeming to have entirely given up on her.

Mrs Bullar screwed up her nose at the odd woman and with the final instruction, 'Coffee for three in my study, and make it snappy!' She blustered past Miss Grenville, gathered Regina and Maria from the corridor and slammed Miss June's office door behind her.

Miss Grenville sniffed. 'Is it on? The coffee, I mean?'

249

Brian reached up for a coffee pot from a shelf over the sink. Miss Grenville didn't move other than to look dreamily about her, until her gaze settled on Letitia.

'Don't I know you?'

Letitia didn't know what to say. Miss Grenville must have seen Letitia about the place, but this was the first time Miss Grenville seemed to have noticed her. It was weird that Miss Grenville didn't know Letitia at the hotel in Southampton, but then she was quite distressed at the time. Had Miss Grenville been involved at all in what was going on? Or had Fitzgerald cruelly played with her affections for his own ends? Whatever the case, Miss Grenville was obviously not well, and Letitia felt very concerned for her.

Truthfully, Letitia said, 'I've been here for a few days now.'

Letitia's answer seemed to satisfy Miss Grenville, who nodded. 'Yes, you have, haven't you?' She sniffed again. 'Coffee, how wonderful. I'll be in the ballroom. I have such a lot to do.' She wafted out, trailing a long silk scarf behind her. It snagged in the door hinge. Miss Grenville tugged it smartly as she left, paying no attention to the rip she'd made in the fine silk.

Letitia supposed that by 'ballroom' Miss Grenville meant the orphanage living room, now a Victorian classroom.

'Coffee sounds marvellous, Brenda my love,' said Mr Shaw, emerging from the kitchen broom cupboard with Ramón.

'I'll bring you a pot, Dad. If you go back to the cottage.' Brian steered him towards the door. 'You will go the right way, won't you?' The right way, according to Brian, was around the back of the orphanage, under the washing lines and through a camouflaged door of sorts in the hedge.

'And please can you take Ramón with you?' Letitia said in Spanish.

Ramón smiled and nodded. 'Si, señorita Letitia, I like,' he said, in a mixture of Spanish and English.

'Yes, yes of course. This way, young man,' said Mr Shaw.

Ramón took his hand as they both snuck out.

When they'd gone, Brian sighed with relief. 'My dad is too ... daring,' she said.

Like father like daughter, mused Letitia.

The kettle whistled on the range and Letitia helped Brian arrange some cups on a tray.

But barely five minutes later, the kitchen door opened again and there stood Mr Shaw once more.

'Oh, Dad!' said Brian.

'We found a poor young woman wandering the grounds,' he said. 'I sent young Ramón on through the hedge, but the young woman was most insistent that she needed to come here.'

Letitia tried to think of any other poor young women who might be returning to Nettlefield Grange and be unaware of Mrs Bullar's return. She'd heard Baby, Fingers and Ida mention some other girls who were busy elsewhere, one in Germany ...

Mr Shaw plonked a large threadbare carpet bag on the kitchen table. 'She was struggling with this, it's very heavy.'

A young woman in round wire-rimmed spectacles, only a few years older than Letitia, entered the kitchen. She was wearing her best Sunday hat. Her well-worn shoes gleamed with polish.

Elsie, Grandma and Letitia's maid from Norfolk, stood just inside the kitchen door, her face shiny with perspiration, some of which had transferred to her spectacles.

'Elsie, you've come!' said Letitia. 'You didn't actually need to come!'

'I wanted to, Miss Letty. I was twiddling me thumbs back home. Threep is nowhere near as interesting without you.'

'Oh Elsie! But how did you find me?'

'You put the address on the letter, didn't you? It wasn't hard. I just went to the station and bought a ticket.

I'd been saving up for an adventure.' Elsie looked about her. 'Is that Miss Grenville here too?'

'Yes, she is.'

'Well, I think I done a good job,' said Elsie. 'There's all your books and bits and bobs. I think I got them all.' She pointed to the old carpet bag on the kitchen table.

'Elsie you've done an amazing job! I'll make sure you get reimbursed,' said Letitia. She wasn't sure how she was going to pay Elsie back for her train fare, but Letitia would have to think about that later.

'Ooh and by the way, this came.' From her coat pocket, Elsie took a thin piece of paper with the title 'POST OFFICE TELEGRAM' at the top.

But before Letitia had a chance to read it herself, Elsie straightened her spectacles and read, 'Will be back by end of week STOP Have someone I'd like you to meet STOP Grandma STOP'.

29

Two Ticking Clocks

Thursday 27th May, Nettlefield

ELSIE ROLLED UP HER SLEEVES and took over at the sink. 'Miss Letty, you shouldn't be doing this.'

Letitia allowed Elsie to steer her away. Grandma being home 'by the end of the week', and whatever was happening to the Spanish children at four o'clock were forcing Letitia to think, hard.

Her first thought was how on earth had Grandma made it to The Bahamas and back in less than a week? It actually felt like many weeks to Letitia, so much had happened, but it was only six days.

Cook took the tray of coffee that Brian had made, a pot and three cups, into Mrs Bullar and those vain girls, Regina and Maria, all making free with Miss June's office. It made Letitia cross to think of them in there.

In less than a minute, Cook returned with the empty tray, putting it away under the sink. 'I'll be off now, girls and thank goodness for this lovely weather.' She pulled her old felt hat on her head and stabbed it with a long pin. 'Cold ham and egg pie for tea, and that plate for those nippers in there at one.' She pointed to a small mountain of corned beef sandwiches under a damp tea towel on the kitchen table. 'Ooh, I don't know what they're about, but the sooner they move on and Doris Tatler is out of our hair, the better. Toodle-loo!' Cook left through the door at the end of the kitchen corridor.

Like Threep's church bells on a Sunday morning, everything came together in Letitia's head. 'Cook just said move on! That's what's happening at four!' said Letitia. 'The children will be moved on but not just anywhere: to places, people, families, where they can be useful in a bad way, like the soldiers who stayed with the families at Glencoe.'

Brian stopped on her way to the bin with the empty corned beef tins.

'The children,' said Letitia, 'as Fitzgerald's spies, in the right families, will learn all sorts of information that would be useful to a foreign power intending to invade. That would be useful to the Nazis for their invasion of Britain. And the fact that the spies are children, especially quiet polite children, children good at being seen and not heard, will mean that their hosts disregard them, be less careful about what they're saying and may well assume the children won't understand anything they do hear.'

255

'Adults can be stupid sometimes,' said Brian.

'You are so right,' said Letitia. 'It all fits, the radio in The Lillie, those vain girls being trained as radio operators and the Enigma machine for encoding the sensitive information.'

A horrible thought then struck Letitia: Fitzgerald wasn't intending to eventually turn the children into murderers was he, like the soldiers at Glencoe? Nothing about the children's so-called schooling suggested that. Though, as Brian said, children grow up. People change.

But those were children from families who were against people like Fitzgerald and the Blackshirts. 'Brian, what do you think? What is stronger – the need to keep your family safe or stopping Nazis?'

Still holding her empty tins, Brian thought for a moment, then very wisely said, 'I think that stopping Nazis would keep your family safe.'

It was clear what had to be done. Letitia had to stop the Nazis and prevent those children going anywhere!

But how was another matter entirely.

A banging from the hallway interrupted Letitia's resolve. She left Elsie with Brian and Mr Shaw, who was unpacking Elsie's shabby old carpet bag.

Miss Grenville, swathed in masses of streamers and her frayed silk scarf, was thumping on the door to the orphanage living room, currently the school room. Inflated balloons bounced round Miss Grenville's feet.

'Let me in, I say,' said Miss Grenville. 'I have waited and waited. How can I get everything ready if you won't let me in?'

The back of Alfredo's head was visible through the window at the top of the living-cum-school-room doors. He turned to glance angrily at the poor woman.

Miss Grenville raised her fist to thump again.

Balloons bounced as Letitia crossed the hall and gently took Miss Grenville's arm. 'Don't you remember? The children are having their lessons here now.'

'But Baby's party? My baby's party? I must prepare. I must make up for all that I've missed ...' She sniffed as if to cry, but her eyes were wide with a strange blankness about them. Had Mr Fitzgerald done something to her mind?

Elsie waded through the balloons and joined Letitia. 'All done in the kitchen, Miss Letty. Ooh, there she is! Miss Oojimaflip from up at The Hall!'

'Elsie, she's very unwell. She's in desperate need of a doctor.'

'Shall I get your case, Miss Letty?' Elsie winked behind her spectacles, looking very keen to see someone else play trainee doctor's dummy. 'I thought she were raring up to something when she come visiting on coronation day.'

'No, I think she needs special care.' Letitia had read about the jackets they made people with Miss Grenville's

257

mental affliction wear, and briefly wondered if bandages might do the trick but quickly dismissed the idea. It was horrible.

But of course, how lucky that Elsie was here! With Miss Grenville out of the way, Letitia could act. She pushed herself between Miss Grenville and the door. 'Why not do the party at home in Threep?' she said. 'You'll have much more space. It's very crowded here. Elsie here can help you take everything home. Can't you, Elsie?'

'Ooh, I don't know Miss Letty, I thought I could stay here with you?'

'... and I'll be home in Threep soon too, won't I, Elsie?'

Letitia gave Elsie a hard, no-nonsense stare.

'I'll be home in time for Grandma's return.' Letitia stared even harder.

Miss Grenville sniffed.

Letitia couldn't tell if Miss Grenville had heard her. Miss Grenville sniffed again, twiddled a few paper streamers between her fingers, and in a small voice she said, 'Baby will come too? She has to come too. You will bring her?' The bedraggled woman looked up. Tears were pooling her eyes.

'Of course we will,' said Letitia, crossing her fingers behind her back. 'Let's go and pack your case ready to catch the train.' Letitia was amazed that Mrs Bullar hadn't come out to see what all the fuss was about.

Elsie trudged back to the kitchen while Letitia took Miss Grenville upstairs to her room.

Letitia spent a frustrating half hour in a room no bigger than a cupboard, lined with empty shelves. Miss Grenville was less intent on packing her case than twirling with her scarf in the tiny space by her bed, singing, 'My baby is coming home, yes she is ...'

When Letitia returned to the kitchen, Mr Shaw was sitting at the table, the largest of Letitia's maths books open in front of him. Brian and Elsie were sitting on either side.

'Miss Grenville is resting,' said Letitia, 'but I have some money for her train ticket. I did feel a little awkward rifling through her bag, but I'm spent out.'

Mr Shaw looked up from an interesting page on fractals. 'This is a useful book of Zaremba's you've got here. Elementary but fascinating to read, though I do wish my Polish were more up to scratch.'

'I did learn,' said Letitia. 'Grandfather was very keen on the Polish mathematicians. He used to say how adversity had forced them to be brilliant. I started German too. Grandfather said some excellent Jewish scientists were being exiled and we should support them. But then Grandfather died and well ... I don't know why

Elsie brought that one.' Letitia could barely remember why she'd asked for the books in the first place.

'All your books look the same to me, Miss Letty,' said Elsie.

Mr Shaw looked up, his eyes sparkling with excitement. 'Brenda says you have an Enigma, I'd be very interested ...'

The kitchen door opened.

Ida, in her mechanic's overalls, came in. It occurred to Letitia that the whole point of Ida's outfit was to 'cover up', but Letitia was learning that Ida was one of the most straightforward people she'd ever met. She was honest and not terribly good at pretending. Fitzgerald was pretending to be a teacher; the Spanish children were pretending to Fitzgerald. And if Letitia couldn't stop Fitzgerald, the children would be pretending to their British hosts, putting the security of the country at great risk.

Miss June's Harry has been pretending too, very much, but to whom has he been pretending the most? Why did he take the Enigma to London before he gave it to Fitzgerald, for instance?

Something else tickled Letitia's conscience. Was she, Letitia, also pretending? Well, she no longer had her doctor's bag, so she wasn't pretending to be a medical student anymore.

Ida quietly closed the door behind her. 'I came to see where you were, Mr Shaw. Is everything all right?' Ida hadn't returned to Southampton on the pretext of a family emergency. Instead, she was staying in the cottage with Mr Shaw, Brian and Bonnie.

'Yes, we're all tickety-boo,' said Mr Shaw as he got up from the table. 'I'll creep back and see to young Bonnie and Ramón.'

'Do be careful,' said Letitia, 'Mrs Bullar could come out of June's office at any moment.'

'Oh, not yet she won't,' said Brian. 'I found one last tin. I thought it might come in useful.' From one of the dustier pans on the shelf above the sink, Brian produced a tin of Ovaltine. 'I put a tiny pinch in the coffee.' Brian grinned, a wide Cheshire cat of a grin.

'Oh Brian, you clever thing,' said Ida.

'What have you done?' asked Letitia, confused.

Ida explained how, before last Christmas, her 'uncle', Arthur Underwood, had used contaminated Ovaltine to drug the blonde children he was preparing to send to Hitler. 'The drug he used,' she said, 'was very strong. Harry used it on Underwood himself when he rescued Bonnie.'

At last, Letitia believed she could see clearly.

'Yes, about Harry ...' started Letitia.

'Do you mind if I have a longer peruse of your book?' asked Mr Shaw.

'No, of course not, I think I have everything I need for the time being,' said Letitia.

'Thank you my dear.' Mr Shaw got up from his chair and stretched his back. 'I am getting old you know.'

'Bye, Dad. See you later.' Brian stretched up to kiss him on the cheek as he left.

'What were you going to say about Harry, Letitia?' Ida still looked miserable about him.

'Yes, about Harry ... Oh, but what time is it? Miss Grenville has to catch the two o'clock train. Elsie, it's time to go. Brian, you didn't put any Ovaltine in Miss Grenville's coffee, did you?'

Brian shook her head as she wrapped greaseproof paper round a pile of sandwiches from under the damp cloth. 'For your journey, Elsie,' she said.

Elsie slumped on her chair. 'But I've only just come.'

'I promise I'll make it up to you when I get home.' Letitia put the parcel of sandwiches inside the old carpet bag which otherwise contained a few of Elsie's belongings suitable for an overnight stay. Letitia did feel a little bad about cutting short Elsie's first adventure, but she had little choice.

Elsie plonked her Sunday hat back on her head, dragged her bag off the table and trudged behind Letitia to the hall.

Miss Grenville wafted down the stairs, her frayed silk scarf fluttering behind her. She carried a small case from which paper streamers were escaping. 'Ah, here we are. I'm just missing one thing but we can get that on the way,' she said.

'You're coming with me … madam,' said Elsie kicking balloons out of the way as she led Miss Grenville across the hall and out the front door.

Letitia watched Miss Grenville skip across the grounds, past the defunct playground towards the gates and the station.

Phew, that was one problem solved.

'About Harry ...' Letitia turned around to find Ida, a frown wrinkling her forehead.

But the sound of crockery smashing and a roar of 'What do you think you're doing?' coming from Miss June's office meant that Mrs Bullar had woken up.

30

'You're Going to Have to Trust Me!'

Thursday 27th May, Stoneham

BABY GRABBED THE CANE HANDLES of Mrs Lovelock's wheelchair and fixed all her determination on Harry Miller 'No. You. Ain't. You 'ain't 'aving her, not her, and not June.' Baby tried pulling Mrs Lovelock backwards, away from him. But the chair, with the old lady in it, was too heavy for her. The handles just creaked and the chair went nowhere.

Harry stood up, his hands in the air in a surrender, blocking the wheelchair so Baby couldn't push it forwards either. 'Baby, it's all right. I'm on your side.'

'But you're German.'

'Yes, but I am not a Nazi. Lots of us aren't. What about Sophie, eh Baby?'

Sophie's German family were put in prison for being against the Nazis. He had all the answers, did Harry.

264

'Yeah, she's her and you're you. You were a Blackshirt.'

'What we wear on the outside isn't always the same as what we are inside.'

'Daisy, Daisy give me your answer do,' sang Mrs Lovelock in the middle of the two of them. Outside, the shouts and screams of the footballers were getting louder. Was Fingers coming this way?

'But what about yer gun? What were you going to do with that?'

Harry smiled at Mrs Lovelock as he walked around her to the back of the chair. 'I had orders to deal with her ...' He sliced his hand across his neck. 'But I didn't, did I? I chose to send her a cup of tea and a sandwich. And because that was a test of my loyalty, things are looking a bit dicey for me here now.'

'That Fitzgerald is as bad as that old devil Underwood,' said Baby.

'Worse,' said Harry. 'And we're trying to get him and his whole network. And you're right, Fitzgerald is not having Junie's mum.'

'Who's we?' asked Baby.

'You're going to have to trust me,' said Harry.

Baby had heard that one before.

And she was sure she had more reasons for not trusting him, but she couldn't think of one at that

265

moment, because the throaty sound of an engine was rumbling out the back of the tent.

'Look, Leonard's here,' said Harry. 'You've told him what's been going on haven't you? Get in the van. I'll bring Mrs L.' Harry tried to shoo Baby through the flap at the back of the tent.

But Baby stayed put. 'What about Fingers? I ain't going anywhere without 'er.'

With perfect timing, Fingers dashed in through the front of the tent, dropped the ball and ran past Mrs Lovelock out the flap at the back and into the waiting laundry van.

Harry picked up the football, stood just inside in the front tent flap, spoke some words in Spanish to the kids who had gathered outside, and kicked the ball. Baby couldn't see where the ball went, but it was a good kick and sent the Spanish camp kids running away after it.

Harry dragged Mrs Lovelock in her chair, backwards over the bumps in the grass, out through the back flap of the tent to the waiting laundry van.

Fingers was still panting on the van floor. 'I think I gave 'em a run for their money,' she said between breaths.

Harry picked up the old lady's chair and put it, with Mrs Lovelock still in it, in the back of the laundry van.

Baby climbed in too. 'What are you going to do?'

'You'll have to hold the chair still in there, I've heard about Leonard's driving,' said Harry.

'But what are you going to do?' said Baby.

Harry was about to slam the second back door shut, when Baby held it open. 'But June,' she said, 'what about June? We can't leave her.'

'I'll take care of June. Don't you worry, she's in safe hands. Nothing bad is going to happen to her while I'm around. Now get in, all the way.'

Like he said, Baby was going to have to trust him.

Harry slammed the van door shut.

Baby felt like a load of moths were fluttering round her insides and, as if on cue, Mrs Lovelock struck up a new song, 'Pack up your troubles in your old kit bag ...'

Through the window in the back door, Baby watched Harry brush himself down, tuck his shirt back in and scrape back his flop of brown hair before disappearing through the flap of the tent.

Leonard revved the engine and, like the worst fairground ride ever, they lurched and bounced across the field between the tents. A heap of pale yellow blankets was piled up messily in the far corner of the van. Next to it, Fingers was sitting leaning against the partition between them and the driver's seat. The blankets looked lovely and soft to dive into, but it was impossible for Baby to do anything other than hold on tight to Mrs Lovelock in her chair.

267

Mrs Lovelock patted Baby's hand. Her voice was extra wobbly with Leonard's driving. 'Isn't this fun, dear? It's a bit like being at the funfair. Do they still have those? I remember swinging in the steam yachts as a girl. Many's a time I swung so high I thought I was going to all out.' And as if someone had come along and switched her off again, she started singing, 'Oh I do like to be beside the seaside ...'

By the large tent near the entrance to the field, Leonard stopped the van. 'Sorry, I forgot a bag. That Mr Miller had me coming over to get you before I'd had a chance to pick up the dirties. I'll be two ticks. It's more than my job's worth if I go back without it. Keep your heads down. I'll be in a right pickle if anyone sees you.'

Baby sat on the floor of the van and leaned against the wheelchair. They'd all be in a right pickle if anyone saw them.

The sun found its way in through the little window in the back doors. The warmth made Baby sleepy.

She heard June Lovelock's voice outside.

'You won't get away with this!'

'Leave her, you've got me,' said Harry Miller's voice. 'She has nothing to do with this.'

Who was he talking to?

'I knew it all along. You have failed us, Miller,' said the cool voice of Easton Fitzgerald. 'You and the woman will pay, but not until I have wrung every last bit of information from you. Moles, drive us back to Nettlefield. This cohort is due to be collected at four.'

A thud against the side of the van, a woman's cry, car doors opening ...

Baby and Fingers took a back door window each and peeped out.

The evil Blackshirt was pressing a gun firmly in the small of Harry's back and pushing him into the cream-coloured car belonging to Moles from the council. Baby could see the back of June Lovelock's head in the car window. The car sped under the Basque Children's Camp banner and out through the main gate.

What were a few dozen moths became a few hundred buzzing and fluttering inside Baby with the worry of what was going to happen to June.

Leonard opened the van back door and flung in a bag of dirty washing. 'Good job I remembered that, Mother's always saying I'd forgot me head if it wasn't screwed on ...'

'They've got 'em!' shouted Fingers.

'They've got June and Harry!' shouted Baby. 'Leonard, follow that car!'

'Ooh-er, right you are!' Leonard ran to the front, got in his seat and started the engine. He wiggled the gear stick with a horrible grinding sound and they lurched away from the camp, down the lane after the Blackshirt's car.

While Mrs Lovelock slept.

'She hasn't, erm ... died 'as she?' asked Fingers, prodding the old lady.

'Not now, June. I'm having a lovely time,' murmured Mrs Lovelock under her breath. She let her head flop asleep again, her body joggling along with the bumps in the road.

That was a relief, but there was still a horrible breathless feeling in Baby's chest. Harry said nothing bad would happen to June, but at that moment she was struggling to believe that. 'Faster, Leonard! Faster!' she shouted over his shoulder.

'Rightio, Baby! He leant over the steering wheel and pressed his foot down on the pedal.

Another lurch and Baby felt a surge of power.

'Ooh, what was that?' said Mrs Lovelock. She opened her eyes for a second before nodding off again.

The van sped on.

The roads got smoother, and through the windscreen Baby looked for the Blackshirt's car. There was a car in the distance, but was it the right one? 'Where are we going?' shouted Baby over the noise of the engine.

'This is the main Nettlefield Road,' shouted Leonard. 'Be there in no time.'

They were crossing a bridge over a river. A few yachts with their sails furled around their masts were anchored there.

270

The van was slowing down.

The engine coughed and spluttered. Leonard banged his foot on the pedal and leant even lower over the wheel as if that would make the van pick up speed again.

The engine noises fizzled to only the creaks of the wheels rolling over the bridge.

'Oh no, I'm really sorry,' he said.

'What's happening?' asked Baby, dreading what he was going to say.

The engine had stopped.

The van rolled off the bridge onto the road on the other side until it stood dead still.

Apart from Mrs Lovelock snoring peacefully in her chair, the quiet was like the world had stopped, not just the van.

Leonard turned around in the driver's seat, gulped, and in a hoarse whisper, said, 'We've run out of petrol.'

At that moment, the messy pile of pale yellow blankets in the corner behind the passenger seat was shifting like a street person waking up under a pile of rubbish.

Something or someone was buried underneath them.

31

Letitia and Ida – What a Team!

Thursday 27th May, meanwhile back in Nettlefield....

THE BULLAR WOMAN'S HEAVY FOOTSTEPS stomped about in the corridor. 'Those children must be fed. The coach will be here for them in two hours!'

'She's coming in. Hide. Quickly,' said Letitia.

Ida, Brian and her dad bundled once again into the broom cupboard as the door flew open and Mrs Bullar filled the doorway. 'Where's the lunch?' she demanded in her booming voice. 'And who are you? Have I seen you before?'

A growl came from under the table.

Frank the dog appeared. He was baring his teeth.

Letitia curtsied. 'I help Cook, mistress.'

With her hand still on the doorknob, Mrs Bullar's eyes narrowed.

'It's alroight,' said Letitia, putting on a small voice and trying to mimic orphan Aggie's accent, 'she don't pay me.'

'Good. Deliver the lunch to our guests. And get rid of that dog. Now!' She pulled the door shut with a flounce.

Less than two hours, now!

Think Letitia, think.

The Bullar woman's heavy footsteps were followed by a shriek of outrage and a booming 'WHAT HAS BEEN GOING ON HERE? You three, deal with this rubbish!'

Ida, Brian and Mr Shaw emerged from the cupboard and all four of them listened to the suppressed giggles, shrieks of frustration and popping balloons, as Alfredo and those Spanish girls 'dealt' with the 'rubbish'.

Playing the part of a humble maid, Letitia carried the only-slightly depleted tray of sandwiches across the hall. The sun poured in the open front door. The shrivelled rubber from the popped balloons scattered over the floor actually made the place look quite cheerful again.

Letitia caught sight of Regina and Maria with three suitcases between them, arguing their way through the main orphanage gate. The simplest mathematics determined that it was impossible to divide three equally into two and end up with a whole number. Regina, or Maria, struggled with two suitcases to the other's one. Neither of the suitcases was big enough for the Enigma, but possibly for the radio. The girls waited for a car to pass by, then crossed the road for the station.

In the orphanage living room-cum-schoolroom, the Spanish children were waiting. They watched Letitia as she placed her tray on the table, clear of any books or pencils or paper. It was easy to read what they were trying to say with their worried looks. Help!

As Letitia, was doing her very best to communicate, I know and I am working on it, don't worry, she caught the eye of the first brave boy who gave the slightest nod of his head, and the girl with two mums, who blinked slowly. Letitia felt the connection and hoped they did. She was not abandoning them.

All the while Alfredo stood on guard, his arms folded across his chest. As Mrs Bullar, lounging in Miss June's story chair, gazed into a small handbag mirror and applied more lipstick.

Letitia returned to the kitchen. 'Brian, take your dad home and take all my books with you, they may come in handy again. Ida, the girls have left The Lillie, we need to check it for clues and retrieve the Enigma. I'm sure it's still there. Are you happy about that?'

'Of course,' said Ida, straightening her overalls. 'Retrieving is not stealing.'

'And by the way,' said Letitia. 'I have a feeling that Harry may be on our side after all.'

'Are you sure? How do you know?'

'I don't know for sure but it is highly probable. What if Harry is one of those Germans who doesn't like the Nazis? Lots of Germans don't – my grandfather's Jewish mathematicians, for instance.'

'And Sophie,' said Ida.

'Baby's friend?'

'Yes!'

'So,' said Letitia, 'considering his heroic actions for you at Christmas, his kindness to the orphans and his affection for Miss June, I think it's more probable that he's pretending to Fitzgerald. Why, I don't know. But there has to be a good reason for him flying the Spanish children in his aeroplane …'

'I knew it!' said Ida, and kissed Letitia on the cheek. 'Come on, let's go and get Harry's machine.'

'I'm not sure it's his, but he definitely had loan of it,' said Letitia.

Brian took her dad by the hand. He shuffled out of the kitchen side door after her, loaded with the whole pile of books.

Letitia and Ida followed through the same door. They waved to Brian and her dad as they made their way through the washing lines of white bedsheets to the cottage under the railway bridge on the other side of the hedge.

Letitia and Ida ran in the opposite direction, past the playground, over West Street and together up the bank to the station. They ran past the stationmaster's office, past the coal heap to the tunnel through the bushes.

In the clearing where it was always sunny, even on cold grey days, sat The Lillie.

And the door was open.

Wide open.

Ida went inside first. Letitia saw Ida's shoulders droop and heard her sigh.

The place was a mess. Dirty clothes, lipstick-stained sheets and coffee-stained blankets were strewn about the place. At the end of the long thin room, dirty dishes and broken glass were scattered over the draining board and the tap was still dribbling water into the sink.

The Spanish girls had definitely gone for good or, as Baby would say, scarpered.

Half-eaten plates of food were stacked wonkily on the table around a space where that radio had sat. Letitia knew they could make radio sets to be quite portable now.

'First, the Enigma,' said Letitia. She turned off the tap and checked in the lavatory. She opened each cupboard door underneath the remnants of Mr Shaw's library.

Ida checked the large mattress-floored room at the far end. 'If it's not here, where is it?'

Letitia sat down at the table and looked up. A different perspective always helped. She stretched out her legs and, under the table, felt something mechanical and hard.

She looked underneath and there it was, without its case, abandoned like a broken toy. Letitia dragged it out, lifted it carefully onto the table. It was quite heavy, but Letitia's arms were strong. 'I'd love to have a really good look at this,' said Letitia.

'I would too,' said Ida. 'I should have remembered my tools.'

'But we don't have time. The girls were radioing from here, or trying to. What did they leave behind? They may have written things down, notes to themselves, notes from Fitzgerald. It's obvious they weren't organised or tidy ...'

'I'll look in the room-bed,' said Ida.

She reappeared with the Enigma's wooden box, carrying it upside down. Inside were little balls of fluff all smeared with more greasy lipstick in various shades of red. 'They've been using it as a bin.'

Letitia picked up one of the balls of fluff. 'I've read about this. It could have medical uses.'

'What I don't understand,' said Ida, 'is why would they leave something as precious as an enigma machine behind?'

'It obviously wasn't precious to them,' said Letitia.

'But won't they get into trouble with Fitzgerald?'

'They didn't seem to be scared of him or in awe of him like the others are,' said Letitia. 'I wonder why? They were certainly more interested in clothes and make-up than espionage. Maybe they just jumped at the chance to come to England, for the fun of it?'

Ida tipped the balls of fluff onto the dirty plates. 'We'll have to come back later and clear up properly.'

Letitia carefully lowered the Enigma into its box, clipped the box shut and picked it up again.

'Hey, that looks important ...' Ida knelt under the table, and from between the table legs and The Lillie's wall, she pulled a sheet of paper.

With the heavy machine more or less comfortable in her arms, Letitia peered over Ida's shoulder to see. 'Oh, well done! That's exactly the sort of thing!' She really wanted to put the Enigma down and have a closer look but they needed to get going.

'It's a list of names and addresses,' said Ida. She ran her finger down the page and counted under her breath. 'Fourteen names and address. Some of them are 'Sir's and 'Lady's ... Where was it you said you came from, again?'

'England, I come from England. I was born here,' said Letitia.

'I don't mean that.' Ida clearly wasn't the sort of questioner that assumed that because Letitia's skin was brown, she came from 'somewhere hot'. 'I mean where

278

you live,' said Ida. 'What's your address? Somewhere up north, isn't it?'

'Threep,' said Letitia. She supposed everywhere was 'up north' here.

Ida held the sheet under Letitia's nose and pointed to a name and address about halfway down the list. 'Is that you?'

Letitia shifted the Enigma to a more comfortable position and looked closely at the rather untidy handwriting.

It was.

There was Grandma's name, Hortensia Maud Ketton, next to the address of their lovely home, The Manor, Threep, Norfolk and next to that, a Spanish Christian name, Consuela with a number: 21.

'This is where they're putting those children, isn't it?' Ida folded up the sheet, put it in the top pocket of her overalls and buttoned the pocket up.

'It has to be,' said Letitia, feeling a bit goosepimply. The fact that her own home was on the list made it so real. But something else was troubling her. Not counting Ramón, there were only fourteen Spanish children at the orphanage, presumably to correspond to the fourteen on this list. So, why was Consuela numbered 21?

'You said your Grandfather was the mayor – that's sort of to do with government, isn't it?'

'Yes, and Grandma still goes to council meetings. This is really important. This means that if we can't stop Fitzgerald taking the children away, we will know where they're going. And will be able to find them.' It saddened Letitia that she couldn't have communicated this to the children, but this was definitely the most important piece of paper either of them had in their possession. 'We must go.' Letitia barely noticed the weight of the Enigma on the way back. Ida offered to take her turn, but Letitia didn't want to stop.

In the cottage under the bridge, all Mr Shaw's Christmases had come at once. His eyes sparkled as he took possession of the Enigma. Though they could have little idea what he was excited about, Brian, Bonnie and Ramón joined in the fun and crowded round him as he started to press keys and turn dials.

Letitia beckoned Ida out into the cottage's overgrown garden.

'Baby mentioned that you could drive a car?' said Letitia.

'Yes, of course I can,' said Ida.

Letitia held back the branches that covered the gap in the hedge and pointed at the dark red car parked outside Nettlefield Grange Orphanage – the Austin Ruby, the property of Mrs Hilda Bullar. 'How do you feel about driving that?'

Ida looked from side to side, breathed in through her nose, bit her lip and flexed her fingers. Everything in her seemed to be wrestling with the greatest temptation she must ever have been presented with. Could Ida Barnes, whom Baby said was the most honest girl in the world, steal a car?

'We need help,' said Letitia. 'We need Baby and Fingers, Miss June, and Harry and José. I have to find José for Ramón.'

'Yes,' said Ida, 'Let's do it!'

'Phew!' said Letitia, and ushered Ida through the hedge.

'It's for a good cause, isn't it?' said Ida, striding towards the car.

'Ultimately yes – rescuing those children and preserving national security,' said Letitia, glancing at the tall windows on the orphanage ground floor where the Spanish children were being made ready to be sent out to important people, like Grandma.

'The greatest cause,' said Ida, opening the driver's door.

'Most certainly,' said Letitia, sliding into the passenger seat.

Ida fiddled under the steering wheel and the engine purred into life. 'Where are we going?'

'The only place that logically and most probably we will find Baby, Fingers, June, Mrs Lovelock, José and ...'

'... Harry?' said Ida.

'Yes,' said Letitia, 'The Basque Children's Camp, North of Southampton.'

32

Meeting on the Nettlefield Road

Thursday 27th May

BABY WANTED TO RUN, to push open the doors on the useless laundry van and chase after those Blackshirts as though her life depended on it. Her life didn't, but June and Harry's did and so did all the orphanage kids and Brian and Letitia and Ida and all of 'em!

But she couldn't leave Mrs Lovelock and Fingers with whatever or whoever it was under the blankets.

A boy's head appeared.

José, last seen last seen in the back of Mrs Bullar's Austin Ruby, looked up at Baby. 'Don't be scared, I am running away too.'

Baby wanted to know how he got there and what had happened to him, but that would have to wait.

The blankets fell away as José sat up. 'I have to find my brother. This van, it goes to Nettlefield, yes?'

'It ain't going nowhere at the minute,' said Fingers, standing over him. 'Unless you can fix it?'

'Nobody can fix it 'til we get some petrol,' said Leonard, twisting round in the driver's seat. 'I'm proper sorry.'

'I can go,' said José, 'I have long legs, I run. You have a ...' he mimed holding a petrol can, 'to carry it in?'

Baby was sure there had to be a faster way. How far away were they from Nettlefield? Couldn't they all just run?

What about Mrs Lovelock?

They were lumbered with folk that needed help.

But wasn't that what all this fighting the Blackshirts was about: not letting the folk that needed help get left behind?

She heard the rumble of another motor car engine getting closer. Perhaps they could hitch a lift?

But when Baby looked out the window, she gasped at the sight of a dark red Austin Ruby speeding towards them.

'Duck!' she shouted. 'Don't let her see you! She's coming for us again!'

But Fingers squeezed past José and sat in the front seat.

'What are you doing? She'll see you!' hissed Baby.

'No, she won't. Look!' Fingers pointed at the car that had stopped, bonnet to bonnet in front them.

When Baby did look properly, she couldn't believe what she was seeing. Ida Barnes sat in the driver's seat, and Letitia next to her. Careful of Mrs Lovelock, who had woken up and was smiling at José, Baby did push the back door open and leapt out into the road.

'How did you know we was 'ere?' Baby flung her arms around Ida before she'd had a chance to get out of the driver's seat.

'We didn't,' said Letitia. 'We were on our way to the camp to get you. It was the most probable place to find you.'

'Well, you've got us. And Mrs Lovelock.'

'And me,' said José, waving at Letitia.

'José, I am very pleased to see you. Ramón is absolutely fine.'

Baby quietly explained about June and Harry being taken by Fitzgerald and Moles from the council. And how Leonard's laundry van had just run out of petrol.

'Fitzgerald and Moles must be taking Miss June and Harry back to the orphanage, mustn't they?' said Letitia.

'That's where his kids are, aren't they?' said Baby. 'It's all about those Spanish kids.'

'Yes,' said Letitia. 'I'm sure the children are being picked up at four o' clock. You know they're being trained as spies against their will, don't you? If we don't stop them, they're going to be sent to important people, host families who have links to government, who know how the country works, who know everything that a foreign power trying to invade Britain would ever need to know.'

'Blimmin' Blackshirts,' said Baby, breathing through her teeth.

'But we won't all fit in the Ruby,' said Ida.

'Perhaps we could take some fuel from her car and put it into the laundry van?' suggested Letitia.

Leonard had joined them on the path next to a grassy slope down to the riverbank. 'I haven't got anything to suck it out, and the nearest petrol pump's a couple of miles away.' His shoulders slumped. 'I've let you down, haven't I?'

Fingers opened her mouth to speak but Baby clamped her hand over it. 'No Leonard, we're grateful that you got us this far.'

'Well,' said Letitia, 'somebody needs to stay here with Mrs Lovelock and your driver. José, I know you'll be anxious to see Ramón, but he really is quite safe in Brian's father's cottage.'

José nodded eagerly. 'Good, I will do what's needed. I trust you. I am not anxious to see Fitzgerald again in a hurry.'

'Letitia, one thing's for certain. We need your 'elp,' said Baby.

'And not for anything medical,' said Fingers. 'You're rubbish at that. We need you because you're clever, you know what's what with that old machine that ain't a typewriter, you can speak the language, and you climb like a cat-woman.'

'Very well,' said Letitia with a gulp, 'I'll go back to Nettlefield and bring Fitzgerald to justice, if I have to run all the way.'

'That's the spirit,' said Baby.

Mrs Lovelock's quavering sing-song voice came from the back of the van. 'Are those nice young men going to keep me company? We could have a lovely sit by the river and nobody will have to run anywhere,' she called. 'You go on, my dears, and sort out those horrible fascists. I'll be quite safe.'

'Blimey, 'er 'earing's good,' said Fingers.

So, it was decided who would get some petrol for the van, who would sit on a riverbank on a sunny Thursday afternoon serenading Mrs Lovelock in Spanish, and who would go back to Nettlefield. Without any more chat, because driving to Nettlefield was at least another quarter of an hour away, Leonard and José lifted Mrs Lovelock in her chair out of the back of the laundry van and set themselves up in a shady spot on the grassy bank of the Hamwell River. Baby, Fingers and Letitia piled into the Bullar woman's motor car and sped off with Ida at the wheel. Baby tried to tell them a plan, because that was what she did, but everything she could think of depended on so many other things that it all sounded rubbish and confusing. Ida was concentrating on driving, anyway.

'The important thing,' said Letitia, 'is keeping those Spanish children safe at the orphanage until the camp people can come and get them.'

'And rescuing June, and Harry you're-going-to-have-to-trust-me Miller,' said Baby.

'And ...' said Ida, 'getting rid of Mrs Bullar again, and getting the Enigma thing to the authorities. The authorities that aren't Blackshirts, that is.'

'Oh my, oh my,' said Baby to herself, 'it's all so flippin' overwhelming.'

Next to Baby on the leather seat, Fingers had the window down and was enjoying the ride with the wind on her face. The horrible woman's car was a big improvement on the backs of rackety old vans, which was how they usually got about.

Baby leaned back on the leather seat and hoped.

Hope was all she had.

But the thing about villains like Mr Movie Star Fitzgerald, the Bullar Woman and all the Blackshirts was that they underestimated the likes of Baby, Fingers, Ida, Letitia and Brian – and that was always their biggest mistake. The Nettlefield Resistance was coming for them.

As Ida drove under the railway bridge, a Black Maria, Nettlefield's police car was turning into the orphanage grounds with its bell ringing. Oh Gawd, that was all they needed.

The church clock in the distance said five minutes to four. Ida followed the Black Maria through the open gates into the grounds. Ida parked the dark red Austin Ruby beside the railings. 'Trust me, I've had an idea,' she said.

The cream-coloured car, belonging to that Blackshirt Moles from the council, was already parked under the playground swing frames where the swing seats should hang. There was no one inside the car.

Ida got out of the driver's seat and ran to the front of Mrs Bullar's Austin Ruby. She lifted the bonnet … and a moment later pulled out a long loop of rubber. 'Fan belt, she won't get far without that!'

Sergeant Ted Jackson heaved himself out of the Black Maria, adjusting his helmet. Constable Spencer joined him by the locked playground roundabout. 'Well I never, Ida Barnes,' said Sergeant Jackson, puffing up his chest. 'And I had you down for a good law-abiding young lady. Stealing a vehicle is a very serious offence. Do you have anything to say?' He reached inside the top pocket of his uniform jacket, took out a small notebook, licked his pencil, and poised to write.

'Yes, please arrest me and take me to the police station. I confess.' Ida dropped the rubber fan belt and stuck out her wrists for handcuffs.

Baby tore out from the back seat of the Ruby. 'No! She didn't steal it! You know Ida, Sergeant. She couldn't steal a ...' In the heat of the moment Baby struggled to think of something. 'A pea! She couldn't steal a pea off a plate! The old woman lent the car to us.'

'No, she didn't. Baby's wrong,' said Ida. 'Sergeant, I stole it. Take me away.' Ida patted the top pocket of her overalls and looked down at Baby with a stare so hard, Baby felt it drill through her brain. What was Ida doing?

The Sergeant was as surprised as Baby. 'Oh, hrmmm, I say, well yes. Spencer, get back in the car.'

'Right you are, Sarge.' The young policeman smirked at Ida.

'Are you going to handcuff me, Sergeant?' asked Ida.

'Well, as you're coming quietly, I don't think that's necessary.'

Ida climbed into the back of the Black Maria and poked her head out of the window. 'Shall we go, Sergeant Jackson?'

Sergeant Jackson, a bit dazed, squeezed back into the passenger seat. 'Yes, yes. Come on now, Spencer, get that engine started.'

How could Ida getting arrested help?

It did get the police out of their hair, though.

Coming down West Street, passing the Black Maria on its way up, was a motor coach. A small one, the sort of charabanc folk might take for a lovely outing to the seaside. Baby was sure this was not for a lovely outing and if she could help it, it wasn't going anywhere.

She peered up West Street for the orphans. Surely they'd be on their way back from school by now. With Miss Lovelock in charge, they'd be running and skipping eager to be home. Not with Mrs Bullar at the orphanage, though. But Baby couldn't see any orphans running, skipping or anything.

Baby hid behind one of the bushes that dotted the orphanage grounds as the motor coach purred through the gates. That Blackshirt Moles from the council was driving.

Perhaps she should lock the gates. If the orphans weren't home yet, they'd be much safer in the street than in the orphanage with those Blackshirts. But how? She needed orphan Aggie and her collection of keys that came in so handy last Christmas.

While the motor coach was taking a few goes at turning around to face the gates again, which must have been tricky with the swing frames and the roundabout in the way, the big front door opened and Mrs Bullar stepped outside. She carried a clipboard like the ladies at the children's camp. Baby could see a child on the step with her. It was a bit too far away to be sure, but she guessed the kid was a Spanish one.

The motor coach had stopped and was pointing at the gates again, its engine still running. Mrs Bullar led the line of fourteen Spanish kids out from the front door while Alfredo stood on guard, watching each one climb the steps on board.

While they were busy with the kids, Baby made a run for it and squatted behind a closer but smaller bush.

The kids all had labels, a roundish shape with corners, pinned to their jerseys and dresses, and a parcel label tied to their wrists. They looked nervous and half asleep, as usual.

Baby was desperately trying to think of something. She guessed where Fingers had disappeared, but she couldn't see Letitia anywhere. What did they think they were doing? Had they all left her to deal with this by herself? She couldn't stop the coach on her own, could she?

But Baby had to do something because as soon as the last kid was on board, the coach driver would surely set off right away. And with everyone she knew who could drive (or fly) kidnapped, arrested, scarpered, or sunning themselves on a riverbank, Baby had no way of catching up with the coach. The Spanish children would be lost. How long would it take to find 'em?

Though she was concentrating on the motor coach, out of the corner of her eye she was certain something small, white and bullet-fast shot out from the West Wing towards her.

The next thing she knew was the raspy lick of a tongue on her ear.

'Frank! Where did you come from, boy?'

Frank's tail was going nineteen to the dozen. But it wasn't just being pleased to see Baby. A parcel label was tied to his collar. There was some printing on one side, but on the other, in pencil, it said ...

We are Locked in

The missus took Aggies keys

June upstairs

HELP!

33

Letitia's Rooftop Epiphany

Thursday 27th May

WHILE BABY AND IDA were dealing with that jolly policeman, Letitia ran after Fingers to the West Wing of the orphanage building.

But in the few seconds it took Letitia to reach the space between the West Wing and the hedge that separated the orphanage from the cottage under the bridge, Fingers had disappeared. Completely. One moment she was there, with her fists on her hips waiting for Letitia, and the next she wasn't.

However, Letitia did find herself standing next to a very sturdy iron drainpipe. So instead of wasting time looking for Fingers, she decided to get some perspective on the whole situation. There was no sign of anything to transport the children. So the children must still be inside with Alfredo, Mrs Bullar and Fitzgerald. Could Miss June and Harry be in there too? If she could just contain them all somehow.

Letitia always found roofs to be the best place for perspective.

She kicked off her shoes and grabbed the drainpipe, next to an area of wall where, if it were the East Wing of the building, the door through to the kitchen would be. When she looked closely, the neat line of cement did suggest there'd been a door at one time, or at least half a door.

With her toes feeling the ledges in the bricks and the ridges formed by joins in the pipe, silently, she climbed. Letitia felt alive when she did this: she lost that knot in her belly she always had when she was trying to live up to her grandparents' various expectations. She supposed it was her destiny to be a doctor like her father and grandfather, but climbing did give her this feeling of freedom and power.

As she climbed, a breeze cooled her face. She leaned back and let it ruffle her hair too.

Two more footholds, two more stretches, and two more pushes on her legs and pulls on her arms and she'd be on the roof.

Letitia tried the gutter – like the drainpipe, it was Victorian cast iron and made to last. She curled her fingers round the warm metal and pulled herself on to the roof. The slates felt hot from the afternoon sun, which shone on her like an approval.

Sitting on the tiles, gripping with her bare feet to stop herself from sliding, she could see the railway line as it curved round from the station behind the orphanage. She could see over the railway bridge and the station buildings to the top of the coal heap and the coppice where the girls' railway carriage, The Lillie, nestled in its sunny clearing.

A train rumbled and chuffed by. It was very loud and the smoke filled her nostrils. She'd heard the trains pass by when she was in the orphanage, which she very quickly got used to. But up here, it was like riding on a train, like Buster Keaton running across the tops of the carriages, leaping from one to the other to catch the dastardly villain.

She stretched for the West Wing's top ridge. She was only just able to reach it. And as on the high wire in the woods at home, the one Grandfather had helped her rig up, just for fun, she pulled herself upright to balance on the ridge.

Free of worry from Grandma watching or sailing up the path with a 'Get down, Letitia! What do you think you are doing?' Letitia felt fully herself.

She was good at this. 'Oh, Grandfather. Why did you have to give me this mission to be a doctor?' She could hear him now. 'Use your talents to help people, Letitia,' he said.

And then it hit her, so hard, she nearly lost her balance.

Use your talents, Letitia!

What had Grandfather encouraged her in? Was it actually to be a doctor?

Not really. He allowed her to help or watch certain procedures, but she had to ask him for her father's medical case, for instance.

However, he had encouraged her to learn new languages – she did pick them up really easily. He had encouraged her with her maths, by buying her interesting books. And he had encouraged her with her climbing and acrobatics – by rigging up her wire, himself, raising it a foot at a time as her balance improved.

She had just assumed that all these things were for having fun. How had she never seen that any talent could be used for good?

All the possibilities, her possibilities, rushed into her brain in torrents. She almost believed that she could fly with the joy of it.

'Pssst! Psssst! Letitia' A hoarse, loud and insistent hissing from somewhere below, followed by someone whispering her name in the same insistent way, snapped Letitia away from her daydream.

Baby was on the ground, hiding behind a bush, waving her arms about, trying to attract Letitia's attention.

Baby pointed at the gates. A small coach was motoring out through them. The children! Oh no! Where was Ida? Fingers? The Orphans? This was a terrible start to helping people. She had failed the Spanish children miserably.

'Letitia!' called Baby in an urgent whispering, as loudly as she could. 'June's upstairs and the kids are inside. I'm going in!'

How did Baby know where the children were? No matter, this was no time to cry over spilt milk. She had to pull herself together and try to recover the situation. She was sure they'd thought of a plan 'B' for the Spanish children but at that precise moment, balancing on a roof about forty feet in the air, she couldn't think of it. But Grandfather certainly wouldn't be proud of a failure who gave up, therefore she would press on with grit and focus.

Letitia stood up, straightened her back, flexed her knees and lowered her centre of gravity. With the breeze in her hair, and the sun on her back, she curled each foot around the ridge tiles as she walked, her arms outstretched for balance.

Thank goodness Letitia didn't have to walk far. The lack of springiness in the orphanage roof was not good. She threw off her blue jacket and sat down on the ridge. She took a deep breath and focused.

On her belly, Letitia slithered down the tiles feet first until she dangled over the edge. Before she slid off completely, she grabbed the iron guttering and hung from it. She swung sideways along the gutter, far enough to peep through the window.

Her heart lurched at what she saw.

The beds and cubicle curtains had been pushed to the ends of the long room, blocking the doors. On the pretty rug in the middle of the dormitory, June Lovelock and Harry Miller were sitting on child-sized chairs, back to back, with the orphans' skipping ropes binding them together.

Easton Fitzgerald was casually circling Miss June and Harry. His white panama hat was not on his head but safely out of the way on a bed near the West Wing door. Fitzgerald, as he prowled, was weighing a revolver from hand to hand.

Fitzgerald smoothed each side of his moustache before he spoke. 'You know I cannot let you go, Miller, until you tell all that you know. And if I have to use the lovely Miss Lovelock here to make you speak, I will.'

'I'll tell you everything if you let her go,' said Harry, wriggling against the ropes that bound him and June together.

'I'm all right, Harry.' Miss June gulped in a big breath. 'Don't tell him anything!'

Clinging to the gutter, Letitia's fingers were beginning to ache. She could see another drainpipe on the other side of the window. She could use that to shimmy down to the sill, perhaps?

Letitia let go of the guttering with her right hand. Rust flakes came away and landed on her tongue. She spat them out, swung her body to the right and reached across. She grabbed the gutter again and followed with her left hand.

But it felt wrong.

Where the gutter had been firm before, now it bounced, and hanging there Letitia bounced with it. She watched in horror as above her head the guttering detached itself from the wall. Like a farm gate, it swung away and Letitia dangled from it, high above the orphanage grounds and the playground.

Letitia did the only thing she could in that situation.

She pressed her legs together like a mermaid tail, she pulled on her stomach muscles, raised her feet, flexed her knees, kicked and swung. The length of guttering bent and creaked.

Letitia kicked, swung, kicked, swung ... until, with all the force, elegance and grace she could muster – and a sprinkling of rust flakes – she let go of the guttering and feet first, torpedo-like, she flew.

34

Baby's Birthday Party

Thursday 27th May

THE HALF-SIZE DOOR, made to look like brick wall, opened. Fingers poked her head out and beckoned Baby inside. 'Where's Letitia, have you seen her?'

Taking a moment to get over Fingers actually using someone's name, Baby said, 'I thought she came with you?' She was trying to swallow the panicky feeling that it was all going wrong already when she felt the brush of fur against her legs. Frank was hurtling down the corridor away from them.

'Were you trying to get arrested an' all?' said Fingers, on her way up a rusty spiral staircase. 'They got June and 'arry up 'ere.'

But Baby was already halfway down the corridor after Frank.

Fingers jumped off the stairs and ran after them both. 'What are you doin'?'

Outside the living room, the little dog settled himself like a draught stopper against the door. Baby reached over him and tried the handle. It was still locked. 'Why haven't you picked this one yet?'

'We need 'er out the way first, don't we?' Fingers meant Mrs Bullar.

Baby peered through the window in the door. The English orphans were all huddled round one table, home from school, but with no tea. Mrs Bullar, on guard by the double doors to the hall, was sitting in June's story chair, the comfiest chair in the room. A suitcase was on the floor beside her.

Robert, with the other kids at the table, spotted Baby. While Mrs Bullar was gazing at herself in a little mirror and smearing on another layer of her red lipstick, Robert pointed at the ceiling.

'Come on,' said Fingers. 'They'll be all right for a bit. It's June and 'arry that won't.'

Baby hated leaving the kids in there. Getting kids out of a peril was what she did, and here she was leaving them in some. But Fingers was right. They should see what's what upstairs first. She called Frank, 'Come on, boy!' But Frank wasn't moving, not again. Of course, Robert was still inside.

Baby followed Fingers up the staircase that the orphans usually took when it was bedtime.

302

At the dormitory door, identical to the door directly below them on the ground floor, Baby grasped the handle.

'It's not locked,' said Fingers.

Through the window, all the beds and flimsy curtains on rails had been pushed higgledy-piggledy to each end of the room. In the big clear space in the middle, June and Harry were tied up back to back on the kids' chairs.

Fitzgerald was with them, leaning like he was playing schoolmaster again.

Except he had a gun in his hand, and it was pointing a whisker away from June's head.

All the panic she felt dissolved into anger, red as the Bullar's lipstick and hot as The Lillie's stove in winter.

June cried, 'You are despicable! Go on then, shoot me! He won't tell you anything, will you, Harry? You'll never get away with it!' June's face stretched in pain.

'We'll see about that,' said Easton Fitzgerald.

'No, we'll see about that!' Baby yanked hard on the dormitory door and, with no thought of what would happen to her, she leapt from bed to bed ready to wring that evil Blackshirt's neck. 'June's right, you won't get away with it!'

But before Baby could get her hands on him, in a shower of broken glass and splinters of rotten window frame, Letitia burst through the dormitory window and landed on her feet; cat-woman, crouched and ready to spring.

And regardless of the broken glass all over the floor, spring she did.

Before Fitzgerald had a chance to realise what was happening, Letitia hooked her arm around his neck, pushed her knee into the back of his knee, and as he lost balance, she pulled him to the ground. 'There, got you!' she said triumphantly.

Fitzgerald dropped the gun. It slid across the floor through the glass and splinters.

And with the bounce from the bed springs, Baby hurled herself at him too. She'd wanted to bring him down ever since the day he slimed his way around The Lillie.

'We've got him,' said Letitia, struggling to hold Fitzgerald on the floor as a he stretched for his gun.

'You savage! Your interfering is punishable by death!' Fitzgerald wriggled like the snake he was.

'I've got him. Untie June and Harry!' said Letitia, ignoring Fitzgerald's abuse and pushing him down again.

Baby pulled at the knots in the orphans' skipping ropes that were holding June and Harry together.

'I'm so sorry we've involved you in all this,' said June with tears in her eyes.

'It's all our job to fight the Blackshirts, June,' said Baby, loosening a knot.

Fingers, as good as her nickname, pulled at another knot on Harry's side.

Harry pulled his arm free. 'We need to get that gun,' he said, and dashed from the chair.

But Fitzgerald, with one enormous wrench of his body, shook Letitia off and barged in front of Harry. Fitzgerald snatched up his gun and fired at the ceiling. 'Enough!' he declared.

Baby's ears rang with the shot.

Fitzgerald grabbed June, yanked her to his chest and hooked his arm around her neck, as Letitia had done to him only moments ago.

Outside, there was a clumping of footsteps. Alfredo charged at the double doors, breaking his way into the dormitory, pushing the rickety beds out of the way with the force of it. The beds scraped across the wooden floorboards. Alfredo blocked the way out with his arms across his chest, his muscles rippling with threat.

Fitzgerald combed his fingers through his hair and straightened his shirt. 'Line up,' he said, waving his gun at the empty bit of wall opposite the windows where the beds had been.

Harry nodded. 'Do as he says,' he said, gently ushering them to the wall, his eyes fixed on June in Fitzgerald's grip.

'You people never learn,' said Mrs Bullar, who appeared at the doors behind Alfredo.

305

Alfredo stood aside to let the woman in.

Mrs Bullar dangled a large ring of keys – Aggie's keys – and sat down on the bed nearest the door. The springs creaked dangerously. 'They won't be disturbing us,' she said.

The woman had come to watch. She had left the English orphans locked in downstairs. They really were prisoners.

Fitzgerald pushed June into the line.

She stroked her neck where he'd almost strangled her.

Fitzgerald tilted June's chin with the barrel of the gun. 'Hands away from that pretty neck,' he said and paced up and down the line pointing his gun at Baby, Fingers, Letitia, June, and Harry in turn, his finger hovering dangerously round the trigger. 'Miller, if you do not tell me exactly to whom in the British Government you have passed on information about Operation Glencoe, I shall shoot one of your bizarre gaggle of friends every minute until you do. He stopped in front of Letitia. 'Starting with this savage,' he said.

Baby heard Letitia gasp, and watched her bravely stretch even taller.

'Well, Miller, what have you got to say?' shouted Fitzgerald, pressing the gun at Letitia's forehead.

Baby was poised, ready to leap and grab that gun, when she smelled smoke. She thought it was from the gun when Fitzgerald fired it. But now it seemed to be

306

coming from the door to the West Wing staircase. It was more like a motor engine smell. Like fuel burning.

And Baby heard singing.

They hadn't brought Mrs Lovelock back already, had they?

But this voice was high and shrill and was accompanied by an 'Ooh, no madam, be careful! You shouldn't be using that! It's dripping everywhere!' and the sound of stout shoes stamping hard on the floor.

Fitzgerald turned to look.

Everyone turned to look towards the West Wing door from where the singing, getting louder and shriller and higher, was coming: 'Happy Birthday to you, Happy Birthday to you, happy Birthday dear Baaaabyyyyyy! Happy Birthday to you!'

At the door, Miss Grenville appeared with black smudges across her cheek and her hair a singed, frizzy mess. She was the wildest Baby had seen her yet.

Miss Grenville trailed fire-tattered scarves, and was carrying the biggest flaming birthday cake it was possible for one person to carry. She clambered unsteadily onto the nearest bed, wobbling with the springs. Long tapers, with flames much fiercer than any birthday cake's candles had a right to be, were falling onto the beds as Miss Grenville bounced across them ...

'I tried to stop her, Miss Letty! I tried to get her on the train, but she's strong, and then she started with the can of paraffin, she said she couldn't get 'em to stay alight otherwise! I tried to put it out downstairs but ...' When the simply-dressed girl carrying an old carpet bag and wearing a soot-blackened hat saw what she and Miss Grenville had walked into, she stopped and gasped.

'It's all right, Elsie.' Letitia pushed the barrel of Fitzgerald's gun away from her face and broke free of the line, while Fitzgerald stood there open-mouthed at the strange arrival of his fiancé.

Baby felt as if her brain was exploding with the madness of it all.

Miss Grenville, the woman who brought Baby to London from India eleven or so years ago. The woman who, so she claimed, stole her from her rightful ma. The woman who had been fixated on Baby ever since she saw her in one of her old green silk jackets, had found her baby. And with what could only be described as an armful of fire, was heading straight for Baby.

But Miss Grenville wasn't a woman used to clambering over beds or bouncing on bed springs with a birthday cake alight with hundreds of paraffin-drizzled tapers. She was drunk with her success at finding Baby and couldn't walk in a straight line. She squashed Fitzgerald's hat, lost her balance and tumbled onto the bed where the cubicle curtains on their rails sucked up flames like water through a straw. Whoosh! In seconds, the curtains at the nearest window were alight and Baby heard the dry window frame crackle as that caught fire too.

An orange glow through the open door to the West Wing was getting brighter as the cries of the children could be heard from the living room below.

Back in the room, Fitzgerald barked at Miss Grenville, 'Rosamund, YOU ARE MAD! Get out! Get OUT!'

Harry seized the opportunity. He curled his hand into a tight fist and swung a right hook at the distracted Fitzgerald.

Fitzgerald fell to the floor, out cold, his nose red and bloody.

Harry grabbed the gun and, running from one end of the room to the other, cleared paths through the two huddles of beds.

Alfredo, a coward in spite of all his muscles, bolted through the doors.

Mrs Bullar tried to get up, but she was stuck in the bed: the thin mattress had sunk between the springs with her weight.

Harry shooed them all, as well as the girl that came in with the madwoman, to the double doors and the main stairs.

'But the madam?' said the new girl.

'I'll get her,' said Harry, 'just go that way!' He pointed away from the fire to the doors where they'd last seen Alfredo.

'No, I'll get her,' said Baby. 'She's my fault.' Baby picked up the pretty dormitory rug from under the chairs where June and Harry had been tied. She threw it on the flaming cake – she'd seen that work before. She grabbed Miss Grenville's arm and pulled her away from the fire.

'Oh, Baby, your cake!' said Miss Grenville.

'No matter,' said Baby, 'come with me.'

'Oh, Baby!' Miss Grenville clasped her burnt and sooty hands together over her heart and obediently let herself be led away.

Mrs Bullar was struggling to get out of the bed as Fitzgerald was groaning on the floor.

The fire had already spread, and flames from the cake were rapidly licking through the rug.

'Go! This whole place will be alight in seconds!' shouted Harry. 'I've got them – JUST GO!'

In the seeping smoke and roar of the fire behind them, they all ran down the stairs.

Mrs Bullar, free of the bed springs, barged past them. She thundered down to the bottom, grabbed a small case off the hall floor, and fled out of the front door.

Letitia slid down the banister. 'I'll get her, she won't get away with it!' she said, and ran after Mrs Bullar, who was already out the front door and sprinting across the grounds.

In the hall, Fingers was picking the lock to the main living room. The sound of the fire raging above them was deafening.

The children locked inside the living room were screaming in terror.

'Children, we're coming!' shouted June through the doors. 'Try not to panic! We're getting you out!'

'Go on outside, I won't be long!' shouted Fingers.

'I'll wait with you,' said Baby, shuddering at the sound of the blaze above them.

'No, get 'er out.' Fingers pointed with her thumb over her shoulder at Miss Grenville, who was clueless as to the chaos she'd caused, only having eyes for Baby.

Baby didn't move.

'SCARPER!' shouted Fingers.

Reluctantly, Baby pulled the madwoman away.

The children tumbled out of the main living room, where the noise of the fire above them was louder than ever. Their eyes were wet with tears from the smoke seeping under the door from the West Wing. June shooed them all out into the grounds, counting them through the door, 'Eleven, twelve ... we're two short!' screamed June. 'Two children are still inside!'

Flames were licking through the roof and round the West Wing. Smoke billowed out of the windows, which were bright orange with the blaze.

Baby looked to see who was missing – more than two.

Harry and Fitzgerald hadn't come out yet.

And she couldn't see Robert, Aggie or Frank the dog.

And she couldn't see Fingers.

35

Tea Time at Last

Thursday 27th May

BABY STARED IN HORROR at the flames burning up the orphanage. Fingers was still inside! Baby should never have left her!

Miss Grenville hovered nearby like some singed jellyfish.

Baby felt June's arm round her shoulders. She tried to wriggle out but June held her tight.

'No, Baby, the fireman have gone in. They'll find her.'

Aggie and Robert appeared at the big front door. Baby peered anxiously for Fingers, but it was Frank who came out with them, his bright white fur now a smoky grey.

The fireman led Aggie, Robert and Frank through the long snakes of water hoses and the fire engines.

With one big twist and pull Baby shook herself free. She grabbed Robert's arms. 'Where's Fingers? Where is she?'

Robert coughed and pointed back at the burning building. 'She got Frank for me,' he said with a wheezy voice.

Baby could see tears in his eyes.

'She did,' agreed Aggie. 'She said if we went and left 'er to it, she promised me and Robit she'd save Frank, and she did.'

Frank woofed and leapt. Apart from his grey coat, he was none the worse for nearly being burned to a crisp.

He circled the three of them, then ran back into the orphanage.

'Wait, boy!' shouted Baby, and ran after him.

'Baaabbyeeee!' called Miss Grenville in a hoarse shrill voice. 'Wait for me!' She hobbled after Baby, her scarves, charred and blackened with soot, trailed after her.

Baby shook her off. 'Get off me! This is all your fault!'

At last, Miss Grenville got the message and one of the fireman moved her out of the way.

But on the front doorstep, Baby ran into another fireman in his big brassy helmet ... with Fingers lolling in his arms.

314

'We forgot Frank ...' Fingers closed her eyes and her head drooped.

Baby shook her awake. 'Stop it! Don't die!'

Fingers groaned and closed her eyes again.

'She'll be all right, love, just a touch of smoke. Brave girl, this one, but looks like you're all brave girls. Though we do say leave it to us, especially for a dog.'

Good thing Frank the dog couldn't understand the fireman. He was circling and woofing again, his tail going round and round like a gyrocopter blade.

June gathered all the orphans, Fingers in the fireman's arms, and the girl, Elsie, who was looking really lost.

'Goodness me,' said June, 'do I have everyone now?'

'Not to worry!' called Mr Shaw. Brian's dad was waiting with Brian out on the street, on the other side of the railings. 'Brenda has counted and assures me everyone is accounted for.'

'Come with us,' said Brian. 'We've made space for everyone!'

'Really?' said June, frantically looking about her at the bedraggled orphans, Robert and Aggie the bedraggliest of the lot.

'We've all got out now,' said Robert. 'No one's hiding in the toilets. Before the missus locked us in, she sent that bully boy, Alfredo, round to check.'

'I think she wanted to lock us in forever,' said Aggie, beside him.

'You're safe now, Aggie.' June put her arm around Aggie's shoulder. 'I don't think Alfredo will be troubling us again, but I do wonder where he has run off to …'

As Brian and her dad led the whole troupe of them across the street and up the slope to the station, Baby noticed a Black Maria drive through the orphanage gates and zoom away up West Street.

'Errr, are we going far? I've got to get back and help the other blokes,' said the fireman carrying Fingers.

'No, not far, my dear man. You'll be back in a jiffy,' said Mr Shaw.

In the Lillie's clearing, catching the last of the evening sun, Baby was relieved to spot a smirk on her sister's face. She was enjoying the attention.

The fireman gently laid Fingers down on a colourful quilt next to Mrs Lovelock in her wheelchair, who Leonard had already delivered back to Nettlefield with José.

Robert, Aggie and the other orphans with José, Ramón, Elsie, Baby, June and Frank the dog, all sat on the mossy soft earth in as big a circle as they could make.

'We didn't have time to tidy up inside yet,' said Brian, setting down a small mountain of sandwiches piled up on a tin tray in the middle of the circle, with some slices of cold ham and egg pie.

Everyone was still a bit dazed from the fire, but at least they were all safe. As they munched, they listened to Mr Shaw explain how Brian, Ramón, Bonnie and himself, had hurriedly evacuated to the old place to be on the safe side. They'd brought as much as they could carry, which included the Enigma machine. 'Fortunately this Polish "double", I think, is quite portable,' added Mr Shaw, knowledgably.

'I made the sandwiches!' said Brian. Of course, she did.

'I carry oranges,' said Ramón, practising his English and offering the oranges, in a small crate, around to everyone. The small crate looked suspiciously like the crates the old greengrocer put on display outside his shop.

'And I've got these,' said Bonnie, holding up two very large, bulging paper bags full of iced buns.

'From the bakers', really?' said Baby, who only knew the baker to be a nasty lady Blackshirt.

'Yes,' said Bonnie. 'She said she's changed her mind and she's sorry, and when she saw the fire engines and found out where they were going, she had to dash back for some buns.' Bonnie frowned as she tried to remember the baker's exact words.

To Baby's mind something about that didn't ring true, but at least they could enjoy her raspberry buns.

'Jolly nice to be back at the old place,' said Mr Shaw, poking his head through the door 'though it could do

317

with a ... titivate. Perhaps, Miss Lovelock, your young man could spare an afternoon to lend a hand?'

June gasped and dropped her sandwich with an 'Oh! My oh my! What was I thinking! I forgot about Harry! Is he still inside the orphanage? Is he even alive?'

36

Nettlefield Creek

Thursday 27th May

FOR A WOMAN HER SIZE, Mrs Bullar could certainly run fast!

Letitia dashed back to the drainpipe, pushed her feet into her shoes and ran at top speed to catch up with her.

But Mrs Bullar was getting in her car!

Even Letitia couldn't run that fast.

The engine revved with angry throaty noises. The car reversed with a grinding and clunking of gears, and turned to point straight out of the orphanage gates!

Letitia imagined an engine inside her too. She was jolly well going to do her best to catch the woman.

But smoke was seeping out from under the bonnet of Mrs Bullar's car, which quickly turned to clouds of it churning from the engine into the orphanage playground. As if there wasn't enough smoke already!

Mrs Bullar flung the driver's door open and burst out of the car. With her case, she bolted across West Street, heading up the slope for the station.

Letitia ran across the road and scrambled up the bank. She excused herself through a small crowd of passengers, railway guards and even the stationmaster, who had all gathered to watch the fire.

But Mrs Bullar was at the top already! Like a rhinoceros, she charged ahead of Letitia and through the ticket office unchallenged.

Letitia sprinted like Jesse Owens and saw Mrs Bullar wave a ticket at the guard on the platform.

'Portsmouth train!' shouted the guard to the one other passenger.

Mrs Bullar barged past the guard to the waiting train.

'Are you alright Madam? Have you come from the fire? We'll have to stop all services if it gets much worse.'

'Of course I am, idiot!' She shoved the single passenger out of the way and pulled the carriage door open.

Letitia dashed across the platform.

But the guard blocked her path 'Can I see your ticket, miss?'

'I haven't got one.'

'You can't get on the train without a ticket,' said the guard.

'But she's getting away!' Letitia pointed at Mrs Bullar's large bottom disappearing behind a carriage door.

'The ticket office is right there, miss,' said the guard. 'Now, if you let me get on ... Portsmouth train ready to depart!' he shouted.

Letitia very much felt like stamping her foot and telling the guard this was a matter of national security, but she didn't have time. She dashed through the ticket office, hurtled past the station buildings to the gap in the fence by the coal heap.

The steam filled the platform in white billows. It was impossible to identify Mrs Bullar's carriage and the wheel rod was moving. The train was on its way.

Letitia hurled herself at the last carriage, pulled the door open and leapt in.

No sign of the Bullar woman as she supposed, but to Letitia's horror no sign of a corridor through to the other carriages either. It was one of those trains that when you got on, you were stuck with whoever you were stuck with. And in this case, Letitia was stuck with the complete opposite to Mrs Bullar, a small slight man reading a newspaper. He looked up, raised one eyebrow above the rim of his glasses, then returned to the paper.

Letitia sat down. She had to think fast. Who knew where Mrs Bullar was planning to get off? Should she wait until the next station or ...

The train crossed the railway bridge, and in no time it was chuffing along the embankment at the back of the orphanage. What a mess the orphanage looked! Flames eating up the roof and grey smoke spewing out. The whole building was fast becoming a charred wreck of a place. She hoped everyone was all right. She'd run without checking. But to Letitia's great relief, as the train left the orphanage behind, she caught a glimpse of a fire truck and the first gush of water at the orphanage roof.

It was now or never.

What would Buster Keaton do?

Letitia opened the carriage door.

The man with his paper stood up, it flapped in the breeze from the open door. 'Wh ... wh ... what do you think are you doing, young lady?'

But Letitia didn't have time to answer him, nor remove her shoes. As the train was fast approaching the viaduct over Nettlefield Creek, she pulled herself onto the roof.

In the steam and smoke, she stood up. The camber, the curve of the roof, helped her grip as she extended her arms for balance. The speed was a thrilling new sensation. The wind thrashed through her clothes, her hair, and her fingers – was this like flying? She could even be on an aeroplane wing! Jesse Owens and now Buster Keaton – two of her heroes! She saw her name, Letitia Zara Ketton, alongside theirs.

She bent, and leaning into the wind, ran along the top of the first carriage, feeling the speed of the train multiply her own. It was glorious! She estimated where the next compartment might be – the vents gave her a clue. She lay down across the carriage roof. Her toes inside her shoes curled round the far edge as, upside down, she peered through a window.

The viaduct was fast approaching.

Letitia refused to panic when there were only two strangely unsurprised elderly ladies waving at her from the first compartment. With a spring that only years of playing in the woods could achieve, she got up and tried again.

What luck! Mrs Bullar was alone in the next carriage attempting to apply more lipstick. She was so surprised at the sight of an upside down Letitia, she applied a thick greasy red streak across her cheek.

Below them, Nettlefield Creek at low tide was giving off a very unpleasant aroma. Letitia swivelled down onto the door, balanced on the ledge below, pulled on the door and swung herself in.

The carriage door flapped open.

Mrs Bullar tried to get away but there was nowhere to go. 'You stupid girl, what do you think you're doing? You and your dirty little friends have wrecked everything!' She lunged headfirst for Letitia in the doorway.

Letitia grabbed the luggage rack and leapt onto the seat.

Mrs Bullar couldn't control her momentum. She pitched through the open train door, tumbled out of the train and off the viaduct.

With a distant splosh, Mrs Bullar, former Matron of Nettlefield Grange Orphanage, landed in the stinking mud of Nettlefield Creek.

As horrible as she was, Letitia did hope that somebody, ideally the police, would get to her in time.

In seconds the train had left the viaduct behind. As soon as it passed a field that looked soft enough, Letitia launched herself out of the train, curled and rolled in the sweet new summer grass.

It took her a minute or two to work out which way was up, and which way was back to Nettlefield.

But as soon as she did, her long legs flew her back to the town.

Half an hour later, she ran around the town hall into West Street, past the church and to the still smouldering, charred and sodden pile that was Nettlefield Grange Orphanage. The grounds were busy with lots of firemen and three fire engines.

Ida was waiting by the railings with that fat policeman, Sergeant Jackson, and his nervous Constable.

Even Letitia had to catch her breath. 'Mrs Bullar …
fell in the mud,' she said leaning over her knees. 'Last I
saw … under the viaduct … in the creek.'

'Off you go Spencer! Pick up reinforcements on the
way and get that woman! She won't get far, covered in
Nettlefield mud. We'll have her once and for all this
time.'

'What if she's stuck, sir?' asked Spencer.

'Initiative, boy! Initiative!'

Constable Spencer seated himself into the driver's
seat of the Black Maria parked in the street and drove
off.

'Hubert Moles has scarpered and left a ton of
evidence,' said Sergeant Jackson. 'More kidnapping and
attempted mass murder, unbelievable what these fascists
get up to.'

'We must believe it, Sergeant,' said Ida.

'But all the children?' asked Letitia. 'The Spanish and
English ... and Baby and Fingers and June and Harry and
Elsie and Miss Grenville! Are they all safe?' All their
names tumbled out in a rush. Letitia held her breath for
the answer.

'They. Are. All. Safe.' Ida laid her hand warmly on
Letitia's shoulder.

Which was enough for now.

Letitia flumped down against the orphanage railings
and suddenly realised how exhausted she was.

She turned her face to the evening sun peeping over the railway bridge, closed her eyes and revelled in its warmth.

That had all been so thrilling. She knew her calling now, or some of it at least, and it was definitely helping. She had definitely helped by using her talents, like Grandfather said. She hoped he'd be proud.

Her face cooled. Had the sun set already?

When she opened her eyes all she could see was the silhouette of an imposing woman in a large, old-fashioned hat, looming over her.

'Letitia, my dear, I have someone I'd like you to meet.'

37

Sir Hugh Sinclair

Thursday 27th May

LETITIA KNEW THAT SHADOW very well, even down to the feathers on the outlandish hat and the handbag big enough to be a small suitcase.

But there was a second, equally imposing shape too.

'Grandma you're ... you're ... here? How did you get back so quickly?' Letitia squinted up at Grandma and the portly gentleman with her. Grandma didn't expect her to walk out with this man, did she? He had to be at least a hundred years old.

'I decided not to make the trip to The Bahamas,' said Grandma. Instead, I scattered your dear grandfather's ashes at Guy's Hospital in London. It was his alma mater, you know. So I spent a few days with Amelia after all, after she'd sorted out her plumbing of course. Thank goodness Elsie is a sensible girl and sent me a note, care of Amelia, as to where you were. Amazingly, it's a part of the world Sir Hugh knows well. Letitia, this is who I'd like you to meet.'

Sir Hugh?

'Of course – Sir Hugh! You came!' Letitia stood up, rubbed her hand on her skirt and offered it to the gentleman.

'Sir Hugh' looked puzzled. 'Is there something I've missed dear Hortensia?'

'I wrote to you,' said Letitia. 'Grandfather gave me your address should I ever need help. It was the last thing he gave me.'

'Well, I shall be delighted to read your letter on my return to London.' He leant in and lowered his voice. 'I trust you haven't passed on my address elsewhere?'

'Oh no, of course not,' said Letitia.

'It's classified, don't you know. But that is how highly your grandfather thought of you, my dear.'

'Sir Hugh is very interested in your talents and would like to offer you a job; an apprenticeship first, of course,' said Grandma.

Letitia was very confused. Even if she abandoned her new plan to use her actual talents and was going to be a doctor after all, she still needed several years training. Did hospitals even do apprenticeships?

'Hmm ... doing what exactly, Grandma?'

Sir Hugh replied, 'Exactly what you've just been doing. While we were waiting for you, we've been chatting to Ida. She's been telling us how you use that brain of yours to uncover villainous plots and pursue enemies of the state – all jolly brilliant stuff. How dashed incredible that after more years than I care to remember, I bumped into your grandmama in London, and we were both on our way to Nettlefield! I went to school not very far away from here – Stubbington, you may know it? A jolly little place a stone's throw from the sea – and far, far back in ancient history, I was born in Southampton.'

Sir Hugh's job offer made Letitia feel quite wobbly. Behind the two old people, Ida was watching the fire engines hard at work in the orphanage grounds. The firemen still training their hoses, gushing torrents of water on the remnants of the fire. Of all the strange days she'd had that week this was the strangest. And there was Grandma not criticising her for her appearance or 'acrobatics' and actually supporting her having a job? And what a job!

Hold on a minute, what exactly did Sir Hugh do?

But Letitia didn't have a chance to ask because Ida was beckoning them away from the soggy, charred husk of a building, over West Street and up the slope to the station. 'Come on. I think everyone's gone to the The Lillie.'

Letitia grabbed Ida's arm. 'What's happened to the Spanish children? Did somebody stop the coach?'

'Don't worry; they're fine. We did it,' said Ida. 'It'll probably cause a diplomatic incident though!'

Letitia, with Grandma and Sir Hugh, followed Ida past the stationmaster's office, the coal heap and through the tunnel in the bushes to that funny little place they called The Lillie.

'After you,' said Ida, as she ushered the three of them into the tunnel.

Sir Hugh quite cheerfully removed his hat and lowered his head. Though he had no need, for Letitia guessed she was the same height as him. Grandma had to remove her hat, which she did less cheerfully.

They were halfway through when Miss June Lovelock barged into them coming from The Lillie. 'Oh, hello! Oh, I'm so sorry, do excuse me! It's an emergency! Oh, Ida! It's Harry, he didn't come out with the others!' said June.

'Oh no!' said Letitia, 'I didn't know.' She felt guilty that after all the excitement, she'd actually forgotten about Harry Miller.

Ida gently took hold of Miss June's hand. 'It's all right. Harry is safe. This is Sir Hugh,' she said, introducing the portly and well-to-do gentleman in the middle of the bushy tunnel. 'He will explain as much as he can.'

'Really? Is that really true?' asked Miss June, not sounding convinced but persuaded to turn around again and rejoin everyone else in the clearing.

'Good evening,' said Sir Hugh to the gathering outside The Lillie. 'What an interesting hideaway – undiscovered for how long, Ida?'

'For a good thirteen years, most of Brenda's life in fact,' said Mr Shaw, who'd stood up to welcome all the newcomers.

Brian fetched two chairs from inside The Lillie for Grandma and Sir Hugh, who picked their way through what had become quite a large group of orphans, adults and younger adults. Mr Shaw kindly brought a chair out for Elsie and put it next to Grandma. And Ida persuaded June to sit down too. As soon as June kneeled down, several orphans draped themselves over her.

Just when Letitia thought that the clearing couldn't get any more jam-packed, the jolly policeman, Sergeant Jackson, appeared. 'Well, let's be having you all, now. We have three Black Marias ready and waiting to take all you nippers to the Southampton Camp.'

'Ooh, it'll be like going on holiday!' said Aggie.

Ramón clung to his brother José's arm. In Spanish, he said, 'You are not leaving again?'

José replied, 'No, we go together. As we were meant to.'

331

Bonnie got up to join the others after kissing Ida goodbye. 'I'll be all right, 'da. I'd really like to try sleeping in a tent.'

'I'm not going without Frank,' said Robert.

On hearing his name, Frank, the grubby little whitish dog, wagged his tail.

'I should have said all you nippers and a dog,' said Sergeant Jackson, 'and we'll be back for the rest of you without a bed for the night, when this lot have got settled.'

June kissed each departing orphan as they followed Sergeant Jackson through the tunnel. 'I know my experience there with that Mr Fitzgerald was not good, but everyone else I met there was really lovely,' she said, after she sent the last one through. 'I so wanted to tell them what was going under their noses, but I was so afraid for Mother.'

As the sun finally went down, every remaining person turned to Sir Hugh, who took some moments to scan each face – Miss June, Mr Shaw, Brian, Ida, Baby, Fingers, Letitia, Elsie, Grandma and Mrs Lovelock, though she was already asleep in her wheelchair. 'Come closer everyone, I don't want to speak any louder than is necessary ...'

'First of all, don't you worry about Miller and Fitzgerald. Everything's under control. Fitzgerald is in the custody of the security services, and the police have

332

picked up Mrs Bullar. And some more of our chaps are tailing their Nettlefield associates. Thanks to Ida's quick thinking, the Spanish children, who were horrifically bullied and threatened into silence and compliance by Fitzgerald, have been rescued before any were deposited with the families they were supposed to spy on. Jolly good idea getting yourself arrested, Ida, and giving the police that list. Which incidentally, Miller has consistently failed to acquire – so a huge well done! Now about that machine ...' said Sir Hugh.

'This one,' said Mr Shaw, fetching it out from The Lillie. 'A 1927 Enigma K, I believe.'

'Yes, it's a commercial one that Miller smuggled out of Germany in '33. His ticket, if you like, into the SIS ...'

Baby frowned.

'The Special Intelligence Service,' whispered Mr Shaw.

'Spies,' whispered Brian. She really did just know things.

'Is Harry a double agent for the secret service?' whispered Ida.

Sir Hugh continued, 'and then this Enigma, or the promise of it, became Miller's ticket into Fitzgerald's network of Nazi sympathisers. Miller identified Fitzgerald as a threat to British security while they were both out in Spain. Miller was forced to fly Fitzgerald's hostage children to Britain to maintain his cover, and then go along with keeping them holed up in Hamwell until the 23rd. They sailed the children up Southampton Water to coincide their arrival at the docks with the Habana.'

'But wasn't it rather risky handing over the Enigma to Fitzgerald?' asked Letitia.

'Yes, that would be so, if Fitzgerald had been accepted into the Nazi fold. If he had, he could have acquired an Enigma or two from them. But he is a maverick, a loose cannon, an unreliable fanatic.'

'Like Uncle Arthur,' said Ida.

'Our friends in the Polish Cipher Bureau helped us secretly adapt the machine so it couldn't actually be used successfully, but would still convince inexperienced operators that it was in perfect working order and any errors were operator errors. Fortunately, Fitzgerald was considerably less up on cryptography and cryptanalysis than he liked to think he was.'

'I saw you on a train, didn't I?' said Letitia.

'Did you, my dear?' said Sir Hugh.

'You had your back to the window, but I recognised the old Polish mathematician and Harry was there too. Are they all connected to the Polish Cipher Bureau?' How thrilled Grandfather would have been to know that Letitia now had a connection to them as well.

'Would that have been that Zaremba, Stanislaw Zaremba?' asked Mr Shaw.

'Yes,' said Sir Hugh. 'He introduced us to some excellent people, who helped us make those temporary adjustments. We were very pushed for time, so some of the work was necessarily done on the train.'

'Ah yes,' said Mr Shaw. 'The wiring in the rotor wheels – it's jolly clever but in many ways very simple too, but the cleverest things are. The operator can create a code every day, but where they believe they are making fresh codes, they are in fact using the same one again and again.'

'One code is much easier to crack than three hundred and sixty-five,' said Letitia.

'One thing for certain,' said Sir Hugh, 'is that this mission to foil Operation Glencoe would have totally failed were it not for all you young ladies.' He again looked intently at each one, Letitia, Brian, Fingers, Ida and Baby in turn. 'Miller is good, not his real name of course, and he will be vital to our efforts if it does come to war ... but we seriously underestimated the manpower for this job.'

'You needed girl power, didn't you?' said Brian.

Sir Hugh laughed. 'Yes, we most certainly did! Ladies, you are wonders!'

'And Dad too,' said Brian, giving her dad's hairy cheek a kiss.

Letitia noticed that Grandma was nodding off in her chair. Elsie was doing her best to prop her up.

'You must all be dashed tired,' said Sir Hugh. 'But one last thing ... there's this little place north of London that I'm thinking of buying, and I'm looking for people to be part of the operation there. I can say no more, and this is top secret, but your skills, Mr Shaw, would be very welcome. I've already made a proposal to young Miss Ketton here, but any of you, if you think you can help your country to fight these fascists in a more formal way, shall we say, I would be very pleased to hear from you.'

They were now sitting in the golden glow of an early summer evening. The sky was streaked with pink and orange, and the moon was up and waiting in the blue. What a day! Only the rumble through the tunnel of a small convoy of Black Marias arriving outside the station, brought it to a close.

One thing troubled Letitia though.

That list.

And, for some peculiar reason, her seven times table popped into her head too.

Some people did have trouble with the seven times table, but for Letitia it was very elementary arithmetic, which she could recite forwards and backwards in Spanish, Polish, German and English. Why was she subconsciously telling herself to remember it?

She'd think about it when she was falling asleep back at the camp.

Though joggling in the back of a police motor car on its way to North Stoneham, sleep came for Letitia before she'd even had a chance to say two times seven is fourteen.

38

Reunion, Revelation & Baby's Resolve

The following days, weeks and months

LUCKILY, THE COTTAGE under the railway bridge was unharmed by the fire. Brian and her dad decided to stay there rather than at the camp. They wanted to be close by to tidy up The Lillie after Regina and Maria's stay. 'Fortunately, it is only tidying up and a good old late spring clean!' said Brian's dad.

Letitia's Gran and Elsie were dropped off together at 'a rather nice hotel near the docks in Southampton.' Letitia's Gran, only a bit begrudgingly, allowed Letitia to stay with the gang at the camp. 'I suppose if international espionage is going to be your career, Letitia Zara Ketton, I'll have to let you go at some point,' she said.

Mrs Lovelock resumed her lovely camping holiday and enjoyed the sing-songs around the campfires. June got stuck in again with camp duties, but under much,

much pleasanter circumstances, and enjoyed telling her story (edited for the sake of national security) to her fellow volunteers. José and Ramón loved being at the camp. Because they actually were orphans, they hoped to stay on in Britain, and Southampton especially.

Miss Grenville was taken to the asylum in Nettlefield to get the care she needed. Leonard from the laundry picked Baby up from the camp and drove her back to Nettlefield to visit. Baby sat in the front of his van this time.

Miss Grenville didn't recognise Baby at all. Was that because of the medicines Miss Grenville had been given? Or because she no longer cared? Baby had her green silk jacket on for the visit. The jacket had been laundered, and instead of the note that she never used to take out – the one with 'Look after Baby' on it next to a lipstick kiss – she put the story that she wrote at the camp in those worrying hours while she was waiting for Leonard to show up. The story was about the woman at the side of the road, her real ma, the one who gave her up. The green silk had been repaired too, by one of the ladies at the camp, with some beautiful new sprigs of embroidery. But even after showing Miss Grenville the story and the new embroidery, Miss Grenville's face was a blank.

Letitia said the Spanish kids were being looked after and the Foreign Office was making urgent enquiries about their families. The thought of it made Baby feel

sick. It was one thing thinking about her own real ma –
and who knows how many actual brothers and sisters
living so poor in India – but the Spanish kids' families
were in prison and at any moment could be murdered by
the fascists ... It wasn't something she did often, but
Baby prayed for their safety.

Mrs Bullar was thrown back into prison, and Baby
very much hoped permanently this time. Mrs Tatler and
the rest of Nettlefield Hands Across the Sea seemed to
go back to their normal jobs, running boarding houses,
shop-keeping, working for the council ... Sergeant
Jackson said he had his eye on them, but Baby knew the
Blackshirts hadn't given up. It would only take another
fanatical fascist to come along. Whatever happened next,
Baby and The Nettlefield Resistance would be ready.

The rebuilding of the orphanage got underway fairly
quickly. Again, townspeople who weren't Blackshirts
chipped in, and in the meantime, they all had a splendid
time at the children's camp. Fingers especially enjoyed
the international football match, England vs Spain,
which she refereed.

Ida went back to college until the end of term, when
she returned to the camp with Gin, back from Germany,
and Sophie from the Bournemouth Art School. Sitting on
deckchairs sipping ice cool lemonade, with rows of sun-
bleached white tents behind them, they all caught up
with each other.

'Heavens above! What larks we missed!' said Gin, swishing her favourite feather boa around her neck to prevent it dipping in her drink.

'I was actually here a few weeks ago, I think I spoke to your Letitia,' said Sophie, who had helped give out the sleeping bags made from the coronation flags.

Sophie only remarked because she recognised Ramón. Letitia herself had been gone for more than a month by this time. She'd returned to Threep to sit her School Certificate and take a further course in German – after that it was all hush-hush as far as Baby and the others knew.

But Letitia had not gone without one final revelation.

They'd only been at the camp for a few days when Letitia had started helping with lessons. Her group was doing their tables. They were reciting the seven times table in Spanish and Basque, which she'd just started picking up when Letitia gasped, and said in English, 'I need a telephone. Where's the camp telephone?' She mimed picking up a telephone receiver. Her little group giggled but one boy understood and took her to a utility tent.

Later, sipping a bedtime cocoa and sitting in a huddle on the grass with Baby, Fingers, Ida and Brian, who was visiting for a couple of days, Letitia explained. 'I thought if I made a mental note of 'the seven times table' I'd remember all my thoughts at the time but so much happened after that, the reasoning somehow got squeezed out ... until now.'

'It was the list that Ida and I found, the list she got herself arrested for, which gave all the details of where the children were supposed to be going.'

'I spotted one child that was actually going to your home, didn't I?' said Ida.

'Yes. And that child had a number twenty-one but there were only fourteen children on the list corresponding to the fourteen Spanish children at the orphanage.'

Baby could see the seven times table connection. 'Once seven is seven, two sevens are fourteen, three sevens are twenty-one ... '

'Exactly!' said Letitia.

Baby was still confused.

'Consuela, I remember her name now. I wonder which one she was? Anyway, Consuela, the child to be sent to us in Threep, and no wonder with Grandma's connections, was halfway down the list. If those were the first, and so far, only Glencoe children, wouldn't she be number seven? Where were the numbers one to fourteen?'

It was Brian's turn to gasp. 'Out there already,' she said, dripping her cocoa from her tilting cup.

'Yes, our Operation Glencoe was not their first attempt.' Letitia drained her cup and slammed it down on the grass. 'Probably against their will, fourteen children are out there, sending secrets to the Nazis.'

There was a moment's silence against the distant, happy background noise of children playing as Baby, Fingers, Brian and Ida took this in.

'I should have noticed when I took the list to the police station,' said Ida.

'No, none of us noticed until now,' said Letitia. 'But the SIS are onto it and I can't wait to start my apprenticeship!'

Baby looked at Fingers, whose eyes had been drawn away to the football game starting up in the middle of the field, and wondered again that with all these exciting things happening for her sisters – Ida the mechanic, Brian the chef, Sophie the tailor, and now Letitia the spy – maybe her and Fingers should think about learning something. Though Fingers could do one very special thing that Baby wasn't allowed to tell anyone about.

Then Baby thought about Gin. What had she really been doing in Germany with her dad?

The thought of America returned.

And left again.

Baby had a very strong feeling that her life's work was on this side of the Atlantic Ocean and had only just begun.

The End until . . .

The Wonder Girls 3 is coming

...

What is the 'special thing' that Fingers can do and Baby isn't allowed to talk about? Will Baby ever let Fingers go her own way? Will either of them ever get to America?

To find out Fingers's *other* special talent and be updated on the progress of *The Wonder Girls 3,* when those other questions will find an answer, please read on ...

A Wonder Girls Short

The
Naming
of
Florrie

J.M. CARR

Join my Readers' Gang

I love sharing my stories with other readers, so I do hope you'll sign up .

Gang members get my monthly-ish newsletter with book news, background snippets to the stories and how I'm getting on with the latest work in progress!
.

I'll also send you **an exclusive to the gang**, *Wonder Girl*s short. You might think you know how Fingers earned her nickname – she is a pickpocketing burglar after all. The truth may surprise you …

Go to jmcarr.com to join the gang and get *The Naming of Florrie.*

You can unsubscribe at any time.

Did you enjoy

'The Wonder Girls Resist'?

You Can Make a Big Difference

Honest reviews do a brilliant job of drawing attention to books. Particularly independently published ones without a huge advertising budget!

That attention is essential for sales.

Sales are really important to me not only because it means more folk are reading my stories, which is thrilling. But also because those sales will help me to publish more. They'll pay for editors, lovely covers, paperbacks and eventually recording studios to turn the stories into audiobooks.

So, I would be hugely grateful if you could take a few minutes to write me a review. It doesn't have to be very long, just a sentence would be great.

Go to jmcarr.com/review-links where you'll find links to take you to the relevant pages. **Thank you very much.**

About the Book

Be careful – these snippets of inspiration and background information contain spoilers!

Allan Glaisyer Minns

Allan Glaisyer Minns was Britain's first black mayor. In 1903 he was elected to the town council in Thetford, Norfolk and served as mayor for two years from 1904.

Allan was born in 1858 in Inagua in The Bahamas, one of nine children born to John and Ophelia Minns.

Allan's grandfather, John Minns, left England looking for adventure in the 'New World' sometime around 1799. When his ship, which was also carrying enslaved African people, began to sink, one of those Africans, Rosette, risked her own life to save John's. Rosette was Allan's grandmother. It's an inspiring story that you can read on John Holdaway's website: https://johnholdaway.wordpress.com.

Allan came to Britain to study medicine at Guy's Hospital in London. He qualified in 1884 and joined his eldest brother Dr Pembroke Minns in Thetford.

Allan was married twice, first in 1888 to Emily Pearson who died in 1892, then to Gertrude Ann Morton in 1896. He had children with both his wives but I could only find out about one of them, his son, Noel Glaisyer Minns, who was also a doctor and my inspiration for Letitia's father. Noel fought in and survived WWI, but died in a motor accident in 1921.

Allan Glaisyer Minns promoted the health benefits of 'fresh air and common sense', which I think works well with my fictional grandfather setting up a tightrope for Letitia in the woods (though you might not think that encouraging tightrope walking shows common sense!). There is no record of Allan experiencing racism, which isn't to say that he didn't face it, but in creating Threep I've imagined a town where racism has no place. The evidence suggests that Allan Glaisyer Minns was well liked and much respected.

He died in 1930 in Dorking in Surrey. He was 71 years old.

Fascists & Fascism

Fascists are on the far right of the left – right political spectrum. They are extreme nationalists, believing that their country is the best to the detriment of all others.

They see violence and war as acceptable ways of increasing their country's power at home and abroad.

Fascist countries are governed by dictators, single rulers who believe that democracy is out of date. For them, the only way to govern successfully is with one strong leader heading up one strong political party governing in a military style. Any opposition to this ruling party is against the law and carries severe penalties.

Fascism's extreme nationalism often leads to a belief in a 'master race', resulting in the terrible persecution of 'others' not identified as belonging to that race.

Fascism still exists in the 21st century. However since calling somebody 'fascist' is now considered an insult, 21st century fascists might not describe themselves as such. But their behaviour is easily recognised.

The Basque Children

In May 1937, the Spanish Civil War had been raging for over a year as Franco and his fellow fascists tried to overthrow the democratically elected republican government. (Unlike in the United States today, the Spanish republicans were politically on the left.)

After a year of terrible civil war and in spite of many volunteers from around the world joining the

International Brigade to fight with the Republicans, Franco was winning.

However, in Spain's industrial northeast corner, the Basque people were proving particularly resistant to Franco. So, in April 1937, helped by Hitler and Mussolini (Italy), Franco bombed them. The strategy was *Blitzkrieg* – a surprise attack using overwhelming force. It's disputed exactly how many people were killed or wounded as a direct result of the bombing. But the probable number is somewhere between 800 to 3000 of the 5000 inhabitants in Guernica alone. The town is famous for having been almost obliterated. That same year, in response, Pablo Picasso painted *Guernica,* a large black, white, and grey oil painting, 3.49m by 7.77m. It's regarded by many as the most powerful anti-war painting in history.

The Basque people begged the international community for help to save their children. France, Russia, Belgium, Mexico, Switzerland and Denmark responded and between them accepted almost 29,000 child refugees.

But the British government said 'No'. They had signed a 'non-intervention' agreement in 1936 – promising not to interfere in the Spanish War. Hitler, Mussolini, and Stalin (USSR) also signed the agreement but ignored it.

Many groups across Britain, part of The National Joint Committee for Spanish Relief, came together to help the Spanish people anyway.

A steam cruise liner, *Habana,* was converted to increase its capacity. While in Britain, preparations were made to receive the children in Southampton. Local scouts, guides and students erected the 500 tents that had to be hired from the British government.

Over 4000 people arrived on the packed ship, 3968 children with 95 teachers, who were all women, 120 assistants, 16 priests, 2 Spanish doctors and 2 Spanish nurses. Southampton welcomed them all on 23rd May 1937.

They were taken by bus to a camp set up in three fields donated by a local farmer, Mr Brown. An *Asda* superstore now stands on the site. People from Southampton, Eastleigh, and the surrounding area stepped up with all kinds of help, from toys to bread, shoes to laundry services, serving meals to digging ditches – everything the children (*los niños* in Spanish) and the camp would need. Others donated too; for instance, Cadbury's, gave one ounce of chocolate per child per day for *pan y chocolate* – chocolate bread, a Basque favourite.

After what had been a rainy few weeks, blighting the coronation of George VI earlier in the month, for *los niños* the sun shone.

Flags that had adorned public buildings for the coronation became sleeping bags, courtesy of students from the Bournemouth Municipal School of Art. People from all round the area were only too willing to share the cost and lend a hand.

Over the following few months, *los niños* were gradually moved on in groups called 'colonies', to less temporary accommodation all over Britain. They were not sent to families, but to specially set up Basque Children's Homes in donated accommodation, or to existing institutions. This was at the request of the Basque government, who wanted the children to stay together as much as possible. Some of them did remain in Southampton. The camp closed on 18th September 1937.

The intention was that the Basque children would return to Spain when the conflict was over. Many did but of course, many others had lost their parents. So they stayed and made their homes in the UK, sometimes being reunited with their families many years later.

Find out more about the Basque children in the UK here: www.basquechildren.org/

Enigma

Arthur Scherbius is most often credited with inventing the Enigma machine in Germany at the end of the First World War. It resembled an early 20th century typewriter. But the Enigma's purpose was to create and decipher codes for confidential information. However, it was recently discovered that two Dutch naval officers, Theo A. van Hengel and R.P.C. Sprengle, had invented the key mechanism that made Enigma work, a few years earlier – the rotor wheels. These wheels were marked around their circumference with the letters of the alphabet. Each wheel turned and aligned with the other rotor wheels, like the numbers on a combination lock, to create or decipher the code.

Between the First and Second World Wars many inventors developed different versions of Enigma, improving on previous versions and making the codes harder and harder to crack. In the 1920s Enigma machines, of one kind or another, were used commercially and diplomatically across parts of mainland Europe, whenever top level confidential information had to be communicated. But when the German military started using them in the mid 1920s, access to Enigma began to be restricted.

Towards the beginning of 1928, a parcel arrived at a sorting office in Poland, followed by an urgent request to return it unopened, *immediately* to Germany.

Perhaps, if the message hadn't sounded so urgent, the Poles might not have been curious. So the parcel *was* returned but not before it had been opened and the contents, an Enigma machine, thoroughly investigated. The parcel was then resealed as if it had never been opened in the first place. It was vital that Germany continued to believe that the Poles had no knowledge at all of Enigma and its operation.

Having an Enigma machine alone was not enough to decipher the codes. It had to be compatible with the sender's machine. And no machine was any use without the heavily guarded *codebook*, which listed how the rotor wheels would be lined up each day to choose the correct new code from the millions of possibilities.

As Hitler grew in power during the 1930s many people believed that the ability to intercept and decipher the coded communications between the Nazi forces was essential for defence. Poland was especially convinced about this.

The Polish Mathematicians

A Polish 'cypher bureau' was formed around 1930 with some very talented young Polish mathematicians. Marian Rejewski was one of these. He worked out the construction and operation of an Enigma from some intercepted messages and a description of the machine – possibly the description obtained from that parcel around New Year 1928.

German people, who hated what Hitler was doing to their country, also bravely leaked vital information that further enabled the Polish mathematicians. Without their work, the British mathematician Alan Turing, the inventor of our modern computers, would not have been able to devise a method for cracking the Enigma codes for every possible alignment of the rotor wheels.

Stanislaw Zaremba was an eminent Polish mathematician from the Polish School of Mathematics. He wrote many university textbooks and, luckily for my purpose, had a distinctive beard. I thought it was plausible that Stanislaw could have met Marian as a student and might have introduced him to Sir Hugh (more on him in a moment). I thought that Marian might have been able to help my character Harry 'fix' his Enigma machine so that even if it did remain in the wrong hands (i.e. Easton Fitzgerald's hands) it would be of no use.

Both Marian's and Stanislaw's mathematics are way over my level of understanding and fortunately not necessary for my story. Stanislaw died in 1942 aged 79 during the Nazi occupation of Poland. At that time many brilliant people like him were cruelly persecuted, often murdered, by the Nazis.

Sir Hugh Sinclair

I have read so many fascinating and inspiring pieces of history in making this story; it has been very easy to get diverted into lots of research. Sometimes, as in the case of The Polish Mathematicians and Enigma, I've only needed fragments.

But it was in one those diversions that I made a brilliant discovery. Sir Hugh Sinclair, the man who bought Bletchley Park, was born in Southampton!

Bletchley Park, a very well-kept secret until the 1970s, is now famous for being the British centre of wartime codebreaking operations. Having been saved from demolition in the early 1990s, the Bletchley Park Trust was born. But it wasn't until 2008, when Professor Sue Black, of Durham University, spearheaded a Twitter campaign to rescue its crumbling buildings. The campaign attracted funding that guaranteed the site's preservation and transformed Bletchley Park into a

National Heritage centre. It's a really interesting and atmospheric place to visit!

That first Bletchley visionary, Sir Hugh Sinclair, was educated at Stubbington House School, near Fareham. Fareham is the model for the Nettlefield of my story.

Hugh joined the Navy when he was 13 years old and by the beginning of WWI was working in Naval intelligence. He was more often known by his nickname 'Quex', but I kept with 'Hugh' for my story. It's plausible to imagine that he and Allan Glaisyer Minns met in London and knew each other well.

At the end of WWI, Hugh founded what is now GCHQ, the UK's Government Communications Headquarters for intelligence gathering, cyber and national security. When Hugh was in charge, it was the Government's Code and Cypher School.

Between the wars, Hugh became the director of the SIS, the Secret Intelligence Service. Today's equivalent is MI6, the foreign intelligence service.

Like the Code and Cypher school, in the 1920s and 1930s, the SIS was underfunded.

By 1936 Hugh knew that the Gestapo, Hitler's secret police, had penetrated several of Britain's SIS stations in Europe. So in response, Hugh set up 'section D' (for Destruction). Its purpose was to sabotage Germany's infrastructure – electricity, railways, food supplies, telephone networks – generally hamper the Nazis' ability to wage war. Find out more about the history of the SIS here: www.sis.gov.uk/our-history.html.

Hugh also prepared a dossier on the danger posed by Hitler, but, because of Britain's policy of appeasement, the dossier was not well-received.

So in 1938, with £6000 of his own money, Sir Hugh Sinclair bought Bletchley Park to house the Government's Code and Cypher School and, in the event of war, to become the centre of British intelligence gathering.

A year later, Sir Hugh became ill with cancer and died in November 1939, just two months into WWII. He was 66 years old.

Noor Inayat Khan

Noor came from a Muslim family heavily influenced by the pacifist teachings of Ghandi. Her mother was American and her father, Inayat Khan, Indian. He was a Sufi Muslim, a musician and a highly respected teacher.

Noor played the harp, was a published writer of children's stories and a descendant of Tipu Sultan, the ruler of Mysore in southern India at the end of the eighteenth century.

Noor was a princess.

The family followed Inayat as his teaching took him around Europe, before settling in Paris. They remained after his death in 1927 but when the Nazis invaded France in 1940, the family left for England. They landed in Falmouth then travelled to stay with Basil Mitchell, a one-time student of Inayat's, in Southampton. Sometimes, it really does seem that all research roads lead home!

With her brother, Vilayat, Noor was determined to help defeat Nazi tyranny. Her pacifism preventing her from killing anyone, she became an undercover radio operator for the Special Operations Executive, a secret WWII British organisation that supported the resistance movement in Nazi-occupied Europe. Noor's job, in occupied France, was one of the most dangerous.

Noor was betrayed early in 1943, held in Dachau concentration camp and murdered by the Nazis in September 1944.

Noor was posthumously awarded the George Cross in 1949 for her incredible bravery. There is a memorial bust of her in Gordon Square Gardens, Bloomsbury, London.

As I write these stories, I think about Noor and young women like her, Sophie Scholl for instance, and try to build their bravery and determination to resist fascism into characters like Baby, Ida and Letitia. Though the real life Noor and the fictional Letitia don't share the same cultural heritage, it is Noor that I'm thinking of when I send Letitia off to join the SIS at the end of this story.

* * * *

A lot of my research, through the lockdowns of 2020 and 2021 has been on the Internet – Wikipedia is an excellent place to start. It led me to some really accessible websites and blog posts – not all research has to be musty and dusty.

Though having said that, my most memorable discoveries were with the original newspaper reports about the arrival of the Habana, that I found in the basement archives of Southampton City Library back in 2019.

I love researching these stories. So it is especially pleasing to include some of the inspiring, important and fascinating things, I have learned, here, rather than weighing the story down with too much information! I hope you find them as interesting as I do and that they inspire you to find out more.

A Note about Refugees

In 1951, the UK signed the **Refugee Convention**, committing to protect people fleeing war and persecution. That commitment has saved hundreds and thousands of lives.

Seventy years later, in 2021, people are still putting their children on boats because the boat is safer than the land. And, as in 1937, some governments are still looking for reasons not to help them.

But, if we are lucky enough to be living free from war and persecution, *we* can help.

Find out how here:

www.unrefugees.org.uk/take-action/

(The United Nations High Commissioner for Refugees (UNHCR), also known as the **UN Refugee Agency,** is the leading global agency for the protection of people fleeing conflict and persecution.)

Acknowledgements

Thank you to Crispin Keith and Jo King who read everything I write, as I write it and give me the encouragement to keep going. Thank you to Tracey Mathias, Sheila Averbuch, Darren Bodey, Sandy Vado, Morgan Delaney and Samantha MacDonald, who gave me the feedback I needed when that early draft wasn't as readable as I'd hoped!

Thank you Sandra Horn, Valerie Bird, Lisa Conway, Penny Langford, Debbie Adamson and Innes Richens, who listened so attentively and insightfully to my chapters as I was revising.

Thank you to Tara Waterman, and Adam Jarvis, who read at such short notice as I was preparing to send the manuscript for a professional edit and to the rest of my 'intergalactic' zoom group, Darren Bodey, Mark Hood, and Lynne Clarke for all your blurb and hook feedback and all round encouragement! Thank you, too, to the 'two Marks' – Mr Stay and Mr Desvaux of the excellent *Bestseller Experiment*, who through their podcast and *The Bestseller Academy,* have introduced me to so many wonderful writers from all over the world.

Thank you, again, to Anne Glenn for another outstanding cover design. It has given me the confidence to sell the book.

Thank you to editor, Julian Barr, and proof-reader, Andy Hodge. The professional skills of both these gentlemen, I cannot recommend highly enough. And a special mention to my Advance Reading Team for encouragement at a vulnerable pre-publication time and that final sweep through the manuscript. Any errors left in the text are all mine as I am a compulsive fiddler and commas, like dog hair, get everywhere!

Thank you to Carmen Kilner of *The Basque Children of '37 Association* for allowing me tell her my story and reassuring me that I wasn't disrespecting the camp or the children. And thank you, too, to Paul Turnbull for his professional fire safety advice or, in this case, *unsafety* advice!

Finally, as always and most importantly, thank you to my own gang – Daisy, Joel, Sam and Ruby and their wonderful partners – Phil, Becki, and Holly, who always cheer me on. I am so proud of you all – everything I do is for you.

And Les, best husband, best dad, best tea-maker, best reader, best technical support and best-ever friend – you're still coping really, really well.

I love you all so much.

Praise for *The Wonder Girls*

"Glorious and life-affirming: girl power 1930s-style.
These girls will wriggle their way into your heart."

Sue Wallman, author, Egmont

"The Wonder Girls is a fast-paced, full-hearted, total
romp of an adventure Any child who loves stories of
adventure, chutzpah and heart will rattle through this
book and be desperate for more. In short, The Wonder
Girls is a real winner of a book."

Georgina Lippiet, in-common.co.uk

"A fast-paced adventure story perfect for readers who
enjoy action-driven plots … The writing is vivid and I
really liked the Nettlefield setting. The villains are
suitably horrid for a middle grade book too. Lovely
happy ending too."

toppsta.com

"This story is full of heart racing moments, incredible bravery and girl power in the face of fascism... It is a fabulous story and I have high hopes for it in this golden age of Children's fiction."

Erin Lyn Hamilton, myshelvesarefull.wordpress.com

"J.M. Carr expertly balances the emotional personal stories of the individual characters and peril whilst maintaining a historical setting that is so real it is almost tangible."

Sally Poyton, Space on the Bookshelf.blogspot.com

".. it is the focus on family, friendship and loyalty that makes a lasting impression ... There is peril, and girl power, and fascist louts – but the core is both humane and full of hope."

K.M Lockwood, kmlockwood.com/writersreviews

Also by J.M. Carr ...

Bert ... so far

Her name's Bert Smith, not Bertina, if only Bert could convince her mum that she likes it that way.

Bert wants to be her dad's first mate forever, taking tourists on boat trips around local beauty spot, Stonewave Cove.

But Bert is forced to live with her Mum and Mum's boyfriend, Ronnie, in his super-clean starter home, only an hour away on the bus but a million miles from Stonewave and Dad.

Bert decides that Dad needs her. Whatever lies Mum tells and whatever Pearl, Dad's new girlfriend, is up to, Dad, Jake Smith, is her dad.

But Mum has more revelations that rock Bert's world and scariest of all, Bert can make or break her growing family.

How far will Bert go for Jake, the dad she wants?

jmcarr.com/books

You're Magic, Duggie Bones

Twelve-year-old Duggie Bones might not be the most popular kid in school but he is magic.

When the mysterious Professor Mosotho sends Duggie, lessons on ancient African wisdom, along with magic spells to give him confidence, Duggie thinks he may have found the answers to some of his many problems, including how to tackle, 'The Baddies', bullies, Brooke, Madison and Clint Baddley.

But is Mosotho really a professor and is it really voodoo magic he's offering? As Duggie's problems increase, he tries to work out whether Professor Mosotho and his 'African Academy of Alternative Arts' is real or somebody playing a horrible trick on him?

Will Duggie ever learn the truth and how will he cope with his rapidly escalating problems in the meanwhile?

jmcarr.com/books

About the Author

J.M. Carr lives in Southampton UK, with her technical support. They share their home with a collie called Cindy, a goldfish called Melbourne and anyone who needs a place to stay at the time. If you would like to find out more about the author, her other stories and the background to this book, head on over to jmcarr.com

In memory of my dear friend and neighbour

Gill Evans

always enthusiastic, always encouraging

Printed in Great Britain
by Amazon

31242101R00219